WHERE THE RIVER RUNS RED

Also by Howard K. Pollack

Everywhere That Tommy Goes

Unmasked

The Fearless Foursome

So You Want to Be an Author

WHERE THE RIVER RUNS RED

HOWARD K. POLLACK

New York

ISBN (ebook): 979-8-9900096-2-2
ISBN (print): 979-8-9900096-3-9

Published by Stonesong Digital, LLC

First Edition: May 2024
Cover image: Erica Simone

One of the book's remarkable strengths lies in its vivid portrayal of high school life, intricately detailing the experiences and emotions of teenagers. Pollack captures the essence of adolescents' lives—their unique language, the fear of tarnishing their reputations, and their engagements in parties, drug experimentation, and alcohol consumption. This portrayal resonates authentically, allowing readers to immerse themselves in the world of these young characters, feeling their struggles, regrets, uncertainties, and the weight of their choices.

—*Online Book Club*

A serpentine and suspenseful mystery about innocence lost and found.

—*Kirkus Reviews*

A complex, suspense-filled murder mystery with thrilling action scenes and engrossing twists. Fans will love its shocking conclusion and its fresh, compelling lead characters.

—*Readers' Favorite*

A suspenseful murder story with the accused's sister trying to prove his innocence years later and falling into great danger. Loved it!

—*Reedsy*

Prologue

He didn't do it. Plain and simple, it wasn't him. But there he was anyway, seventeen years old, sitting in a jam-packed courtroom, waiting for the jury to come back and render its verdict.

The trial didn't go well.

Everything moved in slow motion. Chad Greer's attorney, sitting to his left, had a dour look on his face. He wouldn't even look at Chad, he just kept sifting through his papers, apparently searching for something buried there that he hoped would magically change the outcome.

Chad was cold.

Further over, Cole Hanratty, the D.A. prosecuting him, had a victorious half-grin plastered on a pock-marked face.

Out of the corner of his eye Chad saw Sheriff Chuck Marshall staring him down. Chad blamed him as the one who railroaded him and set him up to take the fall. Someday, Chad promised to himself, he was going to make him pay.

Behind Chad, his baby sister had her head on his mom's shoulder. She dabbed tears from her eyes with a tissue. Dad wasn't there and Chad knew he couldn't give a shit. There wasn't an empty seat in the courtroom. Hushed whispers and accusing eyes burned at his back, giving him the creeps.

The door at the head of the courtroom opened and a court officer appeared.

"All rise," he said in a deep, gravelly voice. A corpulent man sporting a black robe, followed behind and moved to the bench. "Presenting the Honorable Leonard B. Markovitch." Everyone stood and the room went completely silent.

"Be seated," the Judge said, as he sat down. He eyed the court reporter, "On the record."

"Yes, Your Honor."

Peering over his glasses, he panned to the D.A., looked at Chad's lawyer, then at Chad, but he avoided Chad's glare, and said, "The jury has reached its verdict." He focused his gaze at the court officer, and gestured towards the other door, "Officer Rios, please bring them in."

Rios walked to the door on the other side of the Judge's bench, opened it, and ushered in seven men and five women who marched in lockstep. Chad looked at them, one by one, but they too avoided his eyes. As they sat, hushed voices rose again from the gallery.

"There will be no talking!" The Judge bellowed. The room went silent once more, as the jurors took their seats. He looked over to them. "I understand you have reached your verdict."

"We have, Your Honor," said the man sitting in the front row, leftmost seat.

Chad shivered.

The court officer walked over and the juror handed him a folded sheet of paper. The Judge motioned to the court officer, who passed him the paper. He unfolded it, raised his chin, and quickly re-folded it, stared directly at Chad, this time looking directly into Chad's eyes. "Will the defendant please rise."

His lawyer turned to Chad, who was wobbly on his feet and couldn't fully stand. He took him by the arm and pulled him up.

The Judge turned back to the foreman. "Verdict please."

The man rose, and, without any emotion, said, "We the jury find the defendant, Chadwick-Steven-Greer, guilty . . . of murder . . . in the first degree."

Chad's knees weakened, and as he collapsed, he screamed out, "I didn't do it!"

1

Fifteen Years Later . . .

Sawyer Greer, late twenties, slender, with sharp features, was conservatively dressed in a pants suit that shouted 'lawyer.' She was early, so she waited in the hallway outside Hearing Room 333, still unsure of what to expect. It had been fifteen years since her brother Chad was incarcerated, and today was his initial parole hearing. She had visited him regularly, even during her stint at law school. Now, only months into her job working for the Marion County D.A.'s office, she was hoping to be able to help with Chad's parole. She believed all along that he was innocent, and had been wrongfully convicted, and so she intended to dedicate her life, and her career, to uncovering the truth. What better way to do that then to land a job at the D.A.'s office?

At 10:00 a.m. the door to the Hearing Room opened and she walked inside. After taking her seat in the gallery, a few other people entered the room and sat down. She didn't recognize any of them, other than Anthony and Audrey Miller, the murdered girl Megan's parents. She expected them, and if they were given a chance to speak, she figured they would demand that the Parole Board keep Chad incarcerated for the rest of his life.

Chad was ushered in dressed in a suit and tie purchased by Sawyer. He looked handsome, but much thinner, and more weathered than when she saw him two months ago. He forced a smile and nodded at her.

The Hearing began and the Parole Board, consisting of three people, two men and one woman, each peppered Chad with standard questions. Finally, Hearing Officer Marsha DeMonte, a large black woman, with heavily braided brown hair, asked Chad if he had anything more to say. Chad turned and looked at Sawyer. She nodded, offering a faint smile of support.

"Thank you all for granting me this parole opportunity," said Chad. "I simply want to say I have suffered a lot. Being here, I've been beaten, stabbed, and assaulted in a way I don't like talking about. I hope you take into consideration that I never caused anybody any problems. For fifteen years I have been reading, learning, and educating myself, so that the day I walk free, I rejoin the community; hold down a proper job, be with my sister and friends from school. Fifteen years have been stolen from me for a crime I didn't commit. That's all I have to say." He wiped tears from his eyes and lowered his head.

After a few minutes of silence, while the three Hearing Officers spoke quietly to one another, Ms. DeMonte addressed the room.

"Mr. Greer, you were convicted of first-degree murder, by a jury of your peers. It was only because you were convicted as a youthful offender, that you were able to get a parole hearing after only fifteen years in jail. So, the fact that you served fifteen years and suffered in prison, is not a concern of ours. Based on the evidence, it is what you deserve and where you belong. We all thought you would have come to your senses by now; fessed up for what you did. That's what troubles us. Still, after fifteen years in prison, you continue to claim some sort of bizarre innocence. You refuse to admit the horrific crime you committed. Because of this, we have no choice but to deny your request for parole."

Chad stood, and shouted, "I didn't do anything to Megan."

"She had your DNA all over her," retorted Ms. DeMonte.

"I was her friend," said Chad.

"You raped her, bashed in her skull, threw her in the river. That's the kind of friend you are, because she didn't give in to you?" asked Ms. DeMonte.

"I didn't do any of that. I didn't hurt her," said Chad.

"You are a liar, Mr. Greer," Ms. DeMonte stated dismissively.

Chad grew angry. "So, you want me to confess to a lie?"

"A word of advice, Mr. Greer. If twelve people saw you eating oats, it's time to admit you're horse!"

"That doesn't even make any sense," said Chad.

Ms. DeMonte put her hand on her hip. "I don't believe this," she said. "A murderer is here to lecture me on what makes sense. Maybe if you had listened to what your father taught you, you would have made better life choices."

"For your information," Chad said, growing angrier, "My father was a lowlife drunk. I wouldn't listen to him to get a pardon from the Governor."

"You don't really mean that, do you, son?" asked Hearing Officer James Abernathy, a pale, balding, older man.

Chad thought about it for a moment, then said, conclusively, "You never met him."

Mr. Abernathy shook his head. "Son, you haven't learned a damned thing in these fifteen years, have you? You have a golden opportunity here to confess to the murder you clearly committed and instead you waste our time talking about being a good friend to the girl you murdered in cold blood. I don't know why we even bothered giving you a hearing in the first place. Clearly, you are incorrigible. You deserve to rot in prison for the rest of your life."

Chad's temper boiled. "This whole hearing is bullshit," he exclaimed. Extending his middle finger at them, he spit at the Board. "You can all go fuck yourselves!"

Quickly, the officer standing nearby grabbed Chad by the arm, cuffed him and dragged him out of the room.

Sawyer was mortified. She stood and approached the Hearing Officers, "Excuse me, but I have something to say on this matter, and I would like to address the Board."

Hearing Officer Abernathy, stood and asked, "And who might you be, ma'am?"

"My name is Sawyer Greer. I am an attorney with the D.A.'s office. I am also Chad Greer's sister."

"D.A. or not, you have no standing in this proceeding, Ms. Greer, so save your breath," said Abernathy. "I'm afraid this is neither the time nor the place. And, as an attorney, you should know that anything you want to say regarding this matter must be brought up in court, not at a Parole Board Hearing. Please, see yourself out."

With that, he and the other Board members turned and exited.

Defeated, Sawyer fell back in her seat and wept. After taking a few minutes to gather herself, she rose and left the room.

Walking through the parking lot, she was approached by a man she didn't know, but whom she recognized from the hearing. He had been seated in the last row.

"Hello, Ms. Greer," he said, "My name is Mason Walcott. I saw you at the hearing and would like to talk to you."

"About?"

"Your brother and his case, of course."

"Well, who are you?"

"I'm a journalist. I wrote articles about Chad fifteen years ago."

Sawyer squinted, eyeing him up and down. "So, why would I want to talk to you?"

"I know some things about Chad, and I also came to a different conclusion than the jury. I also don't believe your brother was guilty, but I didn't have any hard evidence of that."

"Really?" She furrowed her brow, still looking at Walcott suspiciously. "In my experience, journalists rarely concern themselves with the guilt or innocence of a suspect. More than likely, you're simply looking for a juicy story to pin a Pulitzer on."

"I *wish* I was working for that kind of fancy paper," said Walcott, almost to himself.

"So, why take an interest in an old case that only the immediate families of those involved care about?" asked Sawyer. "It doesn't make any sense."

"It's a long story. Perhaps you'd be willing to grab a cup of coffee with me, so we can talk about it?"

Looking him up and down, and noting his warm smile and demeanor, she was intrigued and reasoned that she had nothing to lose by listening to the man. After all, she was only hitting dead ends today. So, she nodded in agreement.

"There's a Starbucks just down the road apiece," he said, "I can meet you there in ten minutes."

2

Holding a steaming cup of coffee in her hand, Sawyer took a seat across from Mason Walcott. "So, let's get right to it. What is it you want to tell me?"

Mason grinned, "You cut right to the chase, don't you, Ms. Greer?"

"I am very busy and highly suspect. So, if you don't grab me with real information at the get-go, I will be on my way."

"Fair enough. Let me start by saying, I was there."

"There? What do you mean by 'there'?"

"At Rainbow River, where the murder occurred."

"You mean you visited the crime scene?"

"Yes . . . and no. What I mean is, I was there around the time the murder took place. I was part of the group of kids who were hanging out that night."

"That makes no sense. I'm an A.D.A. in the county where it happened. I've seen a list of the witnesses from the file, and your name is nowhere in it."

"Well, there's a lot that isn't in that file."

Sawyer's eyes widened. "Okay, you've got me."

"I thought that might interest you."

"It does, so tell me more."

"I knew Chad . . . I mean, I knew of him. We weren't friends. He didn't know me. I was in college and dating one of the girls from the high school. We went to Rainbow River that night. I knew Chad from his basketball prowess. He was an all-star point guard, and I was a fan. I thought he had the potential to play college ball, and maybe even turn pro."

"Yes, I do remember that. I was just a thirteen-year-old kid, but I went to a lot of his games. He was a good brother to me, he looked out for me and took care of me, because Mom always worked and Dad was never around."

"Seems like you share your brother's low opinion of your father," said Mason. "Sorry, maybe that was too harsh."

"No, it's fine," she said. "Go on, tell me about that night."

"Yeah, so after the game that night, a bunch of us got together; they were mostly friends of my girlfriend, Sandra. Some kid who worked at a pharmacy stole a bunch of Oxy pills and we all took them, including Chad."

"Wait, none of that is in the file either."

"Of course not. After everything hit the fan, the rest of them got together and agreed to never tell about the drugs. Everyone was drinking too, and as kids, no one wanted to get into trouble. And since the drugs didn't have anything to do with the murder, or so they thought, they figured it was best not to say anything to anyone. So, when the police interviewed them, no one mentioned that everyone was wasted."

Anger now getting the better of Sawyer, she reached across the table and grabbed Mason's wrist. "So, why didn't you own up to this when you saw that Chad had been convicted? Why did you wait fifteen years, until now, to even come and tell me this?"

"Like I said, no one wanted to get in trouble, and a pact was made. Besides, it wouldn't have mattered."

"Why not?"

"You're a lawyer. You know better than that. They had DNA evidence. It was on his face." "What's the difference if everyone was high?"

"Look, I don't know. It may have had an impact, but the fact is, this is a major development. I need to speak with everyone who was there that night. Perhaps there are other things that the group withheld from the police?"

"That I don't know. But I do know that Chad was also wasted. He was drinking Vodka heavily while celebrating the victory." He took a sip of his latte.

"So then tell me, what makes you think that Chad didn't kill Megan?"

"Well, during the night I saw them together, they were all kissy-face and sloppy all over each other. And they went off into the woods. A while later, my girlfriend told me she ran into Megan and she was all alone, and I didn't see him for the rest of the night. I didn't know where he went, or what happened to him after that, so I assumed he went home."

"But he never came home that night. I remember that my dad, as much of an asshole as he was, went out looking for him. It was my mom that made him do it. She even told Dad to look by the river. Dad was quite drunk himself, but he took off, and came back a few hours later without Chad. It came out at the trial that Chad had stayed over at his friend Travis's house to sleep it off. No one knew he took OxyContin though, they just thought he was drunk. I guess by the time they took his blood, the drugs were out of his system."

"Makes sense."

"I'm going to need the names of all the people that were there that night. Can you give that to me? I'd like to match it up with the names I took from the case file. Then I'm going to track them down."

"As long as you let me tag along when you interview them."

Sawyer pushed back her seat and stood, handing him her card. "Here, take this and text me the list of names. I'll call you after I've had a chance to look at my notes."

Sawyer sped back to her apartment, barely staying within the speed limit. Once home, she raced inside. She was only able to copy a small part of the file without getting caught, but she got the witness list, and a brief summary. She knew it was improper, but she had to start somewhere. She figured she could always go back and requisition the file from archives again when she needed to. She didn't want to raise eyebrows with her bosses after only working there for a few months. Quickly sifting through her notes, she compared the names of the kids that were interviewed. It was a short list. Mason Walcott was not on it. She wondered how he managed to stay off of it. She then matched up the names against the text she received from Mason and scratched her forehead.

She called Mason. "There are two people missing."

"What do you mean?"

"Your list, not counting you, it has two kids more than what I have in my notes."

"Really? That's strange. Who's missing?"

"There's a girl named Sandra Payne, and a boy named Winston Marshall, both of whom are on your list, but not in what I have."

"Well, they were at the river that night, I can swear to that. As I said, Sandra was my girlfriend at the time, but we broke up when I transferred to school in California and we lost touch."

"Then these two should be our first interviews."

"I agree."

"And does that mean you haven't had any contact with Sandra lately."

"No, I haven't spoken to her in about fourteen years. Do you think you can use the resources of your office to track them down?"

"That I can't do. I have to be very careful. If there's a reason these two were left off the witness list, I don't want to alert the D.A. that I'm investigating."

"Good point."

"And while we're on the subject," Sawyer said, a distinct edge to her voice, "How did *you* manage to stay off the witness list?"

Mason mulled that over for a few seconds. "I recall being interviewed by Chad's attorney, but the prosecution never spoke to me."

"Strange. You'd think they'd have wanted to talk to everyone."

"I guess, but it was long ago and I don't really remember why they didn't."

"Ok, well, right now I need to start a Facebook search for these two. And maybe you can help with your journalistic prowess and try to find them as well. Why don't you look for Winston Marshall on Facebook." Sawyer sat down at her computer and started tapping the keyboard. "I'll look for Sandra Payne. Let's touch base in an hour and see what we've come up with."

3

Mason tossed his phone on the table, shook his mouse and opened Facebook. Aside from the musician Winston Marshall, who, of course, came up first, there were many Winston Marshalls, so he tried to narrow it down more locally, hoping that Mr. Marshall didn't stray too far from home over the past fifteen years. The search was tedious but after a time he was able to find who he was looking for, and as it turned out, the boy became a man and remained in Marion County. While there was no address, his public Facebook page contained pictures of him with friends at local hot spots very close to Rainbow River. Mason was familiar with the places and reasoned it wouldn't be too hard to get an actual home address.

He headed for the fridge, grabbed a Corona, popped the tab with a bottle opener, and took a long swig. He ran his fingers through his thick, dark hair, looked around the room and thought, *I can't bring Sawyer to my place with it looking like this.* He didn't know exactly why he was thinking about her this way. He hadn't been on a date in a while, and this strange attraction to her was making him uneasy. He hadn't felt this way in *forever* and he didn't know if it was good or bad, nor did he have any idea if Sawyer would have any interest in him, but he liked the thought of it.

Sitting back to his computer with renewed energy, he felt that he needed to impress Sawyer. So, he kept digging until he located an address for Marshall. He jotted it down, then started cleaning up his apartment, tossing the clothes he had lying on the couch into a basket. Taking the dirty dishes from the table he placed them in the dishwasher.

Sawyer dug in quickly and, of course, there were dozens of Sandra Paynes on Facebook. She breezed through the first thirty or so until she came upon one entitled 'Sandra Payne Memorial' which was about a girl who was killed fourteen years ago at the age of nineteen. Her bio fit the basic description of the Sandra Payne she was looking for and as she read further, she learned that Ms. Payne died a resident of Rainbow River, Florida. The circumstances of her death were suspect, and for a time the police couldn't commit to suicide or murder. So, with no suspects and questionable facts, the case was left open and unsolved. There had been no activity in the past twelve years. Sawyer logged on to her office account to get the official record but was unable to access records from Tallahassee where the death occurred. A cold case to be sure; over a full decade cold. Sawyer got up, walked over and stared through the kitchen window thinking that maybe this wasn't just a coincidence. One of the things that made Sawyer a good, young attorney was that she was suspicious by nature, so when her gut told her she smelled a rat, she knew that there must be one close by.

She wandered around her apartment, her mind in hamster-wheel mode, and then she sat back down and began a Facebook search for Mason Walcott. He was much easier to find because he wanted to be seen. Pictures of him without a shirt revealed a firm physique with just the right amount of body hair, and, coupled with a solid, muscular build, he looked just her type. A faint tingle between her thighs was quickly suppressed when she hit on another picture of him in a hospital bed bandaged around his chest and head. It was a newspaper clip, and beneath it was a short caption: 'Local Marine Severely Injured in Afghanistan, Returns Home.'

Continuing on, she learned he wrote a few articles for a small circulation war correspondent magazine called "The Actual Facts." The articles he wrote were anti-government and anti-war pieces that almost got him a D.D., more commonly known as a Dishonorable Discharge, but the injury apparently saved him because the military didn't want any bad press over a wounded warrior.

Sawyer also found articles he wrote more locally, some from before he went overseas and a few since. She couldn't find anything about Chad's murder conviction so she switched over to Google and did a name search. After eliminating other Mason Walcott's, she was able to find that he wrote for a now out of business local rag called "The RR Post." Most of the articles were from fifteen or so years ago that were primarily sports related. Some contained stories about Chad S. Greer, a local high school basketball player who showed promise but was brought down by a criminal conviction for murder. There were no details about the crime, just references that he missed a golden opportunity to play college ball and perhaps even pro ball. She continued digging but found nothing more and when all related searches turned up dead end, she began to wonder about Mason.

As she finished a glass of Cabernet, Sawyer's cell rang. "Hello Mason."

"Hey Sawyer, I've got some good intel on Winston Marshall."

"Great, let's hear it."

"Let's meet and take a drive. I'll explain as we go."

"Where are we going?"

"I've got Marshall's address. I think we should go visit him. He lives nearby. Maybe we can get him to talk."

"Oh, so you actually found him *and* his address? I'm impressed."

"You should be . . . so how about you, Sawyer? Did you find Sandra?"

She bit her lower lip. "Yes, and no."

"Care to elaborate?"

"We can talk about it when I see you. I'll text you my address. Come and pick me up in a half hour. I need a few minutes to get ready."

4

Mason picked up Sawyer in his black 2015 Land Rover wearing a red t-shirt with black jeans and grey high-top Sorel sneakers. Grinning, he looked at Sawyer from head to toe. "Well, you dress down quite nicely."

Sawyer blushed behind her Aviator sunglasses. She wore a loose-fitting light-blue top and blue jeans. White sneakers finished off the ensemble. "I'm glad you approve," she said, as she placed a white baseball cap over her long blonde hair. "So, where are we headed?"

"Winston Marshall lives in Silver Springs. It'll take about twenty minutes."

"Good job. So, what else can you tell me about him?"

"Well, for starters, he seems like a redneck from the photos. And he's quite enamored of himself. I only had access to his public page and there are shots of him flexing for the camera, posing on a horse, posing at a shooting range, and he's got one with a cap on that says 'Sheriff' across the top, so I think he's a cop."

"Just great, another civil servant to deal with."

"Yeah, this should be fun," he said, sarcastically. "So, what did'ya find out about my ex, Sandra?"

Sawyer let that question hang in the air for a moment. Mason turned to her and pulled his sunglasses down to the tip of his nose. "Sawyer?"

"Not good news, I'm afraid."

"Why, what is it?"

"Uh, well, she died, about fourteen years ago . . . under suspicious circumstances."

Mason sighed and dropped his shoulders. "Oh no, are you sure? That can't be right. And what do you mean by suspicious circumstances?"

"Trust me, it's her. And from what I was able to uncover, she was found hanged in her dorm room at Florida State University. And they were never able to determine if it was murder or suicide. The case is still open, but has obviously gone cold. No suicide note, but no evidence to suggest homicide either."

His eyes flashed with anger. "I don't believe this! We didn't date for too long, but I knew her fairly well. And frankly, she didn't seem like the type who would take her own life." Mason frowned. "She was bright and had a spark to her. She was always smiling, too. This really stinks to me."

"It sounds suspicious to me, too. Is there anything else you can tell me about that night at Rainbow River?"

"I've told you everything I remember. But suicide? Seriously? Less than a year after Megan's murder? And *before* Chad was convicted. Smells fishy to me."

"I know, and I'm just speculating. But it's too coincidental. Let's hope Marshall is willing to be more forthcoming about the events of that night, and anything he might know about Sandra."

"I wouldn't get my hopes up."

They fell silent for a time as Mason fiddled absentmindedly with the radio unsure what he was searching for. Sawyer looked out the side window deep in thought as her mind raced. Finally, she turned back and said, "So, you were in the military?"

That caught Mason off guard. "How'd you find that out?"

"It wasn't hard. You do have a Facebook page. So tell me, what happened over in Afghanistan that made you write those articles vilifying the government? And how did you get wounded over there?"

"Let's save that for another time. We're about to arrive and we need to figure out how to approach this guy."

"Fair enough, but you *are* going to tell me."

"When the time is right." Mason eyeballed his cell phone GPS and turned off the main road. "I think you should wait in the car while I try to talk to Marshall alone. I'll tell him I'm a journalist and I'm writing a story about Chad and how his parole was denied and ask him if he has any comments about it."

"What if he recognizes you from that night?"

"He won't. I barely had two words with any of the guys. They were all hanging around a campfire and I was off in the near woods with Sandra. I could see them and hear the laughter but couldn't quite make out what they were talking about. I was more interested in making out with my girlfriend."

"And if that doesn't get you anywhere?"

"I'll text you and you come around and play little sister A.D.A. looking to get the truth to set your brother free."

"I don't know. I think we should both approach him together and be up front from the get-go. Assuming he's a cop, he's going to have his guard up and be suspicious anyway. And with your tactic he might just tell us to take a hike."

"I suppose," he said, pulling the car to a stop at the curb. "I guess we can try it your way."

Sawyer pointed with her chin. "Is this the place?"

"Over there," Mason fingered a weathered-looking, grey house with a black front door. A security camera pointed down the driveway, while another stood sentry at the front door. "Looks like this guy is either very cautious, or paranoid." He pointed to the cameras.

The two walked up the drive and over to the front door. Before they could knock, it opened, and Winston Marshall came out. No uniform, just jeans, a brown checked flannel shirt, gun belt, gun and holster by his side, along with a cowboy hat and boots to finish off the look. "Who the hell are you two?" He demanded, in a heavy southern drawl. He pursed his lips, scratched the week-old stubble on his chin, and closed the door behind him, leaving the three of them standing on his porch.

Sawyer spoke first. "Good afternoon, you must be Winston Marshall?"

"That I am. And again, who the hell are you?"

"My name is Sawyer Greer. I'm with the Marion County D.A.'s office." She showed her badge.

"Greer . . . Greer," he repeated the name while removing his hat. That sounds familiar."

"You knew my brother, Chad Greer, back in high school."

"Yeah, that's right." He hesitated, as if in thought. "The kid they got for murder at the river way back when."

"That's right," said Mason.

Marshall turned to him. "And who might you be, Mister?"

"My name's Mason Walcott."

"Don't sound familiar." Marshall spat a wad of tobacco juice onto the ground.

"You wouldn't know me."

Sawyer interjected. "We're here to talk about my brother. We were at his parole hearing this morning and it didn't go well."

"I wouldn't suspect that it would, ma'am. I was there, and I'm sorry to say, but the boy was guilty as sin. Killin' his own girlfriend that night. Damned if I knew what he was thinking."

"I'm sorry, Mr. Marshall, but there are facts that have come to light which suggest he didn't commit the murder." She stretched the truth. "That's why we're here."

"And this is coming from the D.A.'s office?"

Sawyer hesitated. "In a manner of speaking."

"A manner of speaking? What the hell izzat supposed to mean?"

"I'm conducting a preliminary investigation at this time. And if it proves fruitful, it will become a full-blown matter with the D.A."

"Sounds a little hokey to me."

"Look, you're a cop. If an injustice was done, wouldn't you want to help correct it?"

"Excuse me, ma'am. Did you say I was a cop?"

"Yes, I thought . . ."

"I ain't no cop," he said with disdain. "Where'd you get an idea like that?"

Sawyer's eyes widened, "My apologies, I just thought that . . . well, with that gun on your hip, it made me think you were a cop."

Marshall growled. "Well, like I said, I ain't no cop. I got me a carry permit. So, don't be confusing me with no lawman. You got that?"

Taken aback by his hostility, she said, "I'm sorry, but let's not get off the subject. We were wondering if you knew anything about that night at Rainbow River? You weren't on the witness list, and just a minute ago you said you were there. Is there any reason why you weren't questioned?"

"Frankly, ma'am, I don't remember much about that night. We was all drinking heavily after that basketball game."

"Yes, I'm aware of that. Which brings me to my next question. Do you know anything about drugs at the river that night."

Marshall put his hat back on, averted her eyes, and took a step back. "Drugs? Wha'dya mean drugs?"

"I've been informed that everyone at the river had taken pills, OxyContin to be specific."

Marshall looked down at his boots. "Well that just ain't true." He hesitated, took his hat off again and looked up at the sky. "I don't know nuthin' bout no pills like that. Someone be tellin' you a story, ma'am . . . so if that's all, I need to git goin'. I'm already late for the afternoon shift."

"Please, Mr. Marshall. Just a few more questions. This is my brother we're talking about and anything you know may help me."

"Look, in my eyes that boy was guilty. So, why should I help you with anything?" He started walking towards his truck."

Mason cut in. "I'm sorry, Winston, but you're lying. You see, I was there that night, and I know everyone, including you, took those Oxy pills, so don't try denying it now."

"Bullshit, you weren't there! I'd a known if you were. I ain't never seen you before in my life."

"Well, I *was* there. I was with Sandra that night. Sandra Payne."

Marshall straightened up and put his hat on again. "Well now, there's a name I haven't heard in a long time. Pretty little Sandra P. Now her I remember. Cute young thing. Very sad about her suicide though."

"Yes, that was awful," said Sawyer.

"What a waste of a pretty face," said Marshall, reflecting on the thought of Sandra. Sawyer paused, feeling the strangeness of Winston's statement.

"Hey, don't avoid the subject, Mr. Marshall. Mason was there. So, why are you lying about the drugs?"

"You know what? I think I've said about all I'm gonna say on the matter. I've got to git back to work." Marshall pulled open the door to his truck, hopped in and drove off, leaving Mason and Sawyer with mouths agape.

"That didn't go so well," said Mason.

"No, it didn't. But did you see how evasive Marshall got when I asked him about the drugs?"

"Yes, it was quite obvious he was rattled."

"The man clearly knows something and is hiding it. And we need to find out what it is. Let's get back to my place. I want to have another look at my notes. I know there's something I'm missing. I can feel it in my bones."

5

Three blocks from his home, Winston Marshall took out his cell phone and made a call.

"Hey Pops, you ain't gonna believe this, but a chick from the Marion County D.A.'s office came to talk to me."

"About what?"

"When I tell you her name, I think you'll figure it out. Sawyer Greer."

"Greer?" He thought for a moment. "You mean the kid from high school?"

"Yeah, Chad's sister."

"The fuck does she want?"

"Sounds like she's trying to reopen the murder."

"Are you shitting me?"

"No, I ain't, Pops. She thinks he's innocent and she's diggin' for answers. And she was with some guy named Mason Walcott; says he was there that night."

"Seems like this bitch is getting too big for her britches. I'll tell you what, I still got friends at the D.A. Imma make some calls."

"But, pops, the evidence all pointed to Greer. Why would anyone think he didn't do it?"

"That's right, Boy. I put that son-a-bitch away, and I don't want no female lawyer twisting my words round, trying to make me look bad. Her brother got what he deserved."

"I agree, pops, but you should know I may have slipped and said I was there that night. And that Greer girl asked me why I wasn't in the file as a witness. And the guy she was with, Walcott, he says he was there that night, too, and he saw me."

"Don't worry, Win. I'll handle it. You just keep your mouth shut and your nose clean."

"You think you can do something?" asked Winston. You hasn't been Sheriff in over five years."

"Winston," Marshall Senior said, sternly, "There ain't no *been* in Sheriff."

Chuck Marshall made a call to his good ole' boy, former D.A. Cole Hanratty. He picked up on the first ring. "Hey Chuck, it's been a while. How ya been?"

"All good, Cole, until today."

"Why? Wha'dya mean?"

"I just heard from Winston. He tells me that some new A.D.A. from your old office is reopening the Megan Miller murder from back in the day."

Hanratty scratched his head and looked around the room as if wondering who might be spying on him. "A new A.D.A.? Who is she, and why would she be looking into an old case like that?"

"As to who she is, get this, her name's Sawyer Greer. She's Chad Greer's sister, and she's trying to clear her brother and get him out of jail."

"That's crazy, I remember the case. The boy did it. You got me all the evidence I needed to bring him to justice."

"I did, and I left the Sheriff's office with a stellar reputation and nothing's gonna fuck up my legacy. You got me?"

"I hear you, Chuck. So how do you want me to handle this?"

"You gotta head this one off. You're still in touch with D.A. Crenshaw, aren't you?"

"I am. That boy owes me big time, I taught him everything he knows."

"Well then, make a call and tell him to get that nosy little bitch off the case, or better yet, have him fire her."

"I'm not so sure that's a good idea, Chuck. In my experience when you do something like that it only makes things worse. My guess is she'll feel like something's up if we try to shut her down. Then she'll go all gang busters. There's gotta be a better way."

"Look, make the call. See if Crenshaw will get on board. And while you're at it, see what he knows about the investigation and what new evidence they've got."

Arthur Crenshaw's office phone rang. Cole Hanratty was on the other end. "Crenshaw, it's me, Cole. How ya doing?"

"Hey Cole, nice to hear from you. What's up?"

Dispensing with the pleasantries, Cole cut right to it. "I need some info and some help with a situation."

"Go on."

"You know that new girl you got working for you. Greer. Sawyer Greer?"

"Yeah, what about her? She's a good kid, sharp, works hard."

"Well, you've got her working on her brother's case, and that ain't good."

"What are you talking about? She's not working on anything like that. She's a newbie. I've just got her working on routine matters."

"Huh, then maybe she's gone rogue on you Arthur? You see, I just got a call from Chuck Marshall. He told me she just visited with his son Winston and told him she was looking into the case and believes her brother is innocent. She started asking all kinds of questions."

"Frankly, I don't know anything about it. She's got the day off today. I do know she was going to attend her brother's parole hearing, but that's it. I'll have to have a talk with her."

"You better. I think you know that just from the appearance of it, that's a conflict of interest. You can't have a member of the D.A.'s office looking to overturn a conviction, especially the sister of the convict."

"I'm well aware, Cole. I'll get on it right away. Let me see what she has to say, and I'll get back to you."

"Much appreciated. And when you do, find out what kind of new evidence she's got. Marshall told me she's been looking at the file."

"Absolutely. Give me 'til Monday to sort this out. I'll get some answers."

6

Sawyer took out her notes and the few pages she was able to copy and spread them out on the table. Because of the circumstances surrounding her requisitioning the file, she didn't have the time to copy it, and she didn't want to invite any suspicion at the D.A.'s office, so there really wasn't much to it.

Mason had his hands on his hips and shook his head. "What exactly are you looking for?"

"If I knew that, we'd have the case solved."

Sawyer started sifting through them and in no time she found a page of notes with a summary of witness interviews. She slapped the table. "I knew it! The name sounded so familiar."

"Who?"

"Marshall, that's who. Chuck Marshall was the Sheriff who investigated the murder. Winston must be his son. He looked to be mid-thirties, which would have made him around eighteen at the time of the murder."

Mason interjected. "So that's how he was able to keep his name out of all this. Dear old dad didn't want his son involved, so he made him disappear."

"The question is why? What was he hiding? We really need to speak to all of the kids that were there that night."

The two spent the evening checking Facebook and Google to try to locate all of the kids that were there that night. Mason kept looking over at Sawyer, impressed by her spunk and wondering if she was available. Sawyer caught him eyeing her a couple of times and tried to hide her blush. She too had been wondering about Mason but now was not the time to get involved. She had a mission to complete and romance would have to wait.

Mason exhaled. "I need a break. I think we need some food. What have you got to eat around here?"

"Actually, I haven't gotten around to shopping for a bit, so there's not much here."

"Well what do you say we go out and pick something up then?"

"Honestly," Sawyer said, brushing her hair off her forehead, "I'd rather keep going. We could order some pizza and have it delivered. And I've got a bottle of wine over in the kitchen."

"That'll work for me."

"Great. I'll make the call, you get the wine."

Mason went into the kitchen, found the wine, made himself at home and started opening cabinets looking for glasses.

Sawyer covered the phone and called out, "Left cabinet at the top."

Finding the glasses, he brought everything back to the table and poured.

Sawyer watched him from behind and after she finished ordering she hung up the phone and said, "I just want to thank you, Mason. I mean, we've only just met and we really know very little about one another, but I'm very grateful that you're helping me out here. I usually do everything on my own and it's nice to have someone else to share the workload."

"Think nothing of it. I want to help." He moved over to the couch and sat down. "I didn't do a good job of it fifteen years ago and maybe this is my way of trying to make up for it."

Following him with her gaze, she said sternly, "Don't think for a second that I'm letting you off the hook. There's still a lot you need to tell me." Sawyer took her glass from the table, thought for a moment, as she tried to decide where she wanted to sit. Thinking it too forward to sit next to him, she moved over to the easy chair cornering the couch. "So, tell me, was it really an exercise in altruism showing up at the hearing today? Or were you simply looking for a story?"

"How long before the pizza gets here?"

"Don't change the subject, Mason. Answer my question."

He took a sip of wine, leaned over and placed the glass on the coffee table. Sitting back he said, "To be honest with you, I came today with mixed intentions. I was hoping that Chad would make parole, because that would have let me off the hook for not doing the right thing back then. I also wanted to write an article about it, but after his parole was denied, and I met you, I realized that a story in the paper would be a disaster."

She looked at him earnestly, "Wise decision."

"And now, after starting to get to know you," he grinned, "I wouldn't want to incur your wrath."

Sawyer laughed out loud. "You *are* getting to know me, I see."

"So, where do we go from here?"

"I beg your pardon," she said, sounding flustered.

Mason quickly realized that she misunderstood. "I mean, with the investigation. When do you plan on going to speak to the witnesses?"

Blushing, she said, "Oh, yes, as soon as possible. Tomorrow is Saturday, so I have all day. I'll need to make the best of the whole weekend, then it's back to work on Monday."

"Sounds like a plan."

"Does that mean you'll be joining me?"

"It does. I want to get to the bottom of this for my own reasons." The doorbell rang. "That'll be the pizza!"

Mason said, "Let me get that."

"I guess that means chivalry isn't dead."

They munched on the pizza and continued bantering until the bottle of wine was empty. Standing by the couch and now a little tipsy, Mason thought he'd play a card. "You know, I may have had a bit too much to drink. I'm not sure if I should be driving home right now."

She looked at him with an expression that spoke volumes. "I'm not that easy, fella. You can call an Uber if you don't think you can drive."

He grabbed his heart with both hands and said sarcastically, "Shot with an arrow at close range." He fell back on the couch in mock death.

Sawyer laughed from deep inside, and it made her feel good. She was happy, not sure exactly why, or what Mason had to do with it, but despite the despair she felt over Chad, she was actually having fun. Then she started feeling guilty.

"Thank you again for everything today, but I really feel like I shouldn't be enjoying myself so much. I mean, Chad is wasting away in jail for a crime he didn't commit. I shouldn't be having any fun right now."

"C'mon Sawyer, give yourself a break. You're doing . . . we're doing . . . the best we can under the circumstances. I'm sure he'd understand. You still have a life to live, don't you?"

"Not until Chad is out of jail I don't. I promised my mom before she died."

"Oh my God, I had no idea. Why didn't you tell me that earlier?"

"Well, it's not something I wanted to lead with, but yeah, she passed away two years ago. She'd had it very rough after Chad went to jail and my dad left. I still don't know where he is, and frankly, I couldn't care less. He can go rot in Hell."

"Hey, I'm sorry. I didn't want to ruin the mood we had going on."

"It's okay, I do that to myself a lot. Whenever things start looking up, I always find a way to bring myself down."

7

The driver of the white late model Ford Escape watched as Sawyer Greer exited her apartment complex and entered Mason Walcott's Land Rover. As the two sped off, the white SUV followed surreptitiously.

Mason handed Sawyer a steaming Starbucks latte. "I thought this might help take the edge off after that class six hooch we drank last night."

"Hooch? Oh, the wine. Thanks. How do you feel? I mean, you literally drank the last drop in the bottle."

"I'm good. No hangover. Ready for anything."

"Good, keep that sentiment. And just so you know what we're up against, I went through the rest of the witness summaries and found a hiccup on a statement Daryl Wright gave, so I'd be prepared for today."

"Okay, so what did you learn?"

"It's pretty straightforward. No mention of OxyContin. They were all drinking around the bonfire. Chad and Megan disappeared. Everyone assumed they left to make out."

"Break it down Barney-style. What do you expect to get out of talking to him?"

"I don't really know, but I remember he was a friend of Chad's when we were kids. They were on the basketball team together.

Maybe after all this time he might be more forthcoming about what went down that night."

"At least he still lives nearby. What about the others? Any epiphanies?"

"There really wasn't much information. When I copied the few pages I was able to, I really didn't know what I was looking for, so I just copied what was on top. I have to get back into the archives and take a much better look at the file. The notes in the summary basically said that all of the kids told the same story. It was almost as if they were either coached or all got together and rehearsed what they were going to say."

"Did any of them implicate Chad directly?"

"No, not at all. But I'm beginning to think Chad's attorney didn't do a good job representing him, and that also led to Chad's conviction."

"Really? You think you can ninja punch your brother out of jail?"

"I think so. I'm going to have to do some research on it though."

They pulled up in front of Daryl Wright's home. The white SUV that had been following them pulled over inconspicuously a few houses back. The driver took note of the address they were visiting. Wright's was a modest one story home with a lone Foxtail Palm centered on the front lawn. The house was indistinct from the surrounding homes. Sawyer took the lead once again and rang the doorbell. A handsome, thirty-something black man, with short-cropped hair answered the door.

Sawyer said, "You must be Daryl."

"And you must be?"

"You probably won't remember me, but I'm Sawyer Greer, Chad's sister."

Daryl smiled, recalling how awkward she'd been. "Oh, wow. I do remember you but you wuz just a little girl back then, never thought you'd grow into such a hottie. You and your boy, come on in."

"I suppose." She looked down at the ground, embarrassed.

He ushered them into his home, closed the door and led them to a sparsely decorated living room. "Take a seat." He motioned them to a sofa set in the middle of the room facing a flat screen TV. He pulled a chair from the table and sat in it. "Your brother, Chad? Last I remember, he got some serious time in the big house for killing his girlfriend. Oh, sorry. That came off kinda cold."

"Chad is still in jail, doing the best he can. Which brings me to why we're here."

Daryl turned to Mason. "How do you fit into this puzzle?"

"My name's Mason, Mason Walcott. Just tagging along."

"You ain't no cop, are ya?"

"No, he's not." Sawyer placed her palms on her lap and continued, "I attended Chad's parole hearing yesterday, and it didn't go very well. Chad keeps telling them he didn't kill Megan, and it's gotta be true." She looked over to Mason, who nodded. "In fact, I am now an attorney, and I work for the Marion County D.A.'s office. I'm investigating the case and looking to overturn the conviction."

"Wow, that'll cause some shit over there. I mean, I never believed Chad did it either, but that DNA was bad news for him."

"It was, but despite that I still believe he's innocent."

"I hear ya, and no disrespect. But what are y'all really here fer?"

"Well, I understand that everyone was drinking, and that Chad and Megan took off into the woods, and that was the last anyone saw of them."

"My guess is they went skinny dipping."

"Do you remember drinking that night?"

"Hell yeah. Your brother was key to us getting into the finals, but then Chad got pinched for the murder, which ruined our chances."

"So, you were all drinking?"

"Sawyer, we put down so much hardcore liquor, I'm surprised no one DOA'd. Except, well. . . ." The moment got somber.

"What about drugs? I heard OxyContin was on the menu."

"Hmm, where did you hear that?" Daryl said, sounding evasive.

"Doesn't matter, I just need to know if it was true. And don't worry, it was fifteen years ago, so the statute of limitations wore out."

"Oh, I know that. And yes," he conceded, "We were popping pills." He hesitated, "But we were all agreed to not telling anybody. Back then, we were all worried about getting in trouble with our parents and the police, so we zipped the lip."

"I see. Do you remember who got the pills for everyone?"

"I have no idea. They were just flying around like flies on shit-faced fools."

"That's got a ring to it. But do you have any idea who handed them out?"

"Ah, jeez, it was so long ago. One of the guys we were with that night."

"If I told you all their names, do you think it would help?"

"I don't know, but try me, maybe it'll jog my memory."

Sawyer ran down the list of names.

"My mind just chalked out. Sorry."

"Okay, let's move on. Could you run the night by me the way you remember it? And would you mind if I record it on my phone?"

"That's all good, go right ahead, I got nothing to hide."

"Great." Sawyer took out her phone and turned on the recorder. "Go ahead."

"Well, in the locker room was pure fiendism after the game. Everyone was jumping up and down, climbing over each other and when Coach left us alone, someone opened a locker and popped the champagne. We just popped these corks and started chugging. We headed to Rainbow River to rack up a bonfire in the woods. A bunch of girls from the cheerleading squad followed us like Catholic girls looking for trouble."

"Who drove?"

"Lemme see. We went in a few cars, I don't remember exactly whose cars, but there were eight or ten of us so maybe three of four cars."

"Who did you go with?"

"That I remember. Me and Chad went in Travis's car."

"Do you know how Megan got there?"

"Probably with the girls."

"Okay, so when did everyone start popping pills?"

"Well, once we got there and lit up some trees? We set up the logs the day before, so we juiced it all with some lighter fluid and the tree torch was all aflame. Then someone started flipping the pills."

"Was it a teammate?"

"It could have been, can't be sure."

"Did the whole team go?"

"No, it was just the starting five. Me, Chad, Erik Vanguard, Travis Conrad and Winston Marshall, the Sheriff's son, a frequent flyer with F.U. Airlines, if you know what I mean."

Sawyer looked over to Mason. "Yes, we figured that out. So, what kind of a kid was he?"

"Well, on the court, he'd give you a hoe check just to make sure you had a pair. Winston was the kind of heat wave you want on your team, not theirs."

"Was there much prejudice at school back then? I mean, I was never aware of it, but, of course, you would know better."

"Lemme tell you something, basketball can make a black man three shades lighter."

"Okay, then. Chad was very psyched and loved to play ball. I remember him practicing all the time in the driveway. We had a basketball hoop there and I always heard the ball bouncing from inside my room." She stared up at the ceiling and wiped a tear from her eye, then laughed. "It annoyed the hell out of me, but what I wouldn't give to see him shooting hoops again, and not in the yard."

Mason remained politely silent, put his hand on her shoulder and smiled. Daryl nodded and said, "I'm all for that."

"Anyway, that was a long time ago."

"Yeah, so we partied heavily that night. I barely even remembered some of it with all the Vodka and Tequila being passed around. And the Oxy made it a dinner and a show."

"Was Chad with you at that point?"

"Yes, both Chad and Megan. And they were oxy'd out, too. Chad took a bunch of them."

"For real?"

"Look, we was all just having a hellava great time, pumping up the victory, celebrating, patting each other on the back, the girls google-eying the guys, then Chad and Megan took off to hook up."

"And they never came back?" asked Sawyer.

"No, I didn't see either of them again that night."

"How long were you there before you left?"

"Two, maybe three hours at best."

"So, how'd you get home?"

"Well, it wasn't with Travis, cause he disappeared. I didn't live too far away, so I just stumbled my way home. In fact, a few of us did the drunken sailor all the way home cause we all lived close by."

"Girls and guys?"

"Yeah. And that was it. We didn't know jack shit until late the next day when Megan went missing, and then they found her at the river. When it came out that Chad did it? That blew my mind. Your brother never beat down nobody, not even on the basketball court."

"And that's all you can recall?"

"Yeah, wish I had more info for you, but that's all I got. Hope you can get Chad out and catch the creep that did it."

"You helped a lot. And between us, I think you should go see Chad. I'll bet he'd be happy to see you."

"Might just do that."

When they departed, there was no sign of the white SUV.

Taking a cautious look around, Mason entered the highway and sped up. Sawyer was abnormally quiet for a time, and he didn't want to disturb her thoughts. He knew she was thinking about Chad and how difficult this whole situation was. He wanted to console her but didn't have the words. He reached for the radio and turned up the volume. Music played for a time. Then Sawyer spoke.

"He seems like a nice guy that Daryl. I hope he goes to visit Chad."

"Yeah, too bad he didn't have more to tell us, though."

"Well, at least he confirmed the OxyContin."

"Uh huh, but honestly, I think these pills are a distraction. My big question concerns my brother's DNA. It seems to me that if Chad didn't commit the murder, how was his DNA at the crime scene?"

"I agree. We need to take a closer look at the medical records."

8

D.A. Arthur Crenshaw, short, mid-forties, portly fellow, with a comb-over that wasn't working and wearing a wrinkled sport coat, was waiting outside Sawyer's apartment complex when Mason and Sawyer returned from their visit with Daryl Wright.

Looking confused, Sawyer said, "Arthur, it's Saturday, what's going on?"

"I need to speak with you privately."

Twisting his head sideways, he focused his gaze on Mason. "And who might you be, sir?"

"He's just a friend Arthur, we can speak in my apartment." She looked at Mason. "He was just leaving anyway." Mason turned and moved towards his SUV.

"Very well. Let's go inside." The two walked through the apartment complex and up the stairs to Sawyer's apartment.

As she opened the door her jaw dropped. The apartment had been ransacked. Cabinets were pulled open, and all contents dumped on the floor. The couch was upturned, and cushions were on the floor. Chairs were overturned and papers were everywhere.

Sawyer cried out in alarm, "What the Hell!"

Crenshaw looked in and said, "Wait, let me go in first. Stay here." He sidled along the wall, peered around the corner, looked into the bedroom and bathroom, moving cautiously as he searched the entire apartment. When he found no one there, he called out to Sawyer, "Ok, you can come in."

Sawyer raced around the room in shock. Throwing her hands in the air she shouted, "Who could have done this?!"

"When did you leave here today?" asked Crenshaw.

"I've been gone about 3 hours. This is insane. Why would someone do this to me?"

"Can you tell if anything is missing?"

"I really don't know, but I don't own anything of value. What could they want?" She bent over to pick up papers, then stopped and turned to Crenshaw. "Wait, so what are *you* doing here?"

"I got here about a half hour ago. I didn't see anyone come or go; it's been very quiet. But I needed to talk to you about your unauthorized investigation of your brother's murder conviction."

"Hold on, how did you hear about that?"

"Look, Sawyer, the walls have ears. I know everything that goes on in my office. And I have to tell you . . . and I'm sorry this has to come with such bad timing . . . but, you've committed serious violations of D.A. protocol. You've used resources from my office and engaged in a conflict of interest. You've improperly requisitioned an archived file and questioned witnesses in a case that has been closed for fifteen years. Frankly, you've compromised the professionalism of the D.A.'s office for personal gain. Not to mention that at your brother's parole hearing you used your position as an A.D.A. to attempt to influence the Board. All of these offenses could result in your termination. You need to tell me what you're up to."

"Well, Arthur, it seems to me that if *you* already know about what *I've* 'allegedly' done, then . . ." She looked around the room, ". . . then this invasion must be about what I've been looking into. And

I must be ruffling someone's feathers. It seems clear to me that someone doesn't want me investigating this. So tell me, who contacted you?"

"I don't answer to you!" He shouted. "You answer to me!"

Placatingly, Sawyer said, "Please, I'm not stupid, I questioned Winston Marshall yesterday. You know him. The son of Chuck Marshall, former Sheriff of Marion County. I'm willing to bet he's the one behind all this."

"It goes deeper than that, Sawyer. Anthony Miller, the father of Megan Miller, the girl your brother killed . . . well, he was not happy to hear that my office has reopened the case. You made me look like a fool when he told me about your actions at the Hearing."

Sawyer stopped pacing and gave him a stern look. "First of all, my brother didn't kill Megan. And I am more convinced of that now than ever before, especially seeing how some people close to this case, including you, are trying to stop me from looking into it."

"You're way out of line here, and you better tell me what it is that has gotten you so convinced that your brother didn't kill that girl."

She swallowed hard and took a deep breath. "Aside from all this," she spread her arms across the room, "In just a short time I've learned that there were witnesses who were at the scene of the crime, who never made it into the report, including one Winston Marshall, son of the Sheriff. Additionally, every one of the kids at the river that night were not only drunk, but under the influence of drugs. OxyContin to be precise. But that didn't make it into the report either."

"So that's all you have?" He snorted arrogantly. "And you think that would be enough to reopen the case?"

"I'm only just getting started Arthur, I intend . . ."

"You intend?" He said, raising his voice and interrupting her, "I'm sorry, but who the hell do you think you are? You've been in my office for less than four months, and now you think you run the place?" He barked a laugh. "You can consider yourself suspended . . .

indefinitely, while I do some damage control. And you are to surrender your badge, and your keys. You are not to use the resources of my office to conduct any further investigation. And I suggest you stop it right now if you want to ever think about coming back to work in Marion County."

She dropped her eyes and then quickly looked back up at him. "Look Arthur, there is obviously something else going on here, otherwise why would the former Sheriff be so concerned about me looking into this case again." She bent over and picked up another piece of paper. "And why would anyone be ripping up my place like this?"

"You don't know that this intrusion has anything to do with the old case." His eyes panned the room. "It looks to me like a burglar was looking for something to steal. So, I suggest you call the police and file a report. I don't intend to ruin the rest of my Saturday arguing with you. Now give me your badge and keys, and I'll be on my way."

"You're a real asshole. You know that, Arthur?"

"Keep that up and I'll fire you right here and now, Sawyer. I suggest you close your mouth and do what you're told. That's what my dad taught me, and that's how I got where I am today. I suggest you do the same."

She reached for her purse, removed her badge, separated the office keys from her key ring and tossed them on the table. Arthur picked them up and left without another word.

Deflated, Sawyer wandered around her apartment feeling violated. She started to clean up, then decided it was best to call the police before touching anything more. She needed a record of everything, as it was. She called and made a report and while she waited for the police, she took her own video, then called Mason and relayed all the events to him. He offered to come back and comfort her, but she preferred to wait alone.

Cole Hanratty spoke into his cell, "Hey Marshall, I just finished speaking with D.A. Crenshaw. He paid little Miss Greer a visit."

"And?" Marshall probed.

"Well, he suspended her. Took her badge and keys."

"That's good, but he should have fired the bitch." Chewing hard on his tobacco, he rolled it inside his right cheek. "So, did he tell you what she knows?"

"She seems to think a few witnesses never made it into the report. She says she's got witnesses that say all the kids at the river that night were high on OxyContin pills."

"And who told her that?"

"She didn't say which witnesses, just that she was told."

"Well, this is all fucked up and needs to be shut down."

"Look Marshall, I'm not saying she knows for sure, just that's what she heard. I think she's fishing for more, but Crenshaw said he cut her off and told her if she continued with the investigation he would have to fire her."

"Anything else I should know?"

"As a matter of fact, someone trashed Greer's apartment. You wouldn't happen to know anything about that, would you?"

Marshall spit out a wad of tobacco juice and laughed. "Really now, that's good to know. That means someone this side of Gunshine has enough sense to stick it to her."

"You sure you don't know anything about it?"

"Course I am. Would I lie to you?"

"I don't know, Marshall, would you?"

"Whose side are you on, Hanratty?"

"Yours."

"Well start acting like it." He clicked off.

9

Fifteen Years Earlier . . .

The wheels on Winston Marshall's Ford pickup spun in the dirt as he raced out of the parking lot by Rainbow River. He was drunk, feeling great, and high on Oxy. The radio blasted an old Lynyrd Skynyrd song, *Sweet Home Alabama.* He sang along with it while chugging vodka from his flask as he cruised down the road towards home. There wasn't a car in sight in either direction when a deer suddenly crossed directly in his path. He swerved to avoid it and the truck skidded off the road plowing into a tree.

Luckily, he had his seat belt on, and since he hadn't been driving too fast, he didn't get hurt. His pickup however, took the brunt of the impact. "Fuckin' deer," he cursed, as he exited the cab and walked around the vehicle to survey the damage. After a full circle, he reached back into the cab, pulled out his cell phone and sat down by the side of the road. Shaking his head, he thought, *he's gonna kill me, but I got no one else to call.*

"Pops, sssorry to call you so late," he slurred, "But I got me a heap a trouble. A fuckin' deer ran out on the road and I almost hit it, then I crashed my truck into a tree."

Startled from sleep, Sheriff Marshall jumped out of bed. "Are you okay, Boy?"

"Yeah, I'm fine, but my truck's wrecked."

"Sounds like you been drinkin.' Where the fuck are ya?"

"I'm on Watts Creek Road, about two miles from the river."

"Just sit tight, I'll be there in fifteen."

Sheriff Marshall arrived ten minutes later and hopped out of his SUV. "Holy shit, Boy!" he said, touching the hood of the pickup. "You sure you're okay?"

"I am Pops, had my belt on."

Pulling open the door to the cab, he said, "Smells like alcohol in here." He reached down to the floor and picked up the flask that had spilled out. "You really fucked up! You been drinkin,' haven't ya, ya moron!" He smacked Winston across the face.

Stumbling backward he cried out, "Shit Pops, that hurt! What the fuck, I only had a little, I ain't drunk. It wasn't my fault, it was the damn deer."

Sheriff Marshall scowled. "Go git in my car and wait for me. I gotta deal with this now. We can't leave this truck here overnight, 'specially with it smellin' like booze."

"Look, Pops, I'm sorry . . ."

Cutting him, off he pointed to his SUV, "Shut the fuck up and git." Winston headed off to the SUV, while Sheriff Marshall shook his head, saying to himself, "The kid looks like he got fucked six ways to Sunday. I don't know what a father's gotta do to get through to a son like that." He shook his head as he pulled out his cell and made a call. "Hey Earl, I need a favor. Bring yer tow truck over to Watts Creek Road just north of the river."

Earl looked at his phone. "You gotta be kidding me, Sheriff, it's the middle of the night."

"No questions Earl, just git over here, and hurry." He clicked off.

Earl knew better than to defy the Sheriff so he quickly dressed and jumped in his truck. Marshall climbed inside his son's pickup, looked around, and opened the glove box. Inside, he found a red-colored bra and a vial of pills. He examined the vial and saw that it contained a dozen or so pills. Cursing under his breath, he stuffed the bra and pills into his coat pocket, along with the flask. Earl pulled up ten minutes later. "Ooowee, what on God's green earth happened here, Sheriff?"

He pushed back a strand of his thinning hair, "A deer ran out in the road and Winston swerved to miss it. I need you to git this truck over to your shop. And keep it quiet."

Scratching his head, as he bent down in front of the truck, Earl said, "I gotta say, from the looks of it, this ve-hicle ain't gonna be fixable."

"I don't give a shit, just git it outta here. I'll figure out what to do with it later. Just keep it hidden. And keep yer mouth shut about it, you hear?"

"Sure thing, Sheriff."

Earl pulled away towing the pickup. Sheriff Marshall climbed back into his SUV to find Winston fast asleep and leaning against the window.

"What the fuck wuz ya doin' out here so late at night, Boy?" He bellowed, as he backhanded Winston on the chest.

Winston jolted awake. "Huh, wha'?"

"You heard me. What wuz ya doin' out here?" He backhanded him again.

"Quit it, Pops." He cringed. "I was just celebrating the win tonight over at the river with my friends."

"You're lucky you ain't dead, Boy"

"Yeah, I know Pops. It was a fuckin' deer, and I'm sore, so can ya just get me home."

Poking him in the chest, he said, "This ain't over, but you make sure to keep yer trap shut about all this. I got ol' Earl takin' care of yer truck."

10

Mason refilled his cup of coffee and sat back down in front of his computer. Sunday mornings were always the same routine for him. Today, however, he was on a different mission. Concerned about Sawyer, he truly wanted to see her last night, but she was adamant about being alone. He planned on surprising her with a visit in a few hours but wanted to have something tangible he could tell her, so he began his search to locate the girls from the cheerleading squad early.

Facebook was always the best way to start any search. He punched in the name Caitlin Yaffe and began sifting through pictures and whatever personal information the limited public pages would allow. He quickly eliminated anyone older than thirty-five and younger than thirty. After an hour he was able to pare it down to a few people and eventually found who he was looking for. The problem was, her page had very little information, and without more, it was going to be very difficult to locate her.

Once he made note of as much information about Caitlin as he could, he started another search, this one for Shannon Harper, hoping for better luck. Again, after about an hour he was able to locate who he was looking for. As it turned out, Shannon had moved to Georgia. Her public persona on Facebook was very detailed. Apparently, she had no reservations about keeping anything private. Her page had pictures from as far back as high school, and fortuitously, there were also pictures of the cheerleading squad. Even better, she had remained in contact with all the girls who had been at the river the night of the murder. She was also married and her married name was Shannon Guibert. *No wonder why she continues using her maiden name.* Mason printed a few pictures and located Shannon's address.

The knock on Sawyer's door was loud and fierce. It made her jump. She moved cautiously towards the door, peered through the peephole and saw that it was Mason.

Opening the door she said, "Did you have to knock so loud?"

"Sorry, I didn't mean to scare you."

She breathed a weary sigh. "Well, after yesterday, I'm a bit on edge, come on in."

Mason looked around the room. "I guess you must have cleaned up a bit, everything looks in order."

"I did my best after the police went through everything." Pointing, she said, "I'm going to need to clean the couch though."

"So, what did the cops say?"

"Not to get my hopes up."

"That's a bummer, but I have some good news," He shook the folder he was holding. Sawyer eyed it. "What do you have there?"

"I tracked down two of the girls who were at the river that night. The first one, Caitlin Yaffe, has very little out there on social media, but the second one, Shannon Harper, likes to make herself known. She's an open book. Not only that, but she's still in touch with the other girls from the cheerleading squad. I've got pictures and even her address."

"Really? That is good news." She bobbed her head twice, then looked down in despair. "But, the D.A. told me that if I continued with my investigation he would fire me."

Mason reached out and lifted her chin so they were eye to eye. "You're not going to let that stop you, are you?"

She felt a warm tingle run through her body and ached for Mason to hold her tight, but she resisted the urge. "I don't want it to, but I don't want to lose my job either."

"Look, we can go together and I'll talk to her myself while you wait behind. At least that way, if anything comes up, you won't be implicated."

"You'd do that for me?"

"Of course. Didn't I say we were in this together."

"Yeah, but now it's getting dangerous. I mean, my apartment was vandalized. Who knows what lengths these people might go to stop us."

"When you say people, let's think about it for a second. We only interviewed two people, Winston and Daryl, and it couldn't have been Daryl, so it had to have been Winston, or someone who Winston knows. That would probably be his father, remember, the former Sheriff."

"My thought exactly. The question is why would either of them care anything about me reinvestigating?"

"Think about it. Winston was there that night. He admitted as much. But he wasn't part of the report, so obviously his father took some liberties."

"Perhaps his father was protecting him from something?"

"It would seem so, and just too coincidental that my boss got wind of what I was doing so quickly."

Mason nodded. "At least we know we're on the right track."

"Yeah, and a dangerous one at that." She bit her lower lip. "The former Sheriff probably has a lot of friends in high places, so we're going to have to be extra careful until we can figure out what they're trying to hide."

"So, you're on board with going to see Shannon?"

"Yep. Let's do it."

Mason smiled and looked deeply into Sawyer's eyes, having a similar urge to hold her close.

She felt it, backed away and dropped her gaze. "Give me some time to get ready."

"You mean you want to go now?"

"No time like the present, Mason."

11

Sawyer and Mason were on the road by 2 pm. They took Mason's SUV which was much more comfortable than Sawyer's car. And she preferred not to have to drive to Georgia. The trip would take them about six hours.

Sawyer said, "So, how do you intend to entertain me during the ride?"

Mason grinned. "Well, with both hands on the wheel there isn't much I *can* do to entertain you."

"Very funny."

"And I don't sing, so . . ."

"You could tell jokes, I suppose. But, better yet, why don't you tell me about your stint overseas and how you got wounded?"

"Well, that won't be much fun for either of us. Trust me on that."

"I guess, but I am very curious. I know so little about you. I mean, I read some of the articles you wrote about the war and how you felt that our government was doing the wrong thing in Afghanistan. You were very adamant that we should have either come in full force or just walked away completely."

"Now we're going into the political realm. I don't know what side of the aisle you stand on, but I certainly don't want to get into a political debate in close quarters."

Sawyer laughed, “Kudos, that could be taken as a joke, but no need to worry, I’m not one of those political types who get all wound up about being Conservative or Liberal, or anything, for that matter. I’m just interested in learning what makes you tick.”

“That could be a watch, or a time bomb.” He turned and flashed a warm grin at Sawyer.

“So, you do have a sense of humor,” Sawyer said, smiling.

“I try. But, to answer your question, and I will be brief, we never had an exit strategy, and as current events have shown us, we left Afghanistan the wrong way and it caused major problems, many deaths, and a loss of assets and money. Had we planned properly, none of that would have happened. So now we look weak in the eyes of our enemies around the world. I knew this would happen, and I wrote about it years ago. But the powers that be, including my superior officers, were quite unhappy about it and threatened me with a Dishonorable Discharge. Then, as luck would have it, we were on a routine patrol and we took fire from above. I shielded myself under a tank but was hit with shrapnel that wounded me in the chest and head. It looked much worse than it was. I mean, so many of us lost arms and legs and suffered horribly. I was lucky, and instead of getting dishonorably discharged, I was sent home with my injuries. That’s the whole story in a nutshell.”

“Well, I respect that, and I won’t bother you with any more questions about it.”

“So, how about you? Did you decide to become a lawyer because you wanted to help get Chad out of jail, or was it something else?”

Sawyer turned and looked at him thoughtfully.

“It’s actually a combination of things. I mean, when I was growing up, and in college, I always thought about Chad and how he was surviving in prison. And getting him out was a dream I had many times. But I also thought about doing something productive with my life, and law just seemed to be the way to do it.”

Mason chuckled, "Yet you chose to work in the D.A.'s office putting people behind bars. To me that doesn't seem productive."

"It was a stepping stone. I only intended to work for the D.A. so that I would have access to the information I needed to get Chad out. I always intended to leave once Chad was released."

"I see. Very noble of you."

"Not really. If anything it was selfish of me."

"I wouldn't call you selfish, you were dedicating your life to your brother."

"Either way, I wanted to make a difference in the world, but now I may have screwed everything up."

"No, don't say that. You're doing the right thing, I feel it in my bones. We're going to figure out what went down that night and get Chad out. Then you'll wind up having a great career helping the disadvantaged."

"Thank you, Mason," she said, as she placed her hand on his shoulder. She quickly removed it and turned towards the window so he wouldn't see her blush.

Mason wanted to reach out to her, but instead he reached out and turned up the radio.

They arrived just after 8 pm. It was dark out and the lights were on inside Shannon Harper's home. Set on a well-manicured lawn in an affluent neighborhood, it was clear that she had done well for herself.

"Nice place," Sawyer remarked.

"Very. Now as we planned, I'll go and talk to her. You wait here."

Shaking her head she said, "No Mason, I changed my mind. I need to be part of this and I really don't care if I get fired. This is much more important to me than a job. Especially working for a jerk like Arthur Crenshaw."

"Are you sure about that?"

"Positive. Let's go. And make sure to turn on your phone recorder before we go in."

The two made their way up a path cut between two sets of hedges leading towards the front door. Mason rang the bell. It had a fancy chime to it. They looked at each other and grinned, each knowing what the other must be thinking.

A tall, well-built man of about forty, barefoot and wearing a tight black t-shirt and jeans answered the door. "Can I help you?"

Sawyer answered, "We're looking for Shannon Harper. Does she live here?"

"Yes, she's my wife," His eyes took offense. "And she now goes by my name: Guibert."

"My apologies. Would we be able to speak with her?"

"What about?"

Mason said, "We're actually from her old neighborhood, down in Rainbow River, Florida."

Sawyer cut in, "We're here about my brother. She knows him from high school. If you may, we can explain it to both of you."

"What did you say your names were?"

"I'm Sawyer Greer, this is Mason Walcott." She reached out to shake his hand. "My brother is Chad Greer." He didn't return the gesture, but merely looked down at her.

"Give me a minute." He closed the door and left them outside. "That was a little weird," said Sawyer.

Mason grinned. "I guess he took offense to the surname thing."

"I guess."

Moments later the door opened again and Shannon stood there perspiring in tight pink workout gear, her long hair draped over her shoulders. "Excuse me, but I just finished up a video exercise session online. My husband says you're here about Chad. That goes back a long time."

"Yes, and we're sorry to bother you so late at night, but we just drove here from Rainbow River."

"Geez, that's a long drive. Come on in."

"Thank you," said Sawyer.

Shannon ushered them inside to a well-decorated, contemporary den with abstract art on one wall, a bar in front of another, a flat screen TV on the third wall and a bookcase on the last. They sat down on a blue couch and Shannon walked over to the bar.

"What can I get you to drink?"

"Water will be fine," Mason said.

"That's good for me as well," said Sawyer.

Shannon placed three glasses on a tray along with a pitcher, sat in the chair opposite them and put the tray on the coffee table between them.

Shawn Guibert stood by the entranceway, leaning against the wall, arms crossed over his chest. He wasn't going to miss hearing anything.

As she poured the water, Shannon said, "So what's this about Chad? Last I remember he was in jail for murder."

"Yes, well, let me start off by saying that I am now an attorney, and I have been looking into Chad's conviction and we have found evidence," she said, looking at Mason, "that leads us to believe he did not kill Megan Miller."

Shannon placed her hand on her heart. "Oh my, now that's just remarkable. None of us wanted to believe Chad was a killer. In fact, we *didn't* believe it, but the way the police made it all sound, it seemed clear that he did it. Caused quite a commotion in our senior year."

"Which brings me to why we're here. I wanted to ask you if you could remember back to the night it all happened."

"We're not being investigated for anything, are we?" Shannon asked, eyeing Shawn.

"No," said Sawyer. "We just want to clear Chad's name."

"I put that out of my mind years ago." Shannon gazed over at her husband, Shawn, for support. "And I don't think I know anything that would help you. I mean, I was there that night, but I didn't see anything. You know what I mean?"

"Well, maybe you didn't realize you saw something, or perhaps you know something that may help. For instance, we have recently found out that all of you were not only drinking but had taken OxyContin pills. We were told that nobody wanted to admit it for fear of their parents and perhaps the police."

Shannon hesitated, picked up her water glass and took a sip. "Yes, that's true. We were in high school. No high school kid wants to fess up to that. We were all afraid we'd get into trouble so we all agreed not to tell. Thank God nobody did."

"I don't care that you took Oxy," Sawyer said. "I just want to know who gave it to you."

"I think, maybe we got it from one of the boys . . . yeah, I think it was one of the boys on the team . . . Winston . . . Winston Marshall." Shannon looked over at her husband again.

"Winston Marshall? Are you sure?" asked Sawyer.

"Sure as the rooster crows. He was dealing drugs, so he was real worried the police would find out. In fact, his father was the Sheriff at the time. That would've gone real bad for him."

"Everyone took the pills?"

"Oh, yeah. I mean, it was kinda a special occasion. We were celebrating the basketball team victory, the boys and all us cheerleaders. Wasn't like pills and thrills everyday."

Mason cut in. "Shannon, do you recognize me?"

She looked him eye to eye and squinted. "I don't know. You do look a bit familiar. . . ."

"Well, my name is Mason, I was dating Sandra at the time, and I was there that night."

"Hmm, I just don't know, but if you say so." She twirled her hair around her index finger.

"That's another thing. Didn't Sandra die at school or something, a short time after all this?"

"Yes, she did," said Sawyer.

Remaining aloof, Shawn moved over to the bar and poured himself a scotch, still listening intently to the conversation as he sipped.

"That was so strange, too. Both girls from the squad. And we were all friends with them. It creeped us out. We were told it was suicide, but Sandra didn't seem like the type. I mean, I wasn't particularly friendly with her, but I hung out with the other girls and stayed in touch. . . ."

Sawyer said, "The case went cold, there was never any definitive proof she committed suicide, but also no conclusive proof of a homicide either."

"So sad. I remember Julie took it real hard. They were real close."

"Julie Jamison?" Asked Mason.

"JJ, yeah. I still talk to her."

Sawyer said, "I'd like to talk to her, too. Can you give me her contact info?"

"Sure, I've got it in my phone."

"Great, but before you do, lets' continue. Do you remember seeing Chad and Megan go off together after taking the pills?"

"It wasn't right after, because we were all hanging out and drinking, making a ton of noise, laughing and celebrating the win. The boys got all us girls to make out with them, saying that they deserved it after winning the game. But hold on, I also remember that Sandra wasn't there. She went off with her guy," twisting up her head, she looked over at Mason. "I guess that was you, am I right?"

"Yes, that's correct," said Mason. "When the guys started suggesting they make out, I grabbed Sandra and pulled her away. We went off into the woods and didn't come back."

"But Chad and Megan were still there at that point?" asked Sawyer.

"No, they had left. I remember that Megan wasn't comfortable making out with all the guys, so when it was her turn, she started kissing Chad and then they took off. So, I don't *think* she ever kissed any of the other guys."

"How many girls were there that night?"

Shannon looked up at the ceiling, "I think there were five of us. Me, Megan, Sandra, Julie and Caitlin."

"Did you girls talk amongst yourselves about what happened that night?" asked Sawyer. "We did, and none of us thought that Chad could have killed Megan. But, as I said, the cops said they had evidence, so . . . I mean, we were teenagers. We believed what adults said. I mean, you know. When daddy tells you something, you believe it, 'cause you're a kid. We believed them. None of us saw anything and we all testified that they left together. That was really all we could say, we didn't *know* what happened. In fact, none of us knew that anything happened to Megan until late the next day when her parents started ringing us."

"And that's all you remember?"

"Yeah, that's about all that comes to mind."

"Okay, well perhaps you can help me get in touch with the other girls. I would like to question them to see what they recollect."

"Anything I can do to help. I have all their info on my phone. Hold a sec while I go get it."

As they sat in the car outside Shannon's home, Mason said, "Well, that was enlightening."

"Now we know what Winston was hiding. The Sheriff needed to cover for his son being at the river. The kid was peddling drugs from the pharmacy he worked at. Can you believe it?"

"I'm wondering what else he may have been up to." He let out a long sigh and forced his fingers through his hair. "So where do we go from here, Sawyer? I don't feel like driving six hours back home this late at night."

"Let's grab a bite. I'll do some searching." She pulled out her phone and located a restaurant and a motel nearby.

Extremely tired, they ate quickly and found a place to stay. At the front desk, they were greeted by a young woman with a pleasant smile.

"How can I help you?"

Mason said, "We need a room for the night."

Sawyer interjected, "Make that two rooms, please."

Gnawing the inside of his cheek, Mason looked over at her. "What's the matter, don't you trust me?"

She chuckled, "I don't trust *me,* and I certainly don't trust you."

"Well at least it's mutual." A flat smile played across his face.

Sawyer said, "Once we get back home tomorrow we can re-energize and make a plan to go see Julie Jamison."

Mason nodded, "Yeah, well, Saint Petersburg isn't too much of a drive from there. So that shouldn't be a problem. Go get some rest."

12

It was four o'clock. They planned their trip so that they'd arrive after work hours, just in case Julie Jamison worked during the day.

"Next stop, Downtown, St. Pete," said Sawyer.

Mason punched the address into his phone and the directions to Saint Petersburg came right up. "Less than two hours away," he said, sarcastically. "You sure you wouldn't rather just call her on the phone? We do have her number."

"No, in person is the way to go. I need to see her face when I talk to her. It's the only way to know for sure if she's being honest."

"I guess you're right, I'm just a little tired of all this driving."

"You'll be fine," Sawyer said. "If you want, I can drive."

"No, no, it's okay. At least I have good company." His smile widened as he looked her over from head to chest and up again."

"I can tell you are using your special x-ray power to look into my soul, and not just checking out my rack," she said sarcastically. "Keep your eyes on the road."

Two hours later they pulled into a driveway in a wealthy suburb of Saint Petersburg called Snell Isle. It had been developed by a man named Perry Snell over one hundred years ago, and many of the homes that populated the isle went for millions of dollars.

As they drove through the neighborhood, Mason whistled, then remarked, "Another cheerleader makes good, huh. I guess I picked the wrong profession."

Sawyer smirked. "Either that, or you're just not a gorgeous, well-endowed blonde who landed a rich guy."

Mason laughed, "I saw the pictures, too. But nothing I found suggested she's married."

"Remains to be seen."

They walked up the drive to the door and rang the bell. A simple ding this time. Julie Jamison opened the door. "Yes."

"Oh, hi, my name is Sawyer Greer. You went to high school with my brother, Chad."

She hesitated for a moment, "That was a long, nasty, time ago." She scrunched her nose and stared at Mason. "You look very familiar. Do I know you?"

"We met, a long time ago," said Mason. "I dated Sandra Payne when she was a senior in high school. I'm Mason Walcott."

"Yes, that's right, I remember. About the time of the awful mess with Chad and Megan. And then Sandra died when she went to college the next year." She dropped her head and cast her eyes down. "I try not to even think about it, but, you know, there's always some reminder. Some really lame show like 'Dateline' comes on and its always murder in some small town, and it always seems like the husband or boyfriend did it."

Sawyer gave Mason a wide-eyed look and quickly turned back to Julie. "Yeah, those shows *are* really lame. But anyway, we wanted to talk to you about that night at Rainbow River. Would you be willing to talk to us?"

"Oh, shit, do we have to? That was the worst time for me."

"I'm sorry, and I do understand, but this is important. You see, it's about Chad. I've been investigating the case and we believe he's innocent and we want to get him out of jail."

Closing the door and remaining outside leaning against it, Julie said, "Look, I don't care what you believe, but the police were clear, Chad did it. They had DNA evidence. I mean DNA doesn't lie. Am I right? At first, I didn't think he did it either, but with the evidence . . . and I remember everything like it was yesterday . . . it was obvious he killed Megan."

"Again, I apologize for opening old wounds, I know you and Megan were very close, but we've uncovered information which will show that there was a coverup. My brother didn't kill Megan. But maybe you can tell us what you remember and that may help to clear it up."

"Ok. If you can convince me that Chad might be innocent, I'll tell you what I know."

"Fair enough. Do you want to do this here, or may we come in?"

"Right here. I'm not comfortable with strangers coming into my home."

Mason said, "We understand. No pressure, Sawyer will lay it all out for you."

"Fine, I'm listening," said Julie.

"Okay, well we know that Winston Marshall passed out Oxy to everyone, and, that after the murder, everyone agreed to keep it quiet. So, the police never had that information. I can also tell you that when we went to interview Winston last week, he was very evasive and said he knew nothing about any pills. We also met with Shannon Harper the other day and she confirmed that everyone took the pills, and that Winston was the one who brought them. Mason also confirmed that pills were given to everyone."

"So . . . even if that were true, how does that exonerate Chad?"

"There's more. Winston's name was kept out of everything. He was never interviewed and never called as a witness. There was no mention of him even being at Rainbow River that night. His father, the Sheriff, covered it up. That makes it suspect."

"Go on."

"And, I don't have to tell you, but the death of Sandra Payne, less than a year after the murder, is also very suspicious. Didn't you ever question that?"

"Yes, I did. It was awful. I never believed she committed suicide, but it happened at FSU over three hundred miles away from home. So why would that have anything to do with Megan's murder?"

"Well, did you ever think that perhaps she knew something about the murder and that maybe someone was trying to silence her. I'm sure you know that she never got to testify at the trial."

"I remember. I was devastated when she died." Tears welled up in Julie's eyes. "She was my best friend, and I couldn't sleep for weeks. I had to get counseling. I was on anti-depression medication for over a year. It took a long, long time for me to get over it, but I finally did, and I really don't want to relive this again."

"We're not asking you to, but if you know anything that may help my brother, maybe we can right some of the wrongs. And I also intend to look into Sandra's death as well. I'm with the D.A.'s office in Marion County." Sawyer looked over at Mason again for support.

Mason said, "Look Julie, I'm also convinced that Chad didn't kill Megan, and that Sandra didn't commit suicide, so please, if you remember something, anything, from that night, please tell us."

"Okay, look, I didn't see anything at all. I was just as drunk and spaced out on the pills as everyone else, and we were all partying and hanging around the campfire. But Megan and Chad as well as Sandra and Mason here," she thumbed over at him, "they weren't with us. We were fooling around, making out. Caitlin, Shannon, and I were teasing the guys, lifting up our shirts and having a blast. At the end of the night, we all went home. I don't even remember how I got home. But the next day, when Megan's mom called looking for her, I called Sandra and she told me that Megan had come to her in the woods crying. She said something about Chad and Travis, but she wasn't specific. She said that Megan was upset and didn't want to talk about it, that she would tell her in the morning. Then Sandra told me that Megan ran off down to the water."

Mason said, "Yes, I remember that, too. I was with Sandra, but I had gone off into the woods to take a leak, and when I came back Megan had already gone. I never saw her with Sandra, but Sandra told me she had seen her crying, and that she ran off towards the river. When I asked Sandra what Megan was crying about, she said she didn't know exactly, just something about Chad and Travis. We decided to leave, and when we got to the parking lot, we saw Travis's car drive off. So, we just assumed Chad was with him, and that's how we knew Chad couldn't have killed Megan. He was gone before Megan was killed."

Sawyer's eyes flashed with anger, "You didn't tell me that. Why is this first coming up now? And if you knew that, why didn't you come forward to the police back then and tell them?"

Mason stammered, "Honestly, I did tell that to Chad's attorney. But, as I just said, I also didn't see who was in the car. I just assumed it was Travis and Chad."

Julie said, "So if Chad was with Travis in the car, that means he couldn't have killed Megan. Is that what you're saying?"

"It would appear so," said Sawyer. "But tell me, did Sandra ever tell you what Megan meant about Travis and Chad?"

"No, she never found out. Megan didn't have the chance to tell her before she was killed."

"Well this is something I'm going to have to talk to my brother about. Maybe he can tell me."

Julie was flabbergasted. "Well, if Chad didn't kill Megan, then who did?"

"That's what we need to find out."

"Wow. I can't believe after all these years. Poor Chad, is he alright?"

"Doing the best he can."

Mason was still shaking his head, "The more I think about it, the more I think we need to look further into Sandra's death."

"That's for sure," said Sawyer. "They must be connected."

13

Fifteen Years Earlier . . .

When he entered the Medical Examiner's room, Sheriff Marshall wrinkled his nose as he absorbed the antiseptic odor of formaldehyde. A cold chill ran through his body. His eyes examined the covered remains of Megan Miller. He lifted up the part concealing her face, shook his head, replaced the cover and looked up at M.E., Dr. Heather Kirk.

She was a tall, slender, mid-thirties woman, with deep blue eyes and an engaging smile. Standing in stark contrast to the body beneath the tarp. Dr. Kirk held a note pad, and with a compassionate gesture pushed a strand of hair away from her forehead. She looked directly at the Sheriff.

Marshall removed his cowboy hat and placed it across his chest. "So, Doctor, what can you tell me about her death?"

"Well, Sheriff, this one's a bit complicated. Aside from the bruising on her torso, and the back of her head, some of which may be attributable to being bounced around and getting banged up as she went over rocks in the river, we've found that she's been raped. Not only that, but her toxicology report shows very high levels of OxyContin and alcohol in her system. Clearly, she overdosed on the drug. We've found evidence of a struggle, blood and skin under her fingernails . . . which suggests she fought back against her attacker. So, whoever did this would have evidence of deep scratch marks somewhere on his body. The DNA says it's a male, but we assumed that from the rape."

"The poor girl, she must have been through a lot."

"Yes, Sheriff, a horrible way to die."

"Well, can you tell me what the ultimate cause of death was?"

"Difficult to say. You see, it could be the overdose, and of course the mixture of drugs and alcohol. But the blunt force trauma to the back of her head may have been the final straw. My best guess, the series of events, starting with the overdose, is what did it."

Marshall's mind started racing. The bra and OxyContin vial he found in his son Winston's truck was troubling, to say the least. But he couldn't imagine his son would ever kill someone. It made no sense, but the evidence was right there in front of him.

"Sheriff, are you alright?"

"Uh . . . yes, I'm just trying to wrap my head around all this. We haven't had a murder here in a month of Sundays. This has really thrown me for a loop."

"I understand. So, at this point, do you have any suspects?"

"Not yet. We're going to have to start questioning everyone who was at the river that night, and see where it takes us. In the meantime, please get the report over to my office. I've got some legwork to do. Thank you, Doctor."

Sheriff Marshall left the M.E.'s office in a daze. He didn't like what the evidence was telling him, but no one else knew about what he found in Winston's truck. So, before he did anything else, he took a ride to the local strip mall that shared a parking lot with the Home Depot. He located a dumpster, made sure no one was around who could see him, pulled the bra and pill vial from his trunk, emptied the vial and tossed everything in with the trash.

He drove around for a while, still unsure of his next move. He debated with himself as to whether he even wanted to have a conversation with Winston about any of this. Ultimately, he chose to look the other way, and ignore what he knew could ruin his son's life before it even began.

14

Former Sheriff Chuck Marshall paid D.A. Arthur Crenshaw an unexpected visit at his home. Crenshaw answered the door in a yellow bathrobe that hung off his stooped shoulders like a bent wire hanger. The robe was loosely tied, exposing a white undershirt and an oversized belly. His combover was unkempt, and some strands of hair stuck up in the air while others spilled over his forehead. Crenshaw's shocked expression when he opened the door to Marshall spoke volumes.

Marshall pushed his way past the disheveled caricature. Crenshaw looked out the door, then back inside as he closed it. "To what do I owe the pleasure of this invasion, Chuck?"

"That's Sheriff Marshall to you, Arthur," he said, condescendingly.

"You haven't been Sheriff for years now, but whatever. Why are you here at such a late hour?"

"For starters, a few days ago I was told that you had the situation with A.D.A. Sawyer Greer handled."

"Yes, all taken care of."

"I beg to differ, son. My sources tell me she's been traveling all over the place and interviewing witnesses from the Megan Miller murder."

"I don't know anything about that Ch . . . Sheriff. I spoke to her this past weekend, suspended her, took her badge, and keys. I told her not to take this matter any further."

"Well, apparently, she just went and ignored ya. I'm told she's tooling around with some journalist named Mason Walcott. They spent the last few days in Atlanta and Saint Petersburg. Aside from her earlier meeting with Daryl Wright, right here in Rainbow River, she met with Shannon Harper and Julie Jamison. I'm sure those names ring a bell to ya."

"And how do you know this?" Crenshaw asked, placing his hands on his hips, thumbs forward. "Please don't tell me you're having them followed."

"I ain't telling ya nothing, 'cept she needs to be stopped. And soon, or else."

"Or else what," Crenshaw said defiantly, trying not to look ridiculous standing up to a man as large and imposing as Marshall.

"I don't want to have to say this again, son, but I won't stand for anyone meddling in an old, closed case that *I* investigated." Marshall stepped within an inch of Crenshaw, his chin almost touching Crenshaw's bald head. "My legacy will not be jeopardized, nor will the Sheriff's office be compromised, by a twit like Greer."

Sandwiched between the wall and Marshall, Crenshaw slid sideways to escape the confrontation. "I hope you aren't threatening me," he said, his voice cracking, "You no longer have any power in this county."

"I have more power than ya think, little man," he poked him with his finger. "Just see to it that she is shut down . . . fer good . . . before I have to take matters into my own hands."

"I wouldn't do that if I were you, Sheriff. I'm still the D.A. in this county, and I won't be bullied. Frankly, I can't quite understand why you are so invested in this. If memory serves me, it was clear cut that the Greer kid committed the murder, and if his misguided sister feels otherwise, why not just let her waste her time?"

"Not so simple, that's all I'm gonna say. Just shut her down, or you'll be raisin' Cane!" He poked Crenshaw again, pulled open the door and stormed out.

Marshall climbed back into his truck, looked over at his longtime pal, former deputy, Morgan Dillard. Removing his cowboy hat from his head, he placed it on the seat between them.

"That little cocksucker has no control over Greer. Fact is, I don't think he has control over anything going on in his office. He was shaking like a leaf, dressed like a momma's boy, all ready fer bed. He ain't gonna do shit to stop her, so I'm gonna need ya to intervene."

"Whatever you say, Chuck. I'm ready to take this as far as you need me to."

"Fer now, just monitor her. Follow her wherever she goes . . . and keep me posted."

15

Sawyer took the trip to the Marion Correctional Institution to visit Chad. It was a mid-sized facility that housed approximately thirteen hundred inmates, with a mix of security levels. Chad had been there since he was convicted.

After going through the usual protocol and searches, Sawyer was led to the visiting area where she met her brother and was able to sit across from him at a table.

Chad smiled when they brought him in. They handcuffed him to a bar attached to the table and left him alone with Sawyer.

"How are you, little sis?"

Sawyer settled back in the chair, offering a faint smile. "The question is, Chad, how are you?"

"Still surviving, and sorry about my outburst at the hearing."

"No need to apologize. I can only imagine how frustrating it is to know you're innocent, and all they want you to do is admit you're guilty."

"Yeah, it sucks. And now I'm screwed even worse."

She reached over, touched his hand and squeezed it. "Well, I haven't given up. In fact, this past week I've been looking much more deeply into your case."

"Really? What? Now that you're a lawyer you think you can get me outta here?"

"I hope so. But I need your help."

"Of course. But what can you even do?"

"I know we haven't ever really talked about it, but I think it's time we did. I've tracked down a bunch of the kids that were at the river that night, and I've even interviewed a few of them. I intend to question all of them, but I wanted to check in with you first and see what other information you can give me, so I'm better informed. I was just a child when it happened, so I don't really remember much, and the D.A. cut me off from looking at the file."

"Those fuckers are all corrupt. They railroaded me, and don't want anyone to figure it out."

"Yeah, well, I think you may be right. Can I ask you some questions?"

"Fine, shoot."

"What do you know about pills being given out that night?"

"Wow, so you found out about that, huh?"

"Yes. It seems that the Sheriff's son, Winston Marshall, was the one who passed them out."

"Yep, that's the way I remember it."

"So why didn't it come out at the trial?"

"We were teens. No one wanted to get in trouble. So, nobody said anything about it."

Sawyer looked directly into Chad's eyes, "And you took the pills too?"

"I did, and I got really wasted."

"You should have told your lawyer."

"At the time I thought it might make things worse, and I didn't want to get my friends in trouble. I really didn't think that I'd be convicted of something I didn't do."

"I understand. So, tell me how you remember the night."

Looking up at the ceiling, Chad said, "I think about it all the time. It started out as one of the best nights. We won the basketball game that got us into the finals. I scored twenty points and was the MVP. We started celebrating in the locker room. Someone hid some champagne in a locker and we drank a couple of bottles before we headed off to the river. When we got there, we started a fire and the pills were handed out. I took maybe three of them, and we started doing shots of tequila and vodka."

Sawyer interjected, "Who was there?"

"All the guys from the team, that is, the starting five, and the cheerleaders. We were whooping it up, laughing and getting wasted. The girls started making out with the guys and Megan and I just cut out on our own. We went down to the riverbank and hung out kissing for a while."

"So how did you get separated? Because she was found by the river."

"That's a little embarrassing."

"Why? What do you mean?"

"Well, uh . . . you see, Megan wanted to have sex, and I just wasn't ready. We were both high, and she got pissed when I didn't want to do it, so she took off."

"You didn't want to have sex with her? Why? I thought all you guys were sex fiends."

"I wasn't as, um, I didn't . . . I never . . ." he blurted out, "I never had sex before! There, I said it. You see, you have to understand that I couldn't let anyone know I never had sex. That would have made it hell for my social life at school. I told my teammates I had screwed a bunch of girls, and that's how I got respect, other than my dribbling."

Sawyer's eyes widened. "So, you had never had sex with a girl before?"

"Never."

"Wow. I can't believe that."

"It's true."

"Ok," said Sawyer, thinking of the next question. "Did you go looking for her?"

"No, I started walking up the hill towards the bonfire, and I ran into Travis. I didn't tell him what happened. We were both really wasted, and I told him that I just wanted to leave. So, we left, and that was it. I didn't find out until the next day what had happened to Megan."

"And you went directly to Travis's house?"

"Yeah, I passed out on his bedroom floor and didn't wake up until morning."

"Was Travis with you the whole time?"

"Yeah, of course. Why?"

"Well, if you passed out and didn't wake up all night, is it possible that Travis left and went back to the river?"

"Why would he do that?"

"I don't know. I'm just asking."

"You can't be thinking that Travis killed Megan?"

"I didn't say that, Chad. I'm just trying to cover all the bases."

"Is that what they taught you in law school?"

"It's just that . . ." she hesitated. "Well, Shannon Harper, you remember her, right?"

"Yeah. She was one of the girls from the squad."

"Right. So, she told me that Sandra Payne told her that Megan ran up to her in tears that night and said something about you and Travis."

He looked hard at Sawyer, "What did she say?"

"I don't know, just something about you and Travis. And then Megan ran off." She hesitated, studying Chad to see his reaction. "And does the name Mason Walcott ring a bell?"

"Not sure. Why? Who is he?"

"He was Sandra's boyfriend at the time. He was also at the river that night."

"I do remember some guy being there who we really didn't know, some college dude."

"Yes, that was him."

"So, what about him?"

"Well, he was with Sandra, or I should say, he was in the woods peeing and came back to Sandra when Megan ran off. He said that the two of them also decided to leave, and when they got to the parking lot, they saw Travis's car drive off. He also said that Sandra told him that Megan said something about you and Travis, which seemed to have upset her."

"I don't know, but if that's the case, why didn't he testify at the trial? He could have said he saw me leave while Megan was still alive. I mean, I know that Sandra had committed suicide before the trial, so of course she wasn't able to testify. But, what the fuck?" Chad stood up and pulled on his handcuffs. "How'd you find out about him?"

"That's another story. You see, he found me. He came up to me after your parole hearing."

"He was there? Why?"

"It's not important."

Demanding, he said, "Yeah it is. I mean, holy shit. This guy was there at the river, never testified and could have helped to prove that I didn't kill Megan, and then he just shows up at my parole hearing. There's something fucked up about that."

"Look, he's here to help, and when I put together enough proof to go to court with, he will testify. I just need more evidence. I'll only have one shot at getting the case looked at again," she took a breath. "So, do you have any idea what Megan was upset about?"

Chad sat down. He put his hand through his hair, then shook his head. "No clue."

"Maybe I should talk to Travis?"

"Well, you could have. He was there at the hearing, too."

"Really, I didn't see him, although I probably wouldn't have recognized him."

"He was sitting in the back. He has a full beard, so I guess you might not have recognized him. I assume you know that Megan's parents were there, too."

"Yes. Them I recognized."

He pursed his lips. "I'm sure they were there to make sure I didn't get paroled."

"Probably, but you can't blame them. As far as they know, you killed their daughter."

"I guess, but . . ."

"So why was Travis there?"

"Honestly, I don't know. He hasn't visited me in ten years, so I was surprised to see him."

"Wait, so if Travis drove the two of you back to his house, why didn't that come out at the trial? I mean if he was with you, that proves you couldn't have killed Megan."

"He did testify, but no one believed him. The D.A. made a big deal about the fact that he was my best friend and that he was lying to protect me, and the jury believed it. But if that guy, Walcott, had testified, that would have made a big difference."

"It would seem. And, getting back to what you said before, I don't believe Sandra committed suicide."

Looking confused, Chad said, "What do you mean? That's what the papers said."

"I'm working on a different theory. Which is why I was hoping you could tell me what Sandra was talking about. I think she might have been killed because she knew why Megan was upset. Do you think she could have told Sandra that you didn't want to have sex with her."

"No way. She would never have admitted to that. She had a reputation to uphold, too. You know how girls are about shit like that."

"In case you haven't noticed, I'm not your typical girl. But, yes, I do know how girls are about shit like that." She smiled. Chad's expression indicated he understood what she meant.

"Anyway, so if Travis was such a good friend, why hasn't he been visiting you?"

"Ah, why'd you have to ruin the moment? That felt like old times, and now you gotta go into persistent lawyerly mode. Law school really changed you, sis."

"I'm just trying to help."

"And how the fuck should I know why Travis hasn't been visiting. Maybe it's cause he's got his life to live. Maybe it's because he gets depressed coming to see me. I mean, I get it, what is anyone gonna say to me? You're the only one who ever comes to visit. No one else could give a rat's ass."

"Oh, I'm so sorry." She reached out and touched his hand again. Chad tried to pull away, but the handcuffs wouldn't allow him to. "Well, I'm going to track down Travis and speak with him."

"Good luck. Frankly, as far as I'm concerned he's a piece of shit, abandoning me like that. And you can tell him I said that. Fucking shows up at my hearing and hasn't said a word to me in ten years. What kind of friend is that?"

Sawyer retrieved her phone from security at the prison and walked to her car. She had two messages. The first was from D.A. Arthur Crenshaw. He urgently requested that she immediately come to the office to meet with him. The second was from Mason. He was checking in to see how her visit with Chad went.

As she headed over to her office, she called Mason and told him what she had learned. The two planned to meet after she finished up her meeting with Crenshaw.

16

Forty minutes later, Sawyer found herself seated in the conference room of the D.A.'s office. Crenshaw sat across from her. A large file lay on the table between them. Sawyer eyeballed the file and knew right away what it was.

"Is this a peace offering, Arthur."

He held her gaze for a bit. "Hardly. But I am trying to help you to avoid making a huge mistake and destroying a very promising career."

"And how do you intend to do that?"

Crenshaw reached out and pulled a small folder from the file. Opening it he said, "I decided to have a look at your brother's file since you were so adamant that he is innocent."

"Really? Well thank you."

"Don't thank me just yet," he frowned. "You aren't going to like what I've found."

"Please, enlighten me."

"Well, I'm not sure how familiar you are with the case, but aside from the witnesses who saw your brother go off into the woods with Megan Miller, the primary evidence which basically convicted him was the DNA."

"I'm aware of that."

"Good, so when I tell you that the DNA came from skin cells found underneath Ms. Miller's fingernails that matched Chad Greer one hundred percent, that wouldn't surprise you either? Clearly, there was no doubt the skin cells came from him. And, to put the icing on the cake, when your brother was arrested, he had scratch marks on his face that matched up with the victim's fingernails. Again, one hundred percent. No doubt, no question. That's what one hundred percent means."

"I don't believe that's all there is," said Sawyer.

"Well, then," said Crenshaw, "please enlighten *me*."

"Look, I'm sure there is a logical explanation for the fingernails. What does the file say about how Chad explained this?"

"That's just it, his lawyer didn't permit Chad to testify, and he made no statement about it prior to his arrest. He remained silent throughout, and since he never took the stand, the jury was entitled to infer whatever they chose to from the evidence presented. As an attorney you know that is just the way it is."

Sawyer's eyes focused on the small folder. "May I see that?"

"Here, I made this copy for you. Keep it."

Crenshaw handed her the folder. She spent a few minutes reviewing its contents.

"I'm sure there's a reasonable explanation for this, because, you see, in the brief amount of time that I have spent investigating, I've uncovered information that suggests that the police and the D.A.'s office failed to interview material witnesses, and failed to uncover facts which may have made a substantial difference in the outcome of the trial."

"Look, Sawyer, I get that you think I'm the bad guy here, but I have a job to do. I also have to protect the integrity of my office, and, unless there is real, probable cause to take steps to overturn a conviction, I cannot waste the time, or resources of this office chasing wild theories, especially when there is a clear conflict of interest."

"Well, at least let me tell you what I've found out and you can then determine if there is probable cause to reopen the investigation."

"You have five minutes. Go for it."

"First of all, the Sheriff failed to interview his son Winston, who was at the scene. He was never included as a witness. But, it was Winston Marshall who passed out the OxyContin pills to all the kids at the river that night. All of them were high from the pills and the mix of vodka and tequila they drank. They hid that information from the police. What else do you think they hid?"

"Go on."

"So, I have located a witness who was also not included, and who saw Chad leave the river with Travis and drive off, just after seeing Megan Miller still alive. So, he could not possibly have killed her."

"And who might that be?"

"Mason Walcott. He's the guy you saw me with outside my apartment last week."

"I see. And so how does he explain why he did not testify to this when it mattered."

"He didn't want to get involved at that time."

"So, that's it? That's all you have?"

"No, there's more. Think about this, why was my apartment ransacked? Ask yourself, who is pressuring you to stop me from reinvestigating? What is there to hide if Chad is truly guilty?"

"There are logical reasons and answers to all your questions, Sawyer. For instance, your apartment may have been vandalized by anyone, and completely unrelated to all this."

"Come on, Arthur, do you really believe that it was just a coincidence? And what about Winston Marshall?"

"I do think it was a coincidence. And as to the Marshall kid, if what you're saying is true, and that he supplied drugs to the group, right there is your answer. The sheriff probably didn't want his son to get in trouble for dealing drugs. That's what some fathers do. They cover for their sons."

"And you're okay with that?!" Sawyer yelled. "I'd like to see the toxicology report on Megan Miller. I'm wondering if the OxyContin could have been a contributing factor to her death?"

"Look, Sawyer, the cause of death was blunt force trauma to her head, nothing about an overdose of drugs in there."

"Well, I'd still like to see what the report says about the drugs."

"Come on, it happened fifteen years ago. There's nothing that can be done about it now." He stood and began pacing behind the table. "Certainly, if I were the D.A. at the time, and I knew about that, I would have looked into it. But it's past history and immaterial to a new investigation. You still can't get past the DNA evidence. Just face it. Your brother did this thing, so stop chasing rainbows."

"I'm not chasing rainbows, Arthur. I'm doing solid investigating."

"And, another thing you haven't thought about, isn't it quite possible that Chad returned a short time later and murdered the girl?"

"I'm telling you Arthur, I know my brother, and he didn't do it."

Crenshaw bellowed an arrogant laugh, "Did they teach you that in law school? Is that evidence you can introduce in court? You *know* him, so he's not guilty? Please Sawyer, you're not thinking clearly, which is the whole point of avoiding conflicts of interest." He walked around the table, came up to Sawyer, looked at her compassionately and spoke softly, "You're too close to this, Sawyer, and not seeing the forest through the trees. You have to stop now before it ruins you." He took a breath. "I'm going to give you another week off, and then I want you to return to your job and never think about this again." He handed her back her badge and keys.

Tears formed in Sawyer's eyes, and for the first time she started to think that maybe Crenshaw was right. Chad never mentioned anything about the scratches on his face, and Mason did say that he never actually saw Chad get into Travis's car. Or, maybe Chad did leave with Travis only to return a while later to track down

Megan. Perhaps he was afraid she would tell her friends that Chad refused to have sex with her. Her head started spinning, too many unanswered questions. She needed to talk to Mason.

Sawyer met up with Mason an hour later at Antonette's, a local Italian restaurant. She was visibly shaken and sat silently while the waiter brought them drinks.

Mason sipped his rum and coke waiting for Sawyer to say something. Sawyer's index finger circled the rim of her scotch and soda before taking a long pull. Finally, she spoke.

"Crenshaw showed me part of the file today. It was the DNA from skin and blood cells found underneath Megan Miller's fingernails. They are conclusively Chad's. Worse yet, they have a picture of Chad's face with scratch marks that match Megan's fingernails."

"I see, so what are you thinking now?"

Shaking her head, she reached for the glass again and took another sip. "I don't want to believe that Chad could have actually killed her, but . . ."

"Look, maybe there's a logical explanation for this."

"Well, if there is, Chad didn't tell me. In fact, he didn't even tell me Megan scratched his face. I mean, why would she scratch his face? They didn't have a physical altercation. Chad would have told me that."

"That's something you'll have to ask him about."

"I suppose."

She stared at a spot on the ceiling until Mason asked, "So where do we go from here?"

"I don't know, maybe we should take a break and think this through some more before we go any further."

"You aren't giving up just because of a minor setback, are you?"

"This isn't minor. DNA is irrefutable!"

"So, let's assume it's accurate, we just need to find out how it happened. But if you want to take a break, how about looking further into Sandra's death? It has been on my mind ever since I remembered that Megan spoke to her that night. I really think she was killed and that it is somehow tied to Megan's murder. Perhaps it may help with Chad, too."

Sawyer motioned to the waiter and asked for another round of drinks. "Right now, I think I just want to get drunk, Mason."

17

Sawyer came awake with a splitting headache. The surroundings were unfamiliar. Mason lay on the bed next to her, still asleep. In a panic, she reached over and shook him.

"Where am I? What happened last night?"

Mason stirred. "Wha . . . huh, oh, you're in my bed."

"Oh my God! We didn't . . . ," she lifted the covers. "Did we?"

Mason sat up and grinned. "We did, and it was fantastic." He climbed out of bed, fully clothed. "Just kidding. Do you really think I would take advantage of you in the state you were in?"

She threw a pillow at him. "Very funny. How did I get here?"

"You mean you don't remember? Boy you really got trashed. Can't hold your liquor, I see."

"Last I recall, we were sitting at the table in the restaurant. How much did I drink?"

"A lot," he laughed.

"My head is spinning. Do you have any aspirin?"

Mason walked over to the bathroom, "Gimme a sec. I have just the thing for you." He returned with Extra Strength Tylenol. "Take two of these."

She reached for the container, "I'll take three. How about some water?" Mason ran to the kitchen and brought back a

Zephyrhills bottle. "This is embarrassing. I don't usually drink like that."

"It's okay, you had every right. It was a tough day for you."

"Still."

"Don't sweat it. Let me make you something for breakfast. That will help clear your head."

"No . . . no. I've got to get going."

"Where are you gonna go? Your car is still at the restaurant."

"Well, drive me back."

"I will, but relax. Let's eat and figure out where to go from here. You said a lot of things last night. I know I said we should look further into Sandra's death, but you also said you wanted to track down Travis. I think we need to do both. The question is, which one first?"

"Alright, let me think for a minute," she ran her forearm across her forehead. "I need a shower. Is it safe for me to clean up?"

"If you're worried I might attack you, don't. And while I would love to join you, I would never disrespect you." He pointed towards the bathroom. "You'll find fresh towels in the closet. I'll cook us some breakfast." He closed the door behind him as he left the bedroom.

The cold water splashing her face brought her fully awake. As she soaped up and began washing her chest, an erotic thought played through her mind. *What if Mason opened the door and stepped into the shower?* Shaking her head, she quickly blurred that idea out, trying instead to focus on her next steps. Yesterday was a rough day, it made her actually question a life-long belief. Again, she tried to shake an unwanted thought from her mind. What was happening to her? In a matter of weeks her life was spinning out of control, and off in so many directions. She could no longer keep track of where her life was headed. Job and career, her brother and two murder investigations, a budding romance? It was almost too much to juggle. She thought back to the many helpful meditations she used to practice but had abandoned after law school. She reasoned that it was time to revisit that mind set.

Sawyer came out of the bedroom to the pungent smell of freshly cooked bacon. The table had been set, and the food laid out as if professionally served.

"My, my, who would have thought that you were a chef in disguise?"

"I'm a man of many talents. Something I left out when I told you about my stint in the army. I worked KP duty for about a year, as part of my training."

She sat down, looked up at Mason, almost smiled, and quickly set her eyes on her plate. Reaching for her fork, she said, "I've thought about it, and I think that we should go up to Tallahassee, pull the file on Sandra's death. Since I have my badge back, I can get access to it, have a candid conversation with the D.A. up there." She swallowed a fork-full of egg and trailed it with a slice of crisp bacon.

"Suddenly decisive, I see."

"That's how I roll."

A day later and after a three-hour drive, the two arrived at the Leon County D.A.'s office in Tallahassee. Brief introductions led to a sit down with Nelson Vasquez, a dark eyed, young A.D.A. with little experience, but a big hunger to sink his teeth into anything scandalous. He was weaned on T.V. shows that dramatized murder and mayhem and joined the D.A.'s office hoping to satisfy his penchant.

"Good afternoon, I'm Sawyer Greer, and this is Mason Walcott." She showed her badge and then extended her hand. Vasquez shook Sawyer's hand, then Mason's.

"It is nice to meet you both," he said with a Spanish accent. "Please, have a seat." He motioned them towards the conference room table, and they all sat down.

"As you requested, I reviewed the cold case file on Sandra Payne. Her situation looks very sad, I must say. But there has been no new information in over ten years. So, what can I do for you?"

Sawyer said, "I was wondering if you could provide me with a copy of the file?"

"I'm sorry, but that I cannot do. I can let you look at it while you remain here. You can ask me questions about the file, but that's all you can do. You are with the D.A.'s office, so I'm sure you understand."

"Very well. Can you tell me if there were any suspects interviewed as part of the investigation?"

"From what I found in this file, the police questioned Sandra's boyfriend and her roommate. Both of them were away from campus at that time. Their alibis were solid."

"Can you tell us more about that?" asked Sawyer.

"Well, the boyfriend," he opened a folder from the file and looked at it, "his name was Roy Thatcher. He was a basketball player for Florida State. He was away that weekend, playing a game against Notre Dame. This was verified by his team, and the roster proves it. He scored 15 points in the game. So, obviously, he was ruled out as a suspect."

"And the roommate?" asked Mason.

Looking into the file again, he said, "Rose Chatman. She was also a freshman. She was home with her family in Texas. She had been sick for a week and she was recuperating there. Her parents verified this fact, and her plane tickets confirmed it, too. As I said before, this was a dead end."

"I see. And so how did they determine that it was likely suicide?"

"The file indicates that it was more likely to be suicide. However, no conclusion was made. That is why the case is still open. The room was not disturbed, like with an altercation. No other students in the hall heard any noise whatsoever. Also, only those two girls had fingerprints found in the room. There were no bruises. The autopsy showed no drugs in her system. But, on the other hand, there was no suicide note and her parents were certain she was stable. They said she didn't do drugs and did well in school. We verified her transcript. She was, in fact, a B+ student, and had no school issues whatsoever."

"Does the file reflect anything about the fact that in her senior year of high school one of her closest friends was murdered, and that she was with her the night it happened?" asked Sawyer.

"Yes, there is mention of that in here as well. That was one factor that leaned toward suicide. However, her roommate told the police that she had spoken with her about it in months before, but she had moved on and was focusing on school at that time."

"Were there any break-ins or student assaults around the time of her death?"

"The file does not say anything like this. FSU is a very safe school. Over the years, there have been very few crimes on the campus."

"Do the dorms have any cameras or other surveillance equipment that was looked at?"

"Nothing of the kind. That's a dead end, too."

"Who found her?"

"Her roommate returned after the weekend and discovered her hanging from a rope. The coroner determined that she had been dead for about two days before being found."

"That's just awful," Sawyer said, as she dug her index fingers into her temples.

Mason shook his head in disbelief. "I know she used to keep a diary. Was one ever located?"

"The file doesn't reflect anything like that. I'm sorry."

Sawyer allowed herself a minute to digest everything. Then she asked, "Would you mind if I went through the file while we're here?"

"Sure. I'll be in my office right around the corner. Please stop in before you leave."

"Thank you."

Sawyer and Mason spent the next two hours poring over the file, but nothing jumped out at them. It just didn't make any sense. They weren't buying the suicide angle, but nothing suggested foul play. Mason did snap pictures of some of the more pertinent papers in the file, making sure that no one saw what he was doing. It appeared to be an exercise in futility, but it made him feel like he was accomplishing something. It also seemed to have been a waste of time to even make the trip, but Sawyer felt she had to make the effort, and so did Mason.

Concluding with a quick thank you and goodbye, the two were on their way.

18

Fifteen Years Earlier . . .

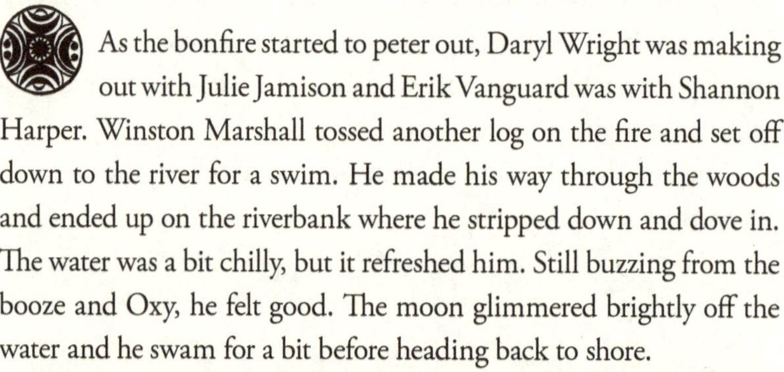

As the bonfire started to peter out, Daryl Wright was making out with Julie Jamison and Erik Vanguard was with Shannon Harper. Winston Marshall tossed another log on the fire and set off down to the river for a swim. He made his way through the woods and ended up on the riverbank where he stripped down and dove in. The water was a bit chilly, but it refreshed him. Still buzzing from the booze and Oxy, he felt good. The moon glimmered brightly off the water and he swam for a bit before heading back to shore.

With no towel, he simply put on his undershorts and pulled on his boots. Taking his pants and shirt in his hands he started walking towards the Big Rock. Everyone knew about the Big Rock. It was a giant bolder standing six feet tall on the bank of the river. Teens would climb on it and party all the time, and they could dive off into the river when it got too hot during the summer months. It was always a cool place to hang out and Winston felt it would be the perfect place for him to dry off and hit his flask for a bit more booze. He even contemplated taking another hit of Oxy.

Off in the distance he spied the Big Rock and could see the silhouette of someone sitting atop it. As he came closer, he saw it was a girl. Getting closer still, he realized it was Megan Miller.

He called out, "Hey there lil' Miss, what ya doin' out here all by yerself? Where's yer boy Chad?" He climbed up on the rock and saw she had been crying. "Aww, what's with the tears, girl?"

Megan shook her head and tried to smile, as she wiped away the tears with both her palms. "We broke up. It's over between us."

"Really? Is there someone else?"

"Yeah. Yeah there is."

"That's too bad." He took out his flask, opened it, and motioned it towards her. "Here, have a sip. This'll cheer ya up."

Megan took the flask from Winston, drank deeply and started to cough. Winston laughed, "Whoa, easy there, girl. Save some fer me."

Looking oddly at him, she said, "Why are you in your underwear?"

"Went fer a swim. You should try it. It'll make ya feel better. C'mon, get naked and let's go fer a skinny dip."

"Nah, it's a little chilly. Besides, I'm not taking my clothes off in front of you."

"Why not? All the other girls were showing their tits at the bonfire. You got nothin' to hide."

"Yeah, well, I'm not like the other girls."

"No, that's true, you ain't. But, I tell ya what, you could probably use another dose of the Oxy. How about you show me your tits and I'll give you another one, on the house. Ya know they're good, and they'll get ya outta yer slump." He grabbed his jeans and reached into the back pocket. "Even better, it'll hit ya faster if we snort it. Lemme show ya." He pulled a pocketknife out of the front pocket, opened it, placed the pill on the flask and ground it up. Then he brushed the powder onto his knuckle and snorted it. "Ahh, there ya go. Now show me yer tits and I'll set one up fer ya." Megan eyed the flask, looked up at Winston, who was practically drooling, and took off her shirt.

Winston quickly ground up another pill. "Bra too, Missy."

She reached behind, unsnapped her bra, and lifted it off. "You better not tell anyone at school about this, Winston, you hear me?"

"I sure do. Lips are sealed. This is just 'tween us."

He brushed the powder onto his knuckle and offered it to Megan. She held one nostril with her index finger and snorted deeply with the other. "Whoo!" she yelled, "That burns."

"That it do, but give it a minute. You'll feel fine. And ya know what, why not chase it with another pill." He took another one out of the vial and offered it.

Megan took it and swallowed it down with another hit from the flask.

"Yeeha, girl, you gettin' yer party on! Now, how's about lettin' me feel those sweet titties of yers?"

"That wasn't part of the deal, Win. You can look, but you better not touch." She giggled.

"Man, oh man, well, how's about takin' care of Junior here?" He placed his hand on the front his shorts.

"That ain't happening either. I'm not that kinda girl."

Winston shook his head. "Well alright, let's just sit here fer a spell and let those pills kick in. Maybe then you'll change yer mind."

"You know, you're a horny boy. Is that all you think about?"

"You bet." Winston grinned and took another hit from the flask. "I like pretty girls, and you're so fine."

"Thank you, but it's not going to get me to have sex with you."

"Hell, I ain't askin' fer sex, just a feel fer me and a squeeze from you. I swear, I won't tell."

"Just keep your hands to yourself and we can sit here and look at the moon."

"Damn, you're a lil' tease, ain't ya."

The two bantered back and forth for a bit and Megan started feeling warm all over. The pills started kicking in and she wanted more. She looked over at Winston, who was staring off over the water. "Hey, Win, gimme another one of those pills and I may let you touch me for a second."

His head spun around so fast it made a pop. "Now yer talkin.'" He reached for the vial again. "And let's snort it," she said.

Winston quickly chopped up two more pills and they snorted them both.

"Now let the fun begin," he said, reaching out to touch her breasts. She pushed her chest forward and looked up at the sky. Winston fondled both breasts for a few seconds, then Megan pulled away.

"I said a second, so that's all you get."

He cursed under his breath. "Tease. So how about you givin' Junior a few strokes then? It's only fair."

"Why don't you just take care of yourself? Isn't that what you boys do, anyway?"

"Hell no! I ain't got no time fer that. Besides, with a hot Missy like you sittin' here next to me with her tits hanging out, it's only natural that you take care of me. Junior is aching right now, show a lil' mercy on him."

"I'll tell you what, show it to me, I'll give it one squeeze, and then you have to stop bothering me about it. I'm not going to finish you off. That's your problem."

"Sure thing, Missy," he said, as he stood and pulled his shorts down.

Megan reached up and gave Junior a squeeze. "Now I know why you call it 'Junior.'"

"Hey, what's that supposed to mean?"

"Just kidding. But it does look kinda small." She giggled.

"Bitch!"

"Hey, don't get nasty with me. I was just joking. Besides, you're the one who wanted me to squeeze it."

"Well now, ya better finish me off."

"Not happening. Now put that thing away before you hurt yourself."

"You're pushing your luck here, girl. Teasing me forever, then leaving me high and dry? How am I supposed to be a man if ya keep me from being one."

"You're no man," said Megan. "Your thing's too small to be a man. Maybe a boy." She started laughing at her joke.

Winston was furious. "Yeah, well. I'll show you I'm really a man."

"And how are you going to do that?" Megan asked between chuckles.

"You owe me, and I may just to take what I'm owed."

"Don't you dare!" exclaimed Megan, her voice turning serious.

He reached out and grabbed her by the hair. She slapped Winston hard across the face. Then she took her shirt and stood up. "That's it. You need to leave."

"Why you lil' bitch!" He raised his hand to hit her, but she cringed and started to cry."

He hesitated, thought better of it, and lifted her bra from the ground. "Ahh, you just ain't worth the trouble. All into it then suddenly not into it. You're just a confused kinda girl. Don't know how to please her man. But I'm keepin' this as a souvenir of our time together. You owe me that." He jumped off the rock and started walking into the woods. Stopping, he called back, "I may just have to come back when ya come to yer senses and realize we could be havin' some real fun here tonight. There ain't no one else around and we really had something going 'tween us, ya hear."

Megan thrust up her middle finger and sat back down to cry. Overwhelmed by too much Oxy flooding her system, she stretched out on the rock and eventually drifted off to sleep.

19

After a two-day break, Sawyer's head had cleared and she was able to locate Travis Conrad. He hadn't moved far from Rainbow River, so she coordinated with Mason to go together and see if he could shed any new light on things.

A thirty-minute drive brought them to an isolated log cabin in the woods. Tucked away at the end of a dirt road, there weren't any other cabins in sight. They made their way towards the small structure. Travis opened the door before they even reached it. Tall, broad, and tattooed up and down both arms, he had an imposing look about him.

"This is private property. I don't entertain solicitations," he said as he turned away. "Wait, Travis, don't you recognize me? I'm Chad's sister. You saw me at his parole hearing. Don't you recall?"

Travis spun around and gave Sawyer the once over. "Yes, you do look familiar." He looked accusingly at Mason. "So, who are you?"

"The name's Mason Walcott, I'm a friend of Sawyer's."

"So why the hell would you come all the way out here?"

Sawyer said, "I wanted to ask you some questions about the night Megan Miller was murdered. I'm looking into it because I believe Chad didn't commit the crime. I've spoken to a number of the kids who were there that night and you were on my list. I'm hoping you'd be willing to talk to us."

"I really don't have much to say. I testified in court and they didn't believe me."

"May we come inside and just talk for a bit?"

"Sorry, but I'm a very private person. I live alone and I don't take visitors. You can do your talking right out here."

Sawyer frowned and turned to Mason, then immediately refocused on Travis. "Very well. I'll make it quick."

"That suits me just fine." Travis put his hands on his hips and stood imposingly. He was tall, about six foot three and quite stocky.

Mason focused on the hat Travis wore but said nothing. He needed to wait until he was alone with Sawyer to tell her.

"So, what can you tell me about that night?"

Off-putting, Travis said, "Why don't you just ask me what you want to know. If I have an answer, I'll give it to you."

"Fine. What can you tell me about the OxyContin that was handed out to everyone that night?"

Travis laughed deeply. "So, you found that out. I'm impressed. Everyone agreed not to squeal. Winston didn't want to get in trouble with his dad, the sheriff, and the rest of us didn't want to get in trouble with our parents either. You know how fathers are."

That hit a nerve for Sawyer. "Actually, I don't," she said to herself.

"So, everyone took the pills?" asked Mason, trying to keep Travis talking.

"Yep, and Chad took a bunch of them. We were doing shots of tequila and vodka and the girls started flashing their tits, then Winston suggested that they make out with all of us, 'cause we won the game. It was about then that Chad and Megan took off."

"Do you recognize me?" Mason asked.

Travis squinted and looked closely at Mason. "Never seen you before in my life."

"Well, I was there that night. I was Sandra's date."

Travis twisted his face up and stared at Mason. "I remember Sandra had a guy with her, but I can't say it was you. She and her date also left the bonfire pretty early."

"That's true, we did. And what about you, when did you leave?"

"I hung out by the fire for a while, made out with a couple of chicks, copped a feel or two then high tailed it out of there."

Sawyer asked, "So, when did you run into Chad."

"Pretty much after I left the bonfire. I was headed to my car. My head was spinning from too much drinking, and those pills. When I got close to the parking lot, Chad showed up. He was coming from the river. He told me he wanted to leave, and I was ok with that, so we left and went back to my house. We were both spent and passed out in my room. That's about all I remember. So, if that's all, you can be on your way."

Sawyer blurted out, "Why did you stop visiting Chad? He told me to tell you to go fuck yourself for abandoning him."

"He did, huh. Well, that does sound like him," he laughed. "You can tell him that I just don't have the time to keep visiting some loser who's gonna spend the rest of his life in jail."

"So, why did you go to the parole hearing then?" she asked.

"Honestly, I don't know, maybe it was a false sense of loyalty. Maybe I was hoping he'd get paroled. Maybe I just wanted to see what he looked like. Fact is, I gave up on him long ago, but something inside me told me to go anyways."

"Do you think he was guilty?" Sawyer asked, snidely.

"You know, that's an interesting question. At the time, no, not at all. And I testified that he left with me, but, as I said, they didn't believe me, or maybe they thought he killed her before he ran into me. I don't know. But the one thing I do remember was the DNA. Once that came out at the trial, everyone figured Chad did it."

"Well, did my brother ever tell you how he got the scratches on his face?"

"He said that when he and Megan were getting all hot and heavy by the water, she accidentally scratched him. I had no reason to doubt that. He'd had girls before. But when I thought about it afterwards, it did seem kinda strange. I mean, what girl scratches her boyfriend's face when they're pumping fur?" He lifted his cap off and scratched his head. "Anyways, are we done here?"

"So, you don't know for sure," Sawyer challenged, "but you don't seem to care if Chad was wrongfully convicted?"

"Like I said, it's been a long time, my life's changed a lot over the years, and I just can't go back there anymore. So, if you'll excuse me, I've got things to do." He turned, pushed open the door and shut it hard behind him."

Mason said, "He's a real prize. What a piece of shit."

"You can say that again."

"He's a real prize. Wh—"

". . . Ok," said Sawyer, chuckling. "I got it."

As they walked away, Mason said, "Did you see it?"

"See what?"

"The cap."

"The cap? What about the cap?"

"FSU! Florida State University."

"So?"

"So, I don't believe in coincidences. I think we need to find out if he went to FSU."

"Mason, you can't be thinking that Travis killed Sandra? He might be a piece of shit, but he hardly fits the profile of a killer."

"Look, I admit, it's a stretch, but it's something to look into. I mean, he's a big, strong guy, he could have easily overpowered her."

"Yeah, but why? What's his motive?"

"No clue. But let's see if he even went there first."

When they returned to Mason's SUV, Sawyer pulled out her phone and placed a call to Nelson Vasquez, the A.D.A. from Tallahassee. She asked him to look into Travis Conrad and see what, if any, connection he had to Florida State University.

20

Sawyer's cell dinged. She received an anonymous message that said: 'I have vital information for you about the Rainbow River murder. Meet me at eight pm in the Rainbow River parking lot at the end of Watts Creek Road.'

The message caught her off guard and she immediately felt that it was some sort of a trap. She didn't want to go without backup. She checked the time, it was seven-fifteen pm, so she had forty-five minutes to get there and she lived twenty-five minutes away. She called Mason, but he didn't pick up. So, she left him a message telling him to meet her there. As an added precaution, she took out the .22 caliber pistol she recently purchased, checked to make sure it was loaded, and placed it in her purse.

Fifteen minutes later she was on her way. She tried Mason again, but still no answer. *Where could he be? Why isn't he picking up?* She left another message.

The first leg of the ride took her up a steep hill. Once she turned onto Watts Creek Road there was a steep drop down. As her car accelerated, she pressed the brakes to slow down. The pedal went down to the floor. She tried pumping the brakes, but it was useless. The car kept accelerating downhill. She knew instinctively that if she didn't veer off the road fast, her car would be going much too fast, and if she hit something, she'd be dead.

Bracing herself, she turned off the road and ran over high grass and foliage before hitting a tree. The airbag didn't deploy and the seat belt didn't lock so the impact propelled her forward. She hit her head on the steering wheel and lost consciousness.

Seconds later, another vehicle drove past and kept going.

Mason got out of the shower, exited the bathroom, and checked his phone. He listened to the message from Sawyer, dressed quickly, and headed out to the river. It was seven thirty pm and he was twenty minutes away. He raced along the road and made it to Rainbow River before eight. The parking lot was empty. He called Sawyer, but she didn't answer. He left a message that he was already at the lot, but no one was there. He waited another ten minutes and decided to head up Watts Creek Road in the direction of Sawyer's place.

It was already almost completely dark outside, but the full moon glowed and lit the sky. Halfway up the road, he spotted Sawyer's car pressed up against a tree. He jumped out and raced to the door. He saw Sawyer. Her face was bloody and she was unconscious. The door was locked. Mason grabbed a large rock and broke the rear passenger window. He reached in and unlocked the door.

"Sawyer! Sawyer!" he called out. "Are you okay?!"

There was no response. He leaned in and gently pushed her head back against the headrest. She was still unconscious. In a panic, he called 911, reported the crash, and his location. He was told it would be at least twenty minutes. That wasn't fast enough, so he undid her seatbelt and carried her to his SUV. He strapped her into the front passenger seat and raced off.

As he drove, she began to come to. Shaking her head, she said, "Where am I? What happened?"

"It's okay, Sawyer, you were in an accident. I'm taking you to the hospital."

"I'm bleeding, my head's killing me. My chest hurts real bad. I think I broke some ribs."

"You'll be okay once we get there. Just stay calm and don't strain yourself. We'll be there in a few minutes. Try not to speak."

She started coughing up blood. She whimpered and began to cry. "I'm dizzy, my brakes failed, I couldn't slow down."

"Okay, we're almost there. Just try to stay calm." He reached out and put his hand on her knee and squeezed it.

Minutes later he pulled into the Emergency Entrance at County Hospital. He raced inside yelling for a stretcher. Attendants came out and rushed to the car. They lifted Sawyer out and wheeled her towards the entrance.

Mason ran alongside, shouting, "She was in an accident, please help her!"

Once inside, they took her for X-Rays and Mason was left behind to speak with hospital staff. A call was placed to the police, and a short time after two officers arrived and took Mason's statement. He explained how he found her and that he brought her to the hospital, but he didn't know how the accident happened, other than that she said her brakes failed. Once finished, he sat down in the waiting room. The officers headed to the scene of the accident.

Hours later a doctor entered the waiting room and approached Mason. Mason jumped up, "How is she? Is she going to be alright?"

"She's going to be okay. She's resting now. Looks like a concussion and three broken ribs, so she'll need to stay here for a few days for observation."

"Can I see her?"

"She's asleep, we gave her some pain medication. She should wake up in a few hours."

"Okay, thank you. I'll be back shortly." Mason headed out to his car and back to the scene of the accident.

He arrived to find the two officers he met earlier talking with a tow truck operator. Sawyer's car was already on the flatbed.

Mason approached the police cruiser and joined the men. "So, what happens next?" he asked.

"We're taking the car to our garage to examine it," Officer Delfino said, looking at the tow truck driver. "We really can't tell what caused the accident from here."

Officer Murphy turned to face Mason. "How is the girl doing?" asked Officer Murphy.

Mason shook his head, "She has a concussion and broken ribs, but the doctor said she'll be okay."

"That's good news," said Officer Delfino. "From the damage to the car, she could have been hurt much worse."

"Well, the car has airbags, I wonder why they didn't deploy?" asked Mason.

"We will have everything checked out and prepare a report."

"How long will that take?"

Officer Murphy said, "A few days, at least, you'll just have to be patient. Oh, and one more thing, we found Sawyer's pocketbook in the car, and there's a pistol in it. Any idea why she would be carrying?"

Mason hesitated before answering. "Well, she's an A.D.A and her apartment was vandalized a few weeks ago, so I imagine that she had some safety concerns and decided to protect herself."

"Sorry, but we have to confiscate it, until she can produce a carry permit."

"Excuse me, Officer, but, as I said, she works for the government. She's an A.D.A. I'm sure she has a permit."

"We looked through her pocketbook, and the glove box, and no permit. She's not above the law, and as an A.D.A. she should know that if she's carrying a gun, she has to carry the permit." He handed the pocketbook to Mason. "And we will need to speak with Sawyer when she is able to talk."

"Understood, I'll check with her and get back to you. Can you give me your number and the location of the station where you're taking her car?"

Officer Murphy handed a card to Mason. "We'll be on our way now. I suggest you get some rest. We'll stop by the hospital tomorrow to speak with her."

Mason pulled out his own card and handed it to the officer. "Please call me if anything else comes up. I'm going to head back to the hospital."

21

Officers Murphy and Delfino arrived at the hospital at 11:00 a.m. the next morning. Mason was sipping a cup of coffee and Sawyer had just awakened. She was still in a lot of pain.

Officer Murphy said, "Good morning, Ms. Greer. We have some questions for you. Are you able to respond?"

After a short silence, she reached for the bed control and raised up the back. Wincing, she said, "Yes, please, ask away. You need to get to the bottom of this."

"Do you remember what happened last night?"

"I do. I received an anonymous text regarding a case I am working on and was asked to meet at Rainbow River."

"We will need to see that text."

"It's in my phone." She looked over to Mason who got up and retrieved her pocketbook. He handed it to Sawyer. She pulled out the phone, unlocked it and located the text. She handed the phone to Murphy. Murphy read the text aloud.

"Ok, please continue."

"So, I got dressed and headed over to the river. As I started down the hill on Rainbow River Road, my speed picked up and when I applied the brakes to slow down, the pedal went right to the floor. I tried pumping the brakes, but they just didn't work. I was afraid

I would not be able to slow down, so I turned off the road and ran into a tree. That's all I remember."

"And you were wearing your seat belt?"

"Yes, I was."

"May I ask you, why were you carrying a pistol?"

"Well, I had an incident a few weeks ago, and I was afraid for my safety, so I bought a gun."

"Okay, and do you have a carry permit?"

"Uh . . . no, I hadn't had time to take the course. I intended to, but I had a lot going on."

Mason interjected, "She was afraid for her life. Someone broke into her apartment." Looking at Sawyer, Delfino said, "Unfortunately, that's not a legal excuse. And as an A.D.A., I'm sure you're aware of that, as well as that the law requires you to have a carry permit in your possession when you carry a firearm."

Sawyer nodded. "I am aware, but why are you focusing on that, rather than looking into what happened to my car. As you know, the airbag never deployed, and my seat belt shoulder restraint never locked up. To me, this sounds like I was set up. Someone must have done this to my car."

Mason said, "Not only that, but I went to Rainbow River to meet Sawyer and whoever it was that sent the text, but no one ever showed up."

"I see," said Delfino, "but that doesn't absolve you of the crime of carrying a firearm without a carry permit. You know it's a felony, and punishable with up to five years in jail."

"Wait a minute, are you actually telling me that your visit here today is to charge me with a crime?"

"We're just doing our job, ma'am. Equal treatment under the law. Now I'm going to read you your rights." Delfino proceeded to read Sawyer her rights. He then reached for his handcuffs, took her wrist and handcuffed her to the bed rail.

Sawyer was incensed. "You've got to be kidding me. I was almost killed. Someone clearly sabotaged my car. I'm in the hospital and you're focusing on a gun possession charge!" she shouted, "This is ludicrous!"

"The law's the law, Ms. Greer."

"Okay, who put you up to this? Did Arthur Crenshaw tell you to charge me?"

"Ma'am, no one tells us our job. It's quite simple, you had a firearm illegally in your possession. And we are officers of the law required to enforce it, and when we see a violation, we must proceed accordingly."

Mason said, "That's bullshit. Apparently, there *is* something else going on here. What you're doing makes no sense, and we will get to the bottom of this."

"Be that as it may," said Delfino as he turned to Sawyer, "you're not to leave this hospital, and once you are well enough to go, we must take you down to the station, formally charge you and then you'll have to be arraigned in court. You know the drill, Ms. Greer."

Sawyer was flabbergasted. "Fine, I want to speak with my lawyer. I have nothing more to say to you, so please leave. In fact, get the fuck out of my room!"

As the two officers were leaving, Murphy said, "We will be checking with your doctor to see when you'll be well enough to travel. Then we will return to take you in."

After they left, Mason came close to Sawyer and took her free hand. "It'll be alright, I can't imagine that this could be so serious. So *what* if you had a gun? You didn't hurt anyone. I mean, you didn't even threaten anyone with it."

"It doesn't matter. The law is pretty clear about carrying without a permit. I've prosecuted a few of those cases. They are correct, although there are some loopholes which I will research again, but beyond it all, I know I'm being set up. This is coming from much higher up. If not Crenshaw, then someone connected to former Sheriff Chuck Marshall."

"So, what can you do about this?"

"Well, I would certainly like to know what they find when they examine my car."

"Yes, agreed, at least that will prove that you *are* being set up."

"Let's just hope they do an honest job. In any event, I'm definitely going to need to have someone who's on my side go over the car."

"Absolutely," Mason bobbed his head. "Do you know someone?"

"Yes. I have a close friend who is a mechanic. But first, I am going to need to get an attorney who can work that out." She managed a flat smile, "And I know just the one."

22

A.D.A. Nelson Vasquez was eager to dig into the Sandra Payne cold case. Armed with the lead that Sawyer Greer had given him, he paid a visit to the Registrar's office at Florida State University. He felt that an in-person request would result in a more expeditious response. While he waited for an assistant to come out and speak with him, he was overcome with emotion, as he recalled his days as a college student there. It had been a great four years, he loved the University, had made many good friends in his fraternity, and remembered the great weekend football games when the 'Noles played at home. It brought him a warm feeling and he couldn't help but smile.

A short time later, Nelson was met by Frances Simmons, a grandmotherly type with shining silver hair and a soft, warm complexion. Her smile matched Nelson's when she greeted him. "Hello, Mr. Vasquez, what can I do for you today?" She thrust out her hand to shake his. He reached out and met her halfway.

"I'm with the local District Attorney's Office. Something has come up regarding an old cold case. I was wondering if you could provide me with some information on a particular person, tell me if he was a student here, and anything else you might be able to tell me about him."

"Well, I'd be glad to help, come with me into my office. I can access student records going back quite a few years. Can you tell me about when this person may have been a student?" She guided him down the hall, and, once inside her office, she offered him a chair.

He sat down. "Thank you. It would have been around 2005. His name is Travis Conrad." Ms. Simmons walked around the desk, sat and began punching the keys on her keyboard. "Hmm, let me see." She watched as the screen started filtering through the program trying to locate the correct year. "Here it is, Travis Conrad. Yes, it looks like he did attend the University. He started here in 2005 and graduated in 2009. Oh, and look at this, he also played basketball for our team."

"Really, can you print all that out for me?"

"Certainly."

"And does your computer tell you anything else about him? His grades? His major? Perhaps if there were any incidents, or trouble he may have caused."

"Give me a minute." She fingered her keyboard again, clicking away with determination.

Nelson smiled eagerly, grateful that he had someone willing to help make his job a little easier.

"Any information you can provide would be greatly appreciated, so take your time, there's no need to rush."

Smiling back, she waited for the screen to reload. "Okay, so he graduated with a 3.4 average, and majored in Communications. Nothing here about any problems. No issues listed here. He did play basketball all four years, and even received a few awards. Apparently, he was quite good."

"I see. Now, is there any way to tell if he ever missed any games, or if he was ever injured?"

"I wouldn't have that information. I suggest that if you are looking for information about his playing record . . . perhaps the library will have some news articles for the dates you are interested in. You could also try the Sports Center, maybe have a talk with the staff over there. They might be able to get you a roster."

"Okay, well you've been very helpful, I think I'll do just that. In the meantime, can you print me the info you've found."

"Of course," she clicked the keyboard again and in seconds her printer started chattering.

Handing Nelson the papers, she smiled again, "I hope this helps with what you're looking for."

He nodded, "I'm sure it will. Thank you, ma'am."

Nelson headed off to the library, and when he reached the large and imposing doors, he had to take a pause. He was ever thankful for the scholarship he had received, because he would never have been able to afford the tuition. His parents had no money to help either. Coming from a very poor upbringing, he always knew that he would have to work hard and struggle to become successful, and it was the schooling he received that got him to where he was today. He had spent many grueling hours in the library studying to succeed, and to make his parents proud.

He knew his way around the library. He immediately located a row of computers and sat down. Access was no problem, and he quickly found the publication 'Noles 247' which reported game results, standings, and all manner of campus sport information. He input the dates he was looking for and found that the Seminoles played an away game at Notre Dame the weekend of Sandra Payne's death. He noted further that they lost the game, and that the loss may have been due to Travis Conrad being injured and unable to play. He printed the article and began thinking more about what Sawyer Greer had suggested. Armed with these new facts, and the fact that Travis Conrad knew Sandra Payne from High School, he felt they may be on to something. Now he needed to find out if Conrad attended the away game, or if he stayed back on campus that weekend. He also needed to find out whether Conrad lived on campus, and, if so, where? Also, he needs to find out who Conrad's roommate was.

Nelson continued his investigation on campus, visited the Sports Center, spoke with staff there and was provided with a roster for the basketball team for the weekend of the Notre Dame game. He then returned to the Registrar's Office and met with Ms. Simmons for another chat. She happily gave him Travis Conrad's housing and his roommate's info as well.

Having obtained all the information he needed, he set off to his office, eager to delve deeper. He also looked forward to a conversation with Sawyer Greer. He felt confident that he was on the right track, and excited at the prospect of solving his first cold case ever.

23

Sawyer spent the next day recuperating and slept most of the time. When she finally felt up to it, she placed a call to her friend and mentor Xander Van Buren, Esquire. Van Buren was a prominent criminal defense attorney in Saint Petersburg. When she attended Stetson University College of Law, she worked for him and learned the tools of the trade at his firm. He was well-regarded and well-respected in the legal community. Even though his office was a few hours away, she knew he would be at her side in an instant.

Van Buren had just completed a week-long trial and his client was acquitted. Proud of the verdict, he didn't concern himself with whether his client had actually committed the crime. But, rather, it was of the utmost importance to him that he did his job effectively.

Sawyer called while Van Buren and his staff were celebrating the victory. His secretary put the call through right away.

"Hey Sawyer, it's been a while. How are you doing?" Van Buren asked.

"Not well, Xan. I need your help."

Van Buren couldn't see the pained expression on her face, but he noted the tone of her voice and immediately took her off speaker phone. "What's the matter? Are you okay?"

"Honestly, I'm not, and it's a long story."

"Well, you've got my attention."

"Okay. I'm sure you remember that I told you about my brother Chad being wrongfully convicted."

"Yes, of course."

"Well, I attended his parole hearing and after he was denied parole, I began investigating the case more closely, to see if I could find sufficient evidence to reopen it."

"And?"

"And I was able to uncover quite a bit of suspicious activity surrounding his conviction. I won't go into all that detail now. But, suffice it to say, I still believe he is innocent, and even more so now because someone just tried to kill me."

Alarmed, Van Buren jumped up from his chair, "Are you serious?!"

"Someone, perhaps more than just one person, doesn't want me prying into the case. And a few days ago, my car was sabotaged. The brakes were compromised, as well as the airbag and the shoulder restraint on my seat belt." She paused and took a breath. "Anyway, I lost control and crashed the car into a tree. I'm in the hospital right now."

"My God. How badly are you hurt?"

"A few broken ribs, and a concussion, but I should be fine. I was lucky." She took a deep breath. "And it gets worse and more suspicious. You see, I was carrying a pistol."

"What, why would you have a gun?" Van Buren was becoming increasingly more concerned.

"I bought it for protection, after someone vandalized my apartment."

"Sawyer, this is sounding crazy."

"It is. That's what I'm trying to tell you. So, now get this: I never obtained a carry permit, and I had the gun with me when I crashed. When the police searched the car after I was hospitalized, they found it in my purse. Now, instead of focusing on the sabotage of my car, they want to arrest me for felony possession of a gun without a carry permit."

"That's ludicrous."

"Yes, they have me handcuffed to my bed in the hospital, and they intend to arraign me as soon as I am able to leave here. And while I'm not sure who is putting these officers up to this, I have my suspicions."

"Sounds to me like this thing is getting out of control. I can be up there first thing tomorrow. In the meantime, don't speak to anyone. Let me do the talking. I'm sure you know that, of course."

"Of course . . . and thank you."

"Don't thank me yet. Sit tight. Text me the name and address of the hospital you're in, and I'll see you tomorrow."

Sawyer's next call was to D.A. Arthur Crenshaw. And, while she heard what Van Buren said, she didn't intend to listen to him completely. She was so furious, she felt compelled to call her boss and have it out with him.

"Hello, Arthur. It's me, Sawyer."

"Hello, Sawyer, are you sure you want to be talking to me?" He rolled the phone from his left hand to his right, switching ears at the same time so he could write down anything she said. "I mean, for now, you and I are on the opposite sides of a case. Your case, to say the least."

"You're a real prick, you know that? Do you really think you can make a possession charge stick?"

"Hold on, Sawyer. You've got this all wrong. This is not my doing. I'm caught in the middle here. The police brought me your case, and if I don't pursue it, it will look like favoritism. I can't look the other way simply because you work for my office. It would make me look bad and I can't afford to have anyone trying to undermine my office and the good work we do here."

"Please, Arthur, I'm in the hospital. Someone tried to kill me. My car was sabotaged."

"That remains to be seen. I havn't received any information with regard to that yet. Your car is still being examined."

"Come on, aren't you getting a little suspicious by now? Ever since I started looking into my brother's conviction, my apartment has been vandalized, my car sabotaged, and my investigation thwarted every time I think I'm getting some valid evidence of a cover up."

"We've been over this already. You are out of control. I think you're losing a grip on reality, and perhaps you shouldn't have been driving that night. Could it be that you simply lost control of your car."

"That's bullshit and you know it. What about the text I received, telling me to meet and talk about the case?"

"You could have sent that to yourself with a burner phone. The officers said there was no way to trace the call, it came from a blocked number."

"So, you really think I'd make up a text? Then what? Go out and intentionally crash my car? Are you out of your mind!"

"Look Sawyer, I really don't know what to believe. But for now, you are suspended again, and you'll need to turn in your badge and keys. Once you're arraigned, we will figure out where to go, but I am leaning towards dismissing you."

"What! This is so unfair. Either you're hiding something that you're aware of, or you're being used by someone who is. And I'm going to get to the bottom of this, with or without the help of your office. I want you to know, I've retained Xander Van Buren to represent me, and I intend to enlist his help to continue the investigation of my brother's conviction."

"Van Buren, huh, your former boss?"

"That's right, and you know his reputation. He won't stand for any of this crap you're pulling."

"I'm shaking in my boots. Goodbye Sawyer."

Despite his aggressive posture with Sawyer, Crenshaw felt bad and even had his own suspicions. He didn't actually believe that Sawyer set herself up, but he was being pressured and did not want to risk compromising his office. Still, he had always been a man of good moral conviction and was not corrupt. He was simply thinking about protecting the sanctity of his office and the men who used to run Rainbow River. It was a small town and word got around. If he were to uncover wrongdoing by the former sheriff, or his former boss, it could open up a can of worms that might bring him down too. After all, he worked the Megan Miller case as a young A.D.A. and if that case were overturned, it would open the door to other criminal defense attorneys to question any other cases he or his predecessor worked on. The way it worked, one bad apple could spoil the whole bunch, which meant that he'd be looking at revisiting, and defending any other case they worked on for the past decade or two. That kind of scenario would limit how many new cases the office could investigate. It might even end his career. Not a result he wanted to think about.

So, rather than dealing with that prospect, he was leaning towards looking the other way, despite Sawyer's predicament. He did, however, want to know if her car was truly tampered with, so he took a ride to the police garage to speak with the men charged with examining it.

He walked in and saw Sawyer's car on a lift. A rail thin mechanic was working beneath it. "Good afternoon. I'm D.A. Arthur Crenshaw. Can I talk to you about this vehicle?"

The man turned to face him holding a wrench in one hand and a rag in the other. He wiped sweat from his greasy forehead and stared at Crenshaw for a few seconds. "I was told not to talk to anyone 'bout this car, so gimme a good reason why I should be talking to y'all?"

"Well . . . Dutch," Crenshaw focused on his name tag, "Since I'm the D.A. in this county, and I'm the one charged with prosecuting the case involving this car, I'm the one you *must* speak to."

"You got a badge sayin' so?" Dutch moved away from the car and over to a tool cabinet.

He threw the wrench into a drawer and began wiping his hands with the rag.

Crenshaw pulled out his badge and showed it to Dutch. Dutch smiled, showing a missing front tooth. "Oowee, so you really is da man. I'da figured you fer much bigger."

"I beg your pardon."

He held up his still dirty hands. "No offense, sir. Just sayin' is all."

"Okay, Dutch, enough with the games, are you going to talk to me about this car, or do I have to find your boss?"

"No, it's all good. Whad'ya wanna know?"

"Okay, so I was told the brakes failed and that caused the crash. Is that what happened?"

Dutch started shaking his head very quickly. "Nah, nah, ain't nothin' wrong with these here brakes. They all good."

"Really, and what about the airbag? Any idea why it didn't deploy?"

"Can't rightly say 'bout that. Sometimes shit just happens."

"Well, what about the seatbelt shoulder restraint. Any idea why that didn't lock up and hold the driver back?"

"That's been checked out, too. Nothing wrong there at all."

Crenshaw walked under the car trying to appear as if he knew what he was looking at. He scratched his head and looked around, then came out to face Dutch again. "Are you the one who will be preparing the report?"

"No, sir. That'll be my boss, Clete Boyer. He ain't here right now, but he'll be back after lunch."

Crenshaw pulled a card from his pocket and handed it to Dutch. "Give him my card and tell him to call me as soon as the report is finalized. And ask him to hurry it up. We have an arraignment coming up shortly."

"Will do, Boss. No sweat." He reached up with the rag and wiped his forehead again.

24

Mason sat with Sawyer in her hospital room watching the news. The newscaster droned on about the border crisis and asked the guest what the Administration intended to do about it.

Sawyer groaned, "Please turn that off. If I hear another news story about the border, I'm going to lose my mind."

Mason took the remote and clicked off the TV. "Other than that, how are you feeling? Do you think you're ready to get out of here?"

"I do, and I don't. I know that as soon as I am able, I'm going to be arraigned. And I don't want to face the prospect of that embarrassment . . . in my own courtroom yet." She rolled her eyes.

"I get it. So, you said your lawyer should be here this morning?"

"Yes, any time now."

"And how do you know him?"

"I worked for him during law school. He's a brilliant attorney and I trust him implicitly."

"Great. I'm looking forward to meeting him."

"You'll get your chance," Sawyer said, pointing toward the door.

Xander Van Buren entered, smiling, carrying a briefcase. Tall and handsome with dark hair, a chiseled chin, and blue eyes, he looked forty but was actually closer to fifty. He bent over to Sawyer and kissed her forehead. "Well, well, you don't look so bad. How do you feel?"

"Getting better. My ribs still hurt," she said as she reached down, touched her side and winced in pain. "But I'm healing."

Van Buren turned towards Mason and shot out his hand to shake, "Good morning. I'm Xander Van Buren. How do you do?"

"Hi, I'm Mason, Mason Walcott." He came out of his chair, stood and shook back. "Nice to meet you." He looked back at Sawyer who had a strange, enamored look on her face.

Focusing back on Sawyer, Van Buren said, "Would you like to speak with me in private? As you know, if we speak with Mr. Walcott in the room, there is no attorney-client privilege."

"Yes, I realize that."

"And it is important to maintain that privilege."

"Agreed. Mason could you give us some time alone." Sawyer smiled at him and looked away.

Feeling immediately like an outcast, Mason stood, visibly concerned, said nothing, and left the room, closing the door behind him.

"Sorry about that, Sawyer. I don't think he was too happy."

"Don't worry, he'll get over it."

"Boyfriend?"

"No, just friends. We only met a few weeks ago when this whole mess started."

"I see, well . . . and this is just my own observation . . . but I suspect he thinks you two are closer than you think. Or at least he wants to be closer."

"It remains to be seen. I've been too wrapped up in what's been going on to focus on romance right now."

Van Buren sat down and took out his iPad. "Right, okay. So please, tell me everything that's happened since this all began. And don't leave anything out."

Sawyer proceeded to tell him everything that had transpired over the past few weeks, leaving no stone unturned. She detailed her suspicions about former sheriff Marshall and her boss D.A. Arthur Crenshaw.

As he clicked away, making notes on his iPad, Van Buren said, "I've dealt with Crenshaw before. He's generally a fair guy, but when he gets his mind wrapped up in his position, and takes things too personally, he loses his perspective. That's when I can crush him. I would be surprised to learn, though, that he's corrupt. Maybe misguided, but not corrupt."

"I agree, but as you can imagine, if it turns out that his office, whether during his tenure or during the prior D.A.'s tenure, committed an actionable offense, and wrongfully prosecuted my brother, that will create a landslide of problems with previous cases, etc."

"Yes, I get that. And I know his old boss, Cole Hanratty, well, even before he was the D.A. here. I first encountered him down in Tampa when he was a defense attorney. Now that guy would make slime look like shoeshine. I never trusted him. He played dirty in court, and whenever he could get away with it, he would. I remember him representing the worst kind of rapists and drug dealers. He got off on getting them off. Then he switched teams and started with the D.A.'s office up here. His reputation preceded him, hence the nickname 'The Rat.' Only a rat would crawl through the gutter looking for loose change. An embarrassment to the legal profession. I can only hope that one day I hear his name bellowed out by Stacey Keech. I wouldn't doubt for a minute that he would prosecute someone whom he knew to be not guilty, or to let someone go whom he knew to be guilty. For 'The Rat,' the world is just a corpse he chews at."

"He sounds lovely. I think he may be the one putting pressure on Crenshaw."

"I wouldn't put it past him, that's for sure."

"So, how are you going to proceed, Xander?"

"Frankly, it's a bogus charge. Based upon what you've told me, not only do we have a defense based on illegal search and seizure, but the gun was in your purse, which was zippered closed, so I can use that to satisfy the "securely encased" exception under the statute."

"Sounds good to me. I'll leave it to you to get in touch with Crenshaw and have him arrange to have me escorted to the arraignment. I want to get this over with so I can focus back on my brother's case."

"Okay, I'll head downtown to court, file my Notice of Appearance, and meet with Crenshaw to coordinate. Just be prepared to have to post some kind of bail."

"Bail? Really?"

"Look, Sawyer, they can't let you off easy. Because you are an A.D.A., they'll try to make an example of you. Otherwise, every defense attorney around will use your case as an example. So be prepared for Crenshaw to act tough on you."

Sawyer held up her hands and shrugged. "This is so wrong, but I get it. Go work your magic." As Van Buren exited the room, he passed Mason in the hallway carrying a cup of coffee.

"She'll be alright, Mason. I'll handle everything in court. I won't let them take advantage of her."

Mason offered a flat smile. "Thank you." Moving past Van Buren, he hurried back into Sawyer's room.

Shaking his head and thumbing at the door, Mason said, "Are you sure about this guy, Sawyer?"

"Absolutely. Why?"

"I don't know, he just looks like a real slick suit."

Sawyer laughed, and then groaned in pain, waiving her hand at him. "Oh please, he's fine. I've seen him in action in court. The man is awesome. In fact, he's already got our defense laid out. I just have to be ready to post bail."

"Really? Bail, why?" He handed the coffee to Sawyer and sat down.

"Appearances. The D.A. can't show any favoritism."

"Wow. That sucks. But you won't have to go to jail?"

"I doubt that."

"Whew, okay, good." Mason smiled, a thought occurring to him. "I am just a little sad, though. I keep picturing you in pinstripes, sitting on my lap."

"If you keep going down this road," said Sawyer, raising her coffee, "you're getting some of this on your lap."

"Ouch," said Mason, falling back into a chair and grabbing his heart, mocking fake death.

Sawyer laughed.

25

Xander Van Buren wheeled Sawyer into the courtroom for her arraignment, flanked on each side by Officers Murphy and Delfino. *As if she were planning on fleeing the jurisdiction.* D.A. Arthur Crenshaw was waiting at his usual table. The courtroom was effectively empty. Both sides wished to keep things quiet, so the Press wasn't there. It was set up intentionally as a late proceeding, after normal court hours. It was 5:00 p.m. and once Sawyer was in place at the defendant's table, Judge Terrence Atkinson was announced by the bailiff. He entered and took his place at the bench.

Judge Atkinson said, "Okay, let's go on the record. Case number 462/2023, People vs. Sawyer Greer, on for arraignment. Ms. Greer, you are charged with carrying a concealed firearm in violation of Florida Statute section 790.01 and related sections. How do you plead?"

Sawyer said, "I plead 'Not Guilty' Your Honor."

"Very well, I'll now hear Mr. Crenshaw on bail recommendations."

Crenshaw rose and addressed the court. "Yes, Your Honor. Arthur Crenshaw for the People. As you know, Ms. Greer is an Assistant District Attorney with my office. She has been in your courtroom numerous times, and she is well aware of the law, in fact having prosecuted a number of gun possession related charges during her tenure with my office. She knows the law and should have known better than to commit this offense. An example must be set here, or we risk backlash from the general public as well as defense attorneys who appear here on a regular basis. We ask that bond be set at fifty thousand dollars. Thank you."

Judge Atkinson turned to the defense table. "Do you wish to be heard?"

Van Buren stood, adjusted his tie, and buttoned his suit jacket. "Yes, Your Honor. Xander Van Buren on behalf of the defendant, Sawyer Greer. As counsel has said, Ms. Greer is a member of the Bar, she works on behalf of the government as an A.D.A. She is not a flight risk, poses no harm to the community. This is her first offense. She resides locally, and as you can see, she is presently wheelchair bound. Moreover, her car is in the possession of the Sheriff's Department and has been totaled. She is not a threat to flee the jurisdiction. Mr. Crenshaw is showboating here. No bail should be required, so I ask that Ms. Greer be released on her own recognizance. R.O.R. is warranted here. Thank you."

"Any rebuttal, Mr. Crenshaw?"

"No, Your Honor."

"Very well. Taking into account the arguments on both sides, it is the decision of the Court to set bail at ten thousand dollars. Ms. Greer shall be held until such time as bond can be posted."

Frowning, Sawyer grabbed Van Buren's arm. He leaned in as she whispered, "It's going to take until tomorrow to get that from the bail bond company. I don't want to be incarcerated. Is there something that can be done? I don't feel safe."

Van Buren rose, "Excuse me, Your Honor, the defendant requests that she be isolated and not put in with any general population of prisoners. After all, she is an A.D.A."

Crenshaw blurted out, "Not for long."

"That was uncalled for, Mr. Crenshaw." Van Buren protested. "And she will have bond posted by tomorrow morning. It would be unsafe and imprudent to keep her with other prisoners. She is an officer of the court. She has prosecuted criminals who may be incarcerated there and her safety would be jeopardized."

Judge Atkinson said, "I am in agreement, Mr. Van Buren, and so I direct that she be held in a holding cell at the Sheriff's Office until bail can be posted."

"Thank you, Your Honor. I have another request."

"Yes, please proceed."

"It is my intention to immediately file a motion to have the evidence in this case suppressed and that the case be dismissed as well. The defendant's rights were violated, an illegal search and seizure was conducted of her vehicle, and the fruits of that search formed the basis for this action."

Interrupting, Judge Atkinson said, "That will be enough, Counselor, save your arguments for your motion. Now is not the time. This is simply an arraignment."

"Yes, Your Honor. I simply wanted to advise the Court and get a scheduling set up."

"That is fine. Prepare your motion for submission and serve it on the People. We can set it down for a week from today for me to review. If I am satisfied with the papers, I will render a decision. If not, I will call for a Hearing in Court. We are adjourned." The Judge banged his gavel, rose, and left the courtroom.

Sawyer turned to look behind her and smiled grimly at Mason, the only other person in the courtroom, other than the two arresting officers.

He leaned in and said, "I'll have the bail bond handled before noon tomorrow. Don't worry."

As the officers came beside her to wheel her out of the courtroom, Van Buren patted her hand, then leaned over and kissed her on the cheek. Mason looked on from behind, then turned and walked out.

Nelson Vasquez phoned Sawyer to discuss what he had uncovered about Travis Conrad. The call went directly into voicemail. Sawyer's battery had run out and the phone was in her purse being held at the Sheriff's Office. He left a message and then called Mason.

"Nelson Vasquez here, Mr. Walcott."

"Hello, Nelson. Please call me Mason. What's going on?"

"I tried reaching Ms. Greer, but she didn't pick up. So, I figured I would call you."

"Yes, she is otherwise detained. So, what have you found out?"

"Well, for starters, I think you two are correct about Travis Conrad. It is looking very suspicious to me, but I have some more I need to check on before I can say for sure."

"Okay, so tell me what you've found so far."

"Right. So, as it turns out, Conrad did attend FSU during the time in question. Not only that, but he played on the basketball team."

"Wow, that's a coincidence."

"Yeah, but it gets better. You see, while the team, along with Sandra Payne's boyfriend, played at Notre Dame the weekend of the murder, Travis Conrad was on the injured list and didn't make the game. Well, let me correct that. He didn't play, and it appears from the news clips that he was not on the bench with the rest of the team. I am still trying to run down his roommate to see if he in fact stayed on campus that weekend. Assuming he did, that makes it even more suspicious. Of course, without more, we don't have enough to indict him, but at least we have a viable lead. That's better than anything we've had over the past decade or so. And, frankly, it's enough for me to get my boss to let me run with the case and continue turning stones."

"That sounds promising. I'll make sure to let Sawyer know. And please keep us both in the loop."

Mason's wheels started spinning and he had a gut instinct that Travis murdered Sandra. He wasn't going to sit idly by waiting for stones to be turned. He suspected Travis all along, and this only confirmed what he had been thinking. Now, he intended to confront the man himself. He figured that if he could get Travis to talk, it might help Sawyer with her brother's case as well. And, since Sawyer was tied up for the moment, he was free to take the ride and surprise Travis with an unexpected visit. He no longer possessed a gun, but he did have a military knife, and he was very proficient at hand- to-hand combat, so he felt confident he could handle Travis, and make him talk. And he intended to use all necessary force.

The drive to Travis Conrad's cabin took Mason less than thirty minutes. He hid his SUV off the road and walked the last half mile on foot. When he arrived, there was no vehicle around. After checking the cabin and barn to make sure no one was home, Mason surveyed the grounds, becoming familiar with the layout of the property, the surrounding woods, and the structures themselves. Once he felt comfortable with his surroundings, he climbed through an unlocked window in the cabin and began searching it. He wasn't sure what he was looking for but felt the need to look anyway.

The cabin had only one bedroom and one bathroom. It was relatively clean and well-kept. In the main area, which was a kitchen and living room set up, a flat screen TV hung on one wall, the second wall housed a fireplace, and the two remaining walls incorporated the kitchen. A table and chairs separated the kitchen from the living room and a couch cornered the TV and fireplace. There were no pictures or other objects of sentiment anywhere in the space, except for two basketball trophies from Florida State University, which were prominently displayed on a shelf above the fireplace.

Mason rummaged through the kitchen drawers and cabinets, searched through the bookcase that stood beneath the TV, and checked out the types of books Travis read. Many of them were survival type instructional books, doomsday prep magazines, NRA magazines, hunting and sports magazines. Under the bed in the bedroom, Mason found a loaded rifle and hunting gear. He took the rifle with him and went out to the barn to check it out. Inside, he found a workbench with mechanic's tools and tools for the yard. Parked in the corner was an X-Pro 4 Wheel ATV. He admired it for a few seconds, then went back and sifted through the tool cabinet. He found nothing of consequence, so he exited the barn and headed back towards the cabin. It was almost dark and as he reached the cabin wall, Travis appeared from around the corner and swung a shovel at Mason's head.

Mason was able to partially block the blade, but it hit him hard enough for him to lose his balance and drop the rifle. He rolled onto the ground, and as he stood, Travis took another swing at him. Mason grabbed the shaft of the shovel before it hit him and pulled it from Travis's hands. Travis kicked him in his side and Mason went down again, but quickly regained his footing. He threw a wild hook and hit Travis on the side of his head. Travis stumbled backwards but didn't fall. Mason charged him and the two grappled and wrestled to the ground.

Travis was bigger and stronger than Mason, but Mason was skilled at hand-to-hand combat. He rolled Travis on his back and shoved his forearm underneath Travis's throat. Travis reached up and grabbed at Mason's face, scratching him and drawing blood. He barely missed clawing Mason's eye, but it was enough to get Mason to lose his positioning and Travis was able to roll him.

The two squared off and Mason yelled, "Hold it Travis, I just want to talk!"

Travis screamed back, "Talking is overrated. You broke into my home and stole my rifle. So, I have every right to kill you where you stand!"

Mason pulled his knife from its sheath and brandished it. Seeing Travis eyeballing the rifle, he shouted, "Don't even think about it!"

Travis dove for the rifle and grabbed its muzzle. Mason jumped on Travis and dug his knife into Travis's thigh, but only grazed him. Travis screeched in pain and released the gun, but managed to roll over and kick Mason in the head. Mason fell backwards and lost his grip on the knife.

The two were on their feet again and faced off. Stepping forward, Mason threw a jab and followed with a right cross that connected and sent Travis backward. He stood strong, raised his hands and assumed a boxing stance. Mason mirrored him and the two began feigning and throwing blows at each other.

Travis had a much longer reach and had clearly trained in self-defense. He threw a combination and finished with a leg kick to the head that took Mason by surprise. Mason was rattled, never expecting Travis to be so skilled in martial arts. He shook the cobwebs from his head and backed up.

Travis laughed, "Come and get it little man, you're going down." He grinned, extended his arms, raised his palms, and motioned his fingers inward in challenge. In a crouch, he began stalking Mason, looking for an opening to attack.

Mason took a fighting stance and raised his guard. He moved as Travis circled closer. They parried again, but this time Mason was cautious and played defense. He blocked the next flurry of punches and avoided a rear leg kick, but Travis was smooth and moved quickly. Despite the leg wound, he managed to connect with a hook to Mason's jaw. Mason went down on one knee. Travis saw the opening and spun another leg kick to Mason's head. Mason fell over and was out cold.

Travis picked up his rifle and went into the barn to retrieve some rope, but when he came out, Mason was gone. Travis caught a glimpse of him running off deeper into the woods behind the barn. He raised his rifle, shot off in Mason's direction and called out, I'm coming after you, and when I find you, you're a dead man. Then he laughed, as he looked down and saw Mason's car keys in the grass where they had been fighting. He picked them up and ran back to the barn to retrieve his ATV.

26

Sawyer brooded in her cell as day turned into night. The wheelchair was gone. She no longer needed it. In fact, she hadn't needed it in court. Van Buren had merely used it as a prop. She could stand and walk around without any trouble and paced for a time before finally laying down on the bottom bunk of the bed. A Sheriff's Deputy appeared on the other side of the bars carrying a tray with a meal and water. He opened the cell and handed it to Sawyer.

Sawyer said, "Thank you, but I'm not quite hungry right now." She placed it on the top bunk and laid back down.

"It won't stay warm for long, ma'am." He closed the cell door. "Better eat it while it's hot." She ignored him and eventually drifted off to sleep.

An hour later, she was awakened by the sound of the cell door opening again. A young woman was escorted inside. Dressed in tight, colorful spandex and a revealing top, her profession was obvious.

Sawyer said, "I'm supposed to have this cell alone. What's going on here?"

"Sorry, ma'am, but we only have two holding cells here, and the other one has two men in it, so she has to be put in here with you."

After the Deputy left, the woman stared Sawyer down, "You got a problem wit' me, bitch!" Sawyer was taken aback, "Excuse me, I wasn't trying to insult you, it's just that . . ."

"It's just nothin' Ms. Fancy Pants. You ain't no better'n me. So ya got nice clothes on, big whoop. You still behind bars. Whad'ya do? Drive drunk in yer Benz?"

"Please, I meant no offense. I'd just like to go back to sleep now. It's late, and I'll be getting out in the morning."

"Yeah sure. Me, too." The woman spied the food tray on the bunk. "Hey now, if ya ain't gonna be eatin' that, I'll let it slide, if ya let me have the grub."

"Help yourself." Sawyer said, as she lay back on her bed watching as the woman took the tray and devoured the food with her hands. She didn't bother even unwrapping the utensils that came with it. She twisted off the cap to the water bottle and guzzled, dripping water down the sides of her mouth. Sawyer was disgusted but tried to ignore it.

When she finished, she climbed up on the top bunk, spread herself out, burped loudly, farted, and giggled.

Sawyer thought to herself, *This is what my life has become. What did I do to deserve this?* She tried to fight off the tears that welled up in her eyes, but to no avail. Finally, she fell back asleep and didn't wake up until morning.

She rose from the bed and looked at her cell mate who seemed to still be sleeping. However, on closer inspection, she realized the woman wasn't breathing. She called out for help, and a deputy raced in, shouting, "What's going on here?" He opened the cell door.

"She's not breathing."

"Did you do something to her?"

"No, of course not, I went to sleep last night and just woke up to find her like this. She needs a doctor. Call 911. Do something!"

The deputy raced out of the cell, locked it, and called for help. Within minutes the area was flooded with police personnel and EMT.

The woman was pronounced dead at the scene.

27

Fifteen Years Earlier . . .

Sheriff Chuck Marshall arrived at Anthony and Audrey Miller's home after receiving a distressing phone call about their missing daughter. Anthony Miller answered the door, disheveled and visibly in a panic. "Sheriff, Megan didn't come home last night, but we didn't realize it until this morning." Looking at Audrey, he said, "My wife has been on the phone all morning calling her friends and their parents." He turned back to the Sheriff. "The last anyone saw her she was with her boyfriend, Chad, down at Rainbow River. The kids were there celebrating the basketball team victory."

Audrey, in tears, came up behind her husband and said, "Please, come in, Sheriff." She motioned towards the den. "I tried calling Chad's mother, Marion, but she never picked up."

The Millers walked into the den and stood by the window. The sheriff remained at the entrance to the den. Audrey stared at the ceiling and dabbed her eyes with a tissue. Anthony put his arm around her as she whimpered.

Sheriff Marshall said, "It'll be alright, I'm sure we'll find her. You know how kids are these days. Did you try her on her phone?"

"We did, and we left a few messages, but she hasn't returned our calls." She pleaded, "Please, you have to find her. She's our baby. She's only seventeen."

"Do you have a picture of her that you can give me?"

Audrey bobbed her head and walked out of the den, leaving the two men alone.

Anthony said, "Sheriff, my daughter is a very responsible girl, she always comes home at night, and Rainbow River is a safe place. I can't imagine what could have happened to her. I'm going to head over to the river as soon as we finish up here. My wife is a mess, and we can't just sit home waiting for Megan to show up. We have to do something."

Nodding, he said, "I understand, and we will get moving on this right away."

Audrey returned with a picture of Megan. The sheriff took it and looked at it closely. He placed it in his breast pocket and said, "Give me the names of the kids who she was with, along with your number. I will get my deputies involved and have them head over to the river right now."

Anthony moved over to a desk in the den and took out paper and a pen. "I can do better than that, Sheriff. I've got the names, addresses and phone numbers of all her friends in my phone. I always keep track of who my daughter shares her time with." He took out his phone and jotted down all the information he had stored in it. Handing it to the sheriff, they moved towards the door. Sheriff Marshall walked outside.

Anthony followed, and, turning back to Audrey, he said, "I'm going to go to the river, you stay here, in case Megan comes home."

Audrey nodded and closed the door. Anthony drove off towards the river.

Sheriff Marshall climbed into his cruiser and made a call to Deputy Rogan Gibson. "Marshall here, Gib. I need you to round up a few of the boys. We've got a missing person to locate. Her name's Megan Miller, teenager who was down at the river last night with a bunch of friends. Get over there ASAP and take a look around. I'll meet you there after I stop by her boyfriend's house. They were last seen together yesterday evening."

"Copy that Sheriff, I'll get on it right away."

Sheriff Marshall raced over to Chad Greer's home, less than ten minutes away. He knocked loudly on the front door. Marion Greer answered. Alarmed, she asked, "Is something wrong, Sheriff?"

"Mrs. Greer, is your son Chad at home?"

"Yes, he came home a few hours ago. What's going on?"

"May I speak with him?"

"Sure, give me a minute." She turned and called out to Chad.

Sheriff Marshall asked, "May I come in?"

She ushered him in as Chad came down the hall. Chad said, "What's the Sheriff doing here?"

"Hi Chad, we know each other from the basketball team. My son Winston plays on it with you. We've seen each other at some games."

"Yes, I know you. What's up?"

"Seems that Megan Miller is missing. You were with her last night, correct?"

Chad raised his eyes, "What? Missing? We were all at the river last night. Didn't she go home with the rest of the girls on the squad?"

"Apparently not. She never came home."

"Well, have you checked with her girlfriends? She's probably with one of them."

"Afraid not," Sheriff Marshall said, as he eyed the marks on Chad's cheek. "How'd you get those scratches?" he pointed.

Fumbling his words, Chad said, "Got that during the game yesterday."

"Really? Did you make the foul shots."

"Nah, the refs didn't call it."

"Hmm, well, when was the last time you saw Megan?"

Chad rubbed at the back of his neck, and wiped off beads of sweat that began to build up. "Uh . . . at some point last night we split up, she went back to the bonfire, and I took off with Travis. He's also on the team."

"Yes, I know him, too."

"Well, Megan's mother called all the girls, and none of them know where she is."

Becoming visibly concerned, Chad said, "Did you try her phone?"

"Her mom did. No answer."

"That's strange, let me get my phone. I'll try and call her."

Chad set off to his room. Sheriff Marshall watched as he walked down the hall, then turned to Marion. "Did he say anything to you about Megan today?"

Marion shook her head, "Not a thing. My goodness, do you think something happened to her?"

"Frankly, ma'am, we just don't know anything yet. That's why I'm here. I've got some deputies going over to the river to look for her, along with her father. But I can tell you this, her parents are very worried." He took off his cowboy hat. "How well do you know Megan?"

Concern spreading across her face, Marion said, "She's been over here many times. Chad's been dating her for a few months now. She's a sweet girl. I think the two are in love. You know how it is with kids. First romances and all."

He smiled, "Yeah, I do, but that was a long while ago for me, ma'am." He turned and looked around. "Say, is your husband home?"

"No, he works today."

"Whereabouts?"

"Home Depot. You know the one, up over in town."

"Yes, ma'am, I do." He rubbed the top of his head. "So, you said before that Chad had just come home a few hours ago. Do you know where he was? Did he sleep home last night?"

"He told me he slept at Travis's house."

"I see."

Chad reappeared holding his phone and calling Megan. "She's not picking up. It's going right into voicemail." He showed the phone to Sheriff Marshall.

He took the phone from Chad and re-dialed the number. It went straight to voicemail. He left a message for her to call him and left his number. He then put Megan's number into his own cell.

"Do you really think she's in trouble?" asked Chad, swallowing hard.

The sheriff put his hat back on, "We all hope not. I'm gonna head over to the river and join the search." He turned to leave.

Chad said, "Wait, should I go too?"

"No, you stay here. If anything comes up, I'll let you know."

"You sure? I mean, I know the river, and all the places we hang out."

"Trust me, son, I know the river better'n anyone. I've lived here almost my whole life. Been down to the river since I was a kid. I know all the hideouts, the Big Rock, and the Hollows, too. If she's down there, we'll find her."

Marion closed the door behind him and looked at Chad. "Did anything happen with you and Megan last night?"

"No, Ma. Why would you ask that?"

"Oh, I don't know, it's just that you didn't come home, she didn't come home. What did y'all do by the river?"

"We were just laughing it up and having a good time, just like usual."

"Were you drinking?"

"C'mon, Ma. We just won the game, of course we had some booze, but nothing too crazy."

"You know I don't approve of your drinking. You're only seventeen."

"Everyone drinks. And look at dad, he's plastered half the time he's here . . . when he's here. Maybe you should tell *him* to stop drinking?"

"That's enough from you. Don't go talking about your father that way. It's disrespectful."

"Whatever."

Marion gave Chad a quick slap on the cheek. "Don't you 'whatever' me. Your father's still your father. He raised you, right, wrong, or whatever, but he still raised you and you'd better show some respect, you hear?"

Rubbing his cheek, Chad moved back a little, then said, "I've gotta go call everyone and see if they know anything. I'll be in my room." He turned and ran off.

Sheriff Marshall met up with his team by the parking lot at the end of Watts Creek Road. They had already inspected the bonfire site, found some trash, beer bottles and empty tequila and vodka bottles.

Sheriff Marshall looked around, picked up an empty bottle of tequila, examined it, tossed it into the ashes and said, "Okay boys, lets spread out and see what we can find." He pointed at Deputy Gibson. "Gib, you come with me down to the Big Rock. That's where all the kids love to hang out."

Gibson followed the sheriff down the hill towards the water. "Did the Greer kid have anything helpful to say?"

"Nah, he says he left her with the other girls, and took off with one of the other boys from the team."

"Nothing suspicious?"

"Not really, though he had some scratches on his face. Said he got them during the game."

"A good kid?"

"Don't know him well, but he's a good ballplayer."

The men made their way to the rock and began searching. Deputy Gibson forced his way through growth behind the rock and shouted, "Over here, Sheriff, I've got a phone." He put on a latex glove and picked it up.

Sheriff Marshall came around to the back of the Big Rock, put on his own latex glove, and reached out, "Hand it over, Gib." He pressed the button, but it was locked. "Okay, let's bag it and keep looking."

A shout came from off in the distance. "Over here! I see a body."

Sheriff Marshall turned towards the voice and started running. Deputy Gibson followed. Downriver, they came upon a naked body washed up on shore. The sheriff went down on one knee and looked at her face.

With a look of dread, he stood, shook his head, took his cowboy hat off, and brought it to his chest. "Oh no, this is her." He reached down, picked up a rock and threw it into the water angrily. Looking at his men, he said, "This is terrible, but we've got to handle this right. Cordon off the area with tape and keep searching. Her clothes have to be nearby. Check upriver. And we need to get a Medical Examiner here." Turning around, he said, "Gib, call it in."

"I'm on it, Boss."

Sheriff Marshall looked back at the body and shouted, "Someone get me a blanket. We have to cover her up." He examined Megan more closely. Rolling her head to the side, he pointed and said, "Look at this bruise on the back of her head."

Gib kneeled over and nodded. "Bad news all around, Boss. It's looking like a murder. First one in five years, I reckon."

"Damn! What a fucking disaster!" The sheriff kicked at the rocks on the shore. Anthony Miller charged out of the woods screaming, "Is that Megan? Is that my baby?" Deputy Hunter held him back. "Please, you don't need to see this."

Trying to get past him, Anthony yelled tearfully, "I do! That's my baby! I need to see her." He pulled away and ran up to her body. He fell to the ground and reached out to touch her face. Sheriff Marshall pulled him back.

"I'm sorry, but you can't touch her. We need to examine her for evidence."

Sobbing, he cried out, "My baby, my baby. Nooo! This can't be. Please, no. It's not her. Tell me it's not her."

Hunter softly pulled him back and held him in a sympathetic hug. His body shook uncontrollably as he wept.

Sheriff Marshall looked back at the corpse of Megan Miller and thought to himself, *Could Winston have done this?*

28

"Sawyer's bond has been posted, Mr. Crenshaw!" Van Buren pounded the desk at the D.A.'s office. "You must direct Sheriff Bursey to set her free."

"I'm sorry, but I can't do that right now, and you know it. A dead woman was discovered in her cell. She was the only one in there, so we can hold her for forty-eight hours while we investigate the cause of death."

Van Buren paced in front of Crenshaw's desk. "This is unacceptable. I spoke to Sawyer, and I agree with her. The girl was poisoned. You may not know it yet, but you can't be that blind. The food was brought in for Sawyer, and she didn't eat it. The girl did. The next thing you know, she's dead. Put that together with Sawyer's car being sabotaged, and it's clear someone is out to get her."

"You don't know that for sure."

Van Buren stopped pacing, spread his hands on Crenshaw's desk, bent over and got as close as he could into Crenshaw's face. "You can't be serious, Arthur. Tell me you aren't the least bit suspicious of all the circumstances here. As soon as she started looking into her brother's conviction, her apartment was vandalized, her car tampered with, and her life threatened. Don't you see a pattern here? Or perhaps it's because you're involved?"

Crenshaw stood and shouted back, "That's ridiculous. I would never!"

"Yeah, well, then get her out of that cell. If they tried to murder her twice already, you know they'll try again. And she's totally unprotected. Anything can happen to her while in custody."

"Look, there's a complete autopsy being done, as we speak. As soon as the results come back, and if it turns out she was poisoned, I will have Sawyer released."

"That's not good enough. Every minute she's in that cell, she's in danger. And if you don't do something about this now, I'm going to go to the media. Rainbow River, and you specifically, will be plastered all over the news."

"You wouldn't!"

"Oh, trust me. I would, and I will."

"Look, it's out of my hands. The Sheriff's Office can hold her for the forty-eight without charging her, just on suspicion."

Van Buren thought for a moment. "Return her to the hospital. They can handcuff her to the bed, like before. When I was with her earlier, she was complaining about severe pains. I think she needs treatment."

Crenshaw nodded, "Ok, look, if you keep this quiet for now, I think I can arrange that."

"Do that, please. And hurry. I'm going to go back and wait with her."

As Van Buren stormed out of the office, Crenshaw phoned Sheriff Scott Bursey. "Sheriff, it's D.A. Crenshaw here. We have a serious problem." He took a breath as he stared at the crack on the ceiling above his desk. "The death of that prostitute is going to make for a lot of bad press, especially with you holding my A.D.A. on suspicion, with no evidence, no motive, and no probable cause. It also doesn't help that the girl was likely poisoned. You know that would raise holy hell for you."

Bursey got up and closed the door to his office. "I hear you, but what am I supposed to do about it? The autopsy isn't complete yet. I'm waiting on it, and I'm investigating to see who was on duty last night. I'm pissed off about this, too. I can't have my office being blamed for something like this. But what can I do?"

"Well, first thing, you need to get Sawyer Greer out of there. You know as well as I do that she didn't do this. But if you need to hold her for the forty-eight, or at least until the autopsy is completed, send her back to the hospital for observation. She's not feeling well, and is still in a lot of pain. You can justify it because of that, and you can still handcuff her to the bed. She won't be going anywhere. Meanwhile, you can continue looking into who had access to her food last night."

Deep in thought, Sheriff Bursey scratched the beard on his chin. And while his appearance could be imposing, he was possessed of an easy manner, coupled with a strong conviction for what was right. So, if there was any corruption in the Sheriff's Department, he would root it out, and crush it. But at the same time, he had to consider how it would look to release a suspect before gathering his evidence. Clearly concerned about showing favoritism to an A.D.A., he remained silent for a time, but finally conceded and said, "Alright Crenshaw, it makes sense. I'll arrange it."

Mason raced though the forest in no particular direction. He just ran as fast, and as far as he could, to escape Travis and his rifle. Finally, out of breath, he stopped and bent over, panting for air. He looked back, and off in the distance he heard the sound of a motor coming towards him. He remembered seeing an ATV in the barn. He shook his head and cursed. He knew he couldn't outrun it. Scanning around, he tried to get his bearings and figure out where he was in relation to the road, and the location of his SUV. Instinctively, he reached for the clip that fastened his key chain to his belt. It was gone. He cursed again and started running through deeper brush, and tighter tree formations, hoping the ATV couldn't make it through.

Travis had wrapped an old shirt around the leg wound and tied it tight. The cut wasn't deep enough to cause much loss of blood, and his adrenaline was flowing. He was in his element. Hunting was in his veins. Normally it was bear and deer, but he could certainly adapt to human prey, and it got him going. He even felt it in his groin. A sadistic grin played across his face. *This is going to be better than sex.* "Fuck yeah!" He yelled out, gunning his ATV as he fired his rifle skyward.

Mason heard the rifle shot. It was too close for comfort. It reminded him of his time in the Marines. He picked up speed, knowing his life depended on evading the enemy. He leapt over a large, dead, tree trunk that lay across his path and kept running.

Travis wasn't far behind. He managed to maneuver his ATV through, around and over all obstacles in his way. He launched himself above the tree trunk that obstructed his way, closing in on Mason. Once he had him in his sights, he stopped, jumped off, aimed, and fired, barely missing Mason, who was now only fifty yards ahead.

Mason ducked behind a tree. Travis shot another two rounds in his direction.

He called out, "I can see you cowering there, it's only a matter of time before I get you. Give up now and I'll end your life quickly and painlessly."

Mason took off again as Travis fired another round. He made it another twenty feet before stepping on a pile of branches that covered a hole. It was a bear trap of some sort, and at least fifteen feet deep. He fell in, twisted his ankle, and banged himself up a bit. But, considering the depth of the fall, he was lucky. He sat quietly for a few minutes while listening to the sound of the ATV coming closer, until it was upon him.

Travis leapt from his ATV and walked over to the hole. "I see you've found one of my bear traps," he laughed. "Most unfortunate for you. But it'll make my life much easier."

Mason called out, "Get me out of here. Let's talk about this, please."

"Nothing to talk about. You broke into my home, you tried to rob me, and I caught you."

"Fine, so call the Sheriff and have me arrested."

Travis guffawed. "I see you have a sense of humor. I wonder how long that will last, seeing as you're stuck in that hole?"

"Look, we can work this out, just throw me a rope."

"Not happening, dude. I think I'm just gonna let you die slowly down there. No food or water for a few days, that should do it. Then, I won't have to worry about being blamed for your death. In fact, I never even saw you here, you must have been wandering around and just fell in the trap."

"Why are you doing this?"

"Why did you come back to see me?"

"Apparently, you know why, Travis, or you wouldn't have attacked me."

"I attacked you because you were trespassing on my property."

Mason shifted around in the hole and rested his back up against the side. He looked up at Travis standing over the hole with the rifle pointed down at him. "I wasn't trespassing, I just wanted to talk to you about your time at Florida State University."

Travis bellowed, "Ahh, good old FSU. Brings back fond memories."

"Any about Sandra Payne?"

"You mean your former girlfriend?" he grunted a laugh.

Mason shouted, "You know exactly what I'm talking about. Why not just confess right now?

If I'm to die here, the least you could do is tell me what really happened to her."

"Perhaps I will, but not right now. I've got something more pressing to take care of." He held Mason's car keys over the hole, then gripped them tightly in his palm. "First, I need to make your vehicle disappear. See you later."

29

Sawyer was back in the hospital and Xander was sitting by her bedside watching as she devoured the burger and fries he brought her. Still chewing, she said, "Thank you so much for the food, and everything else. If you weren't in my corner, I doubt that Crenshaw would have let me go."

"Well, you *are* still in handcuffs." He patted her hand. "I'm just glad I could help. But, now that I know you're safe, I have to get back to my office and prepare your motion papers. I want to get this farce of a case dismissed as quickly as possible." He placed Sawyer's cell phone on the table beside her bed. "I think it's charged up enough for you to use it. Please stay in touch, and if you need me, just call."

"You're the best. Thanks again." She took a pause. "You know, it's strange that I haven't heard from Mason. I think I should call him."

"You do that. I'll touch base with you later." Xander smiled as he walked out the door. Sawyer put down her burger and called Mason, but it went to voicemail. She left a message, then checked her voicemail and listened to the one from Nelson Vasquez. She immediately called him back.

"Nelson, this is Sawyer Greer, I just received your message."

"Hi Sawyer, I'm glad you're getting back to me. I gave Mason some information yesterday. Did he relay it to you?"

"Mason?" she furrowed her brow. "I haven't spoken to him. What did you say to him?"

"That Travis did attend FSU, and he was even on the basketball team there. He also didn't play in the Notre Dame game the weekend that Sandra was murdered. And now, I do believe it was murder, and I am seriously considering that it was Travis who did it. You see, I was able to locate Sandra's boyfriend, who also played on the team. And he confirmed that Travis, not only didn't play in the game, but that he didn't travel with the team. He absolutely was not in South Bend, Indiana that weekend. So he clearly had the opportunity. And I can't imagine that everything we've learned is just coincidental."

Sawyer was nodding as he spoke. "Hmm . . . wow, this is all so crazy, but it's starting to make sense. Are you going to go after him?"

"Well, I've got a few more seeds to sew up here before we can secure a warrant, so let's chat again in the next day or so."

"Sounds good, and thank you. Now I've got to find Mason."

"What do you mean? Is he missing?"

"I really don't know. I've been dealing with some personal issues, but he didn't pick up when I called." She took a breath, "Whatever . . . I'm sure it's nothing. If I don't hear from him soon, I'll try him again in a little while." Hungrily, she grabbed a bunch of fries and stuffed them in her mouth.

Sawyer's phone rang. It was her mechanic friend, Brad Pawluk.

"I just finished going over your vehicle, Ms. Greer, and what I found is quite disturbing. From what I can see, it looks like someone tampered with the brakes. I'm thinking that whoever it was, drained the system of the brake fluid, so your brakes would fail, but then after the accident they refilled the system. There's fresh fluid in the master cylinder, and throughout the lines, so unless you recently had your brake fluid replaced, someone did a number on you."

"And you're sure of this? Because I haven't had anything done to my brakes since I've owned the car, and that's over three years ago."

"Well then, yes, I'm sure. That fluid is brand new."

"Wow, and so what about the airbag and the safety belt?"

"Those are a different story. I can't tell if they were tampered with, but the seat belt is operative now. As to the airbag, all the sensors are operational, but I can't tell if someone disengaged it and then reset it."

"I see, well, at least I know I'm not crazy, and someone did tamper with my brakes."

"That's for sure, ma'am. You best be careful. It sounds like someone has it in for you."

"Thank you, Brad. I'm looking over my shoulder all the time now."

Sawyer placed a call to D.A. Crenshaw. His secretary picked up and routed the call through to his office.

"Arthur, it's Sawyer. I just received a call from my mechanic, and he confirms that my brakes were tampered with."

Crenshaw shook his head rapidly, "That's not what the shop mechanic at the Sheriff's Department told me. I spoke to him and he swore up and down that the brakes were fine."

"Yeah, well then why is there fresh brake fluid in the system. My guy confirmed the fluid was brand new, and he surmised that someone drained the system, and after my accident, filled it up again with new fluid."

"I'll have to go back and speak with his boss."

"You do that," Sawyer said, firmly. "And since I have you on the phone, has the autopsy come back yet?"

"No, I'm still waiting on it, but so far, the forensics team has indicated that there was no poison in the water bottle, or in the leftover food on the plate."

"Well, I hope you know that I didn't do anything to that poor girl."

"I never thought you did, but we have to abide by protocol and procedures. Again, we can't show favoritism to anyone simply because of their position with the County."

"I get that, but shouldn't you be focusing on who is after me? I mean, it's clear that someone wants me dead, and out of the picture."

"Trust me, Sawyer, I am looking into that. I just need some time, and I have to do it quietly, but I have my suspicions."

"Finally!" She raised her fist in mock triumph, then winced in pain. "And so, if you believe that, then you have to consider that my brother could be innocent."

"Honestly, Sawyer, I feel terrible about what you've been going through, and I do think there is something suspicious going on."

"Well, I really need to get a look at the complete file, not just the tidbit you gave me the other day."

"I understand. I tell you what, I'll pull the entire file and bring it over to the hospital so you have something to do while you're convalescing."

"Thank you, Arthur, and thank you for getting me out of that cell."

Two hours later, Crenshaw arrived with the D.A.'s murder file. He sat down and placed it on the table beside Sawyer's bed.

"How are you feeling?" he asked, displaying a sympathetic frown on his face.

Sawyer tried to smile. "Well, considering what could have been, I guess I'm doing okay."

"That much is true." He gestured towards the file. "That should be everything. I'll leave it for you to go through." He rose and walked to the door, and asked the Sheriff's Deputy to come in and remove her handcuffs.

"What's going on Arthur?" she asked.

"The autopsy came back. The girl died of a fentanyl overdose. So, it's clear that you had nothing to do with it. What we don't know yet, is whether she was brought in having already ingested the drug, or if somehow it was put into the food."

"But you said the food was checked?"

"It was, but that isn't conclusive. It's highly doubtful, but it could have been sprinkled on the top and she just ate it. There wasn't much leftover food on the plate, so it's a dead end. But odds are she came in high, and died of a heart attack overnight."

"That's awful."

"Yes, and Sheriff Bursey is looking into it, he's reaching out to her friends to see if she was a user. Either way, you're in the clear."

"One down, and one to go."

"On that note, I'll be on my way. I'm headed over to see the lead shop mechanic at the Sheriff's Department."

30

Sawyer spent an hour going through the file before reaching for her phone and calling Mason. On the other end, buried in a small pile of leaves on the side of Travis Conrad's cabin, the phone rang where it had fallen during the scuffle. She left another message.

Mason had spent the last few hours trying to wedge himself between the walls of the hole and inch his way up. His efforts were futile as the walls were too far apart. He then took out his knife, which he had wisely picked up when he ran off earlier, and began digging foot holes in the wall, hoping he could use them to wedge his feet in and climb up. He stopped when he heard the sound of the ATV coming closer.

Travis returned, bent over and looked into the pit. "Gettin' comfy down there, dude?"

"Fuck you Travis. Get me out of here and we can pick up where we left off. You landed a lucky blow before, it won't happen again. I'll take you down."

"Now, now, little man. You're no match for me, but I have no intention of letting you out. But, I did do some more thinking while I was eating dinner. And I realized that moving your vehicle would only implicate me, so I left it where you hid it." He tossed the keys into the hole. "I don't think you'll be needing these, but they're better off with you than with me." Travis chuckled loudly.

"You won't get away with this." Mason shouted.

"I've gotten away with much more." He laughed again. "So, this will be easy."

"Really, then since I'm going to die down here, the least you can do is let me know what happened to Sandra . . . you owe me that."

Travis sat down by the side of the hole, took out his flask of tequila and sipped. "I don't owe you a thing, but it would be fun to tell someone after all these years."

"Good, so let's hear it."

Travis took another long swig from his flask. "Sit tight."

"Do I have a choice?"

"Still with the jokes, huh? Well, you won't be laughing much longer. You see, I had no *choice*, I had to kill Sandra."

"Why? What did she ever do to you?"

"It wasn't what she did to me, it's what she knew. But first, tell me why you're so interested? I mean, other than that she was your girlfriend, that is."

"Isn't that a good enough reason?"

"Not after all these years. Where was your concern when it first happened?"

"Frankly, I didn't know about it. We had broken up, and I transferred to college across the country, and lost touch. I didn't come back to Rainbow River until last year, and by then it was old news, no one was talking about it."

"So, why now?"

"You tell me what she knew, then I'll tell you why now."

"Sorry, dude, but I'm the one calling the shots, or did that go over your head?" He snorted a laugh. "You see what I did there?" He took another sip of tequila. "Having fun yet?"

"You're a real prize, Travis, you know that?"

"Whatever, but if you don't want to tell me why, I think it's time for me to go." He stood, opened his pants and began peeing into the pit while he laughed.

Mason stood and pressed himself against the wall to avoid getting wet. He shouted up, "Alright, quit it and I'll tell you."

"That's more like it." He shook himself off and closed his fly. "I showed you mine. You show me yours." He laughed again.

"I started investigating Megan Miller's murder because I became convinced Chad Greer was innocent."

"And what made you think that?"

"I remembered that night when Sandra told me Megan came up to her crying. She was alone, and when we left, we saw you pulling out of the river parking lot, presumably with Chad. So, he couldn't have done it."

"That much is true, we did leave at that time."

"And you even testified to that at trial."

"As I said, they didn't believe me. So, go on."

"Well, I started working with Sawyer to help her uncover what really happened, and as part of it, Sandra's death came up. I didn't believe she would commit suicide. I thought she was murdered. And both Sawyer and I suspected that the two deaths were connected."

"Ahh, I see. And so that's what led to your downfall." He chuckled.

"Okay, now it's your turn. Why'd you kill Sandra?"

"Wait, we aren't finished with Chad yet. What makes you think he didn't return to the river a little later on and kill Megan?"

"That, I don't know. Are you saying that's what happened? Did you come back with him? Did you help him kill her?"

Travis barked a laugh, "No, I'm not saying that, and no, I didn't help kill Megan. I just went home and passed out as soon as my head hit the pillow. I slept through the night and woke up with Chad in my room. But who knows, he could have slipped out while I was asleep, and did the deed."

"Makes no sense, what would his motive have been?"

Travis flashed an obnoxious grin. "That's the big question. Did he have a motive?" He took another sip, "He may have. Let me ask you this; did you know if Chad had a hankering for boys?"

"What? What are you saying? That Chad is gay?"

"I didn't say that. I just asked if you knew?"

"Stop playing games with me." Mason thought for a moment, "Wait, is that why Megan was crying to Sandra that night? She told me that it was something about you and Chad. Did she see something?"

Travis threw a few rocks into the pit. "You catch on pretty quick."

"So, you and Chad were . . . ? And you didn't want anyone to find out?" Travis remained silent. "And you thought Megan told Sandra?" Still no response from Travis. "But Megan never told Sandra, or she would have told me. Sandra didn't know, and you killed her anyway."

"Couldn't take the chance. It would have ruined my reputation with the basketball team. Work before play, after all."

"You sick bastard."

"You try living with something like that!" Travis exclaimed. "Besides, it's kind of funny how you wound up in my hole." He chuckled at his remark.

"I did *not* need that picture," Mason said to himself, trying to shake the mental image out of his head.

"See, you're not the only one who has a sense of humor."

"You think Chad killed Megan because she found out he was gay?"

"That's what I would've done, if I had done it."

"I really think we can talk this over," said Mason. "I was in the army, you know. I don't see color or sexual orientation. I just see green."

"Nice try," said Travis. "I'm going out of town for a few days, and by the time I return, I suspect you'll be dead. Then I can cover your ass with dirt, so no one will ever find you."

31

Fifteen Years Earlier . . .

She was wasted. She was sitting alone looking out over the river. The water shimmered against the glow of the moon. Megan Miller couldn't tell if it was fifteen minutes or an hour since she took off and left Chad. Frustrated with him because she wanted to have sex and he didn't, she just stomped away in anger. He said he wasn't ready for it, and when she tried to undo his pants, he had pushed her away. She couldn't believe he was turning her down, but she was very high and if she couldn't have sex, she really just wanted to be alone. She wandered around along the riverbank for a time before she set off back to the campfire.

As she walked through the woods, and up the hill, she discerned some movement ahead and followed the sound. Looking off in the distance she saw two figures, one kneeling in front of the other who had his pants down around his ankles. As she got closer, she could see it was Chad standing up and Travis kneeling down in front of him. Chad was groaning softly, and as Megan tried to get closer, she stepped on a tree branch, snapping it and making a loud sound. The two boys heard it, turned and could see Megan watching them. Chad quickly pulled up his pants and ran towards her. She started running, but Chad caught her, pulled her back by the shoulders and wrestled her to the ground.

She wanted to scream, but Chad covered her mouth. She writhed around trying to get loose. "Calm down, Megan. Please, I can explain."

Megan kept shaking her head from left to right, trying to break free, but Chad's grip was too strong. She reached up and scratched his face, drawing blood, then finally relented. Chad took his hand away from her mouth.

"Let me go," she cried out. "What were you and Travis doing over there?"

"Nothing, let me explain?"

"There's nothing to explain, I know what I saw."

"Please, you can't tell anybody."

"So, is that it? Is that why you didn't want to have sex with me?" Megan began to cry. "You told me you loved me. How could you do that? It's gross."

"Stop, it isn't what you think," Chad pleaded. "It's the Oxy. I don't know what happened. I lost control. You have to believe me. You can't tell a soul."

"Just let me go," she kept slapping his chest. "I can't look at you right now."

"Please, Megan. Promise me you won't tell anyone."

Through her tears she whispered, "Okay, but let me go, I can't be near you right now."

Chad released his grip and she took off. Travis looked on from behind a tree and followed her as she ran. She made her way through a clearing in the woods and as she got further up the hill and away from the water, she ran into Sandra Payne who was sitting on a large rock, waiting for Mason to return. He had taken a break from their make-out session to relieve himself in the woods. Shy about taking a leak in front of her, Mason had wandered off so he couldn't be seen.

Travis watched as Megan tearfully spoke to Sandra. He couldn't make out what she was saying, but when Mason reappeared, Megan had already gone and ran off towards the river. Travis, not wanting to be seen, quietly turned and went back to find Chad.

Mason said to Sandra, "Was someone just here?"

"Yes, it was Megan, and she was crying and said something about Chad and Travis, but didn't want to talk about it. She said she'd call me in the morning."

"Well, things are getting pretty weird around here. I think it's time we booked."

"Yeah, I agree."

Travis caught up to Chad near the parking lot and called out, "Wait up." Chad turned and watched as Travis ran up to him. Out of breath, Travis said, "She saw us. You know that, right?"

"She promised me she wouldn't tell anyone."

"And you believe her?" Travis's jaw dropped as he raised his palms to his cheeks. "I saw her talking to Sandra, then she ran off and her boyfriend showed up. We can't let her tell anyone. We'll be destroyed at school."

"Look, she promised she wouldn't say anything. Let's just get out of here and figure it out in the morning."

"Are you fucking kidding me? Do you realize how bad this could go for the both of us. I've got an FSU scholarship, you know. I've got a future. So do you. We can't let what she thinks she saw ruin our future. We should track her down."

"No, trust me, I know her. She'd be just too embarrassed to talk. We should just go."

"You had better be fucking right about this, Chad."

Travis's car drove off just as Mason and Sandra reached the parking lot. They watched as the taillights disappeared into the darkness.

32

Sawyer needed to get out of the hospital, and now that she had been freed, she made arrangements for a rental car and took an Uber from the hospital to pick it up. Once back home, she set her mind to going through the file in earnest.

She waded through the incidentals, flipping page after page, still unsure what she was looking for. Finally, she came across the full toxicology report and began to read. She made notes in her pad as she read along, until she reached a point in the report that talked about the cause of death. The report, written by Dr. Heather Kirk was very detailed, however, when Sawyer flipped to the following page, the language and typeface appeared to change, ever so slightly. And while the preceding page seemed to indicate that there may have been multiple, accumulated causes of death, the final conclusion zeroed in on rape, and blunt force trauma to the back of the head, apparently caused by the force of the rapist smashing Megan's head against a rock. The report also noted that the skin and blood found underneath her fingernails showed clearly that she struggled with her assailant. A footnote in the report indicated that a separate toxicology report, done after the fact, contained a DNA comparison that showed a perfect match to Chad Greer. That was the report Crenshaw had showed her previously.

Still troubled with the report, she began to wonder why there was no reference to the rape kit, or the DNA, which would have been extracted in the testing. She placed a call to the M.E.'s office and learned that Dr. Kirk still worked there. So, she made an appointment to meet with her first thing the next morning. She then called Mason. Voicemail again.

Growing ever more concerned, she decided to take a ride to his apartment. As she cleared the top of the hill where her brakes had failed, she was hit with a nauseous rush and her body began to shake. She pulled over to the side of the road. She took a few long, deep breaths, trying to overcome her fear, but the pain in her chest kept reminding her of the last trip she took downhill. She couldn't move and just sat there for a while, staring ahead as she relived the accident, over and over. Unwilling, or unable to put the car in gear again, she got out, knelt on the ground, and vomited. Still in pain, she rolled over, sat up and began to cry. It was then that she realized how much she needed Mason, and how she had begun to count on him. *Where was he?* she wondered.

Knowing that there was no one else she could call—Xander had gone back home . . . which was at least two hours away—she forced herself to get up and get back in the car. Once inside, she placed her hands on the steering wheel, gripping it tightly. Acknowledging her palms were sweaty, she wiped them on her jeans before reaching for the gear shift. Still shaking, she was finally able to put the car into drive.

Slowly, she returned to the road. Going downhill there was no need to accelerate, but rather, she kept light pressure on the brakes as she rolled downhill. When she reached the spot where she had crashed, she had to stop again and get out. She walked over to the fallen tree and surveyed the damage, thinking to herself, *poor tree, you didn't deserve to die like this. I'm so sorry.* She ran her hand across the downed tree trunk and sobbed again.

With much effort, she returned to the car and proceeded to Mason's apartment. Driving through the parking lot, she didn't see his SUV, so she made her way to his apartment and rang the bell. No answer. She knocked hard and called out his name. Still nothing. She went to the window and looked in but couldn't see anything. She tried calling him again. Voicemail.

Not knowing what to think, but feeling drained from the day she had, she returned home and went to sleep.

33

Sawyer awoke the next morning, anxious at the prospect of meeting with Dr. Kirk. She made some coffee, sat down and reviewed her notes before leaving for the M.E.'s office. Not leaving anything to chance, she took the entire file with her, still worried that someone might try to break in again. Once underway, she called Mason. Voicemail again. Worry had turned to dread, but she needed to meet with the M.E. first.

Upon her arrival, she was directed to Dr. Kirk's office. Now a seasoned professional, she had matured into a fine-looking woman who carried herself with a confidence that matched her position. She motioned to Sawyer, "Please, have a seat, Counselor, and tell me how I can help you."

"Thank you, Doctor. I'm here about an old case of yours, going back fifteen years."

"Oh my, that goes back a ways. I was just starting out then, and I've come a long way since."

Sawyer looked around the office. "I can see that," she smiled.

"So, to what case are you referring?"

She glanced at the doctor, then reached for her file and opened it. Handing the toxicology report to her, Sawyer said, "This is yours from a murder case where my brother, Chad Greer, was convicted, and remains in jail."

Her soft expression changed to one of realization. "You know, I knew your last name sounded familiar, I just couldn't quite place it." Nodding, she said, "I have a vague recollection of it. My first autopsy when I started working here."

"I see, well please take a look at the report and re-familiarize yourself with it. Then I'd like to ask you some questions."

Dr. Kirk took the file and began reviewing it. She flipped through the pages, scanning without looking in detail. "It's been a long time. I have a slight recollection of the matter, but the specifics don't come to mind. Perhaps you could jog my memory?"

"Of course. You see, when I went through the report I saw that you concluded that the cause of death was a blow to the back of the head, but there appeared to be other intervening causes. Also, I didn't see anything in the report about drugs, only that she had alcohol in her system. However, in my conversations with witnesses, I was told that Megan had taken OxyContin, along with all the other kids at the river that night. So, I was wondering why that never made it into the report?"

Dr. Kirk began flipping pages again, located the page she was looking for and read silently. "I'm beginning to remember this case now, and something doesn't make sense here." She rubbed her forehead. "Some of this writing doesn't appear to be my mine. And it appears as if there were changes made. I see lines eliminated from the report.

I do remember I made reference to a number of possible causes of death. She had overdosed on OxyContin, but none of that is reflected here."

"Are you saying that someone revised your report?"

Nodding, she said, 'It doesn't make sense, but yes. It looks like entire paragraphs were changed. You can even see the font is slightly different. I don't know who would have done that."

"Back then, did you have a boss, or superior, who reviewed your work?"

"Yes, I did. But no one would have changed it or eliminated facts. That would have been brought to my attention."

"So, you're saying that the report was altered without your knowledge or permission?"

"It appears so."

"Who was your boss back then?"

"That would have been Dr. Liam Cavanaugh. He hasn't worked here in a very long time."

"Hmm. Well, did you testify at the trial regarding your report?"

"No. That I remember. I was called out of town the day before I was supposed to testify. My mother had been in a serious accident. I went to see her in the hospital in New York. So, Dr. Cavanaugh took my place."

"Oh, how awful. Was your mother okay?"

"Yes. After a few months of rehab, she was fine. It was a hit and run, and they never caught the driver of the other vehicle."

Sawyer was deep in thought. "Pardon me for saying this, but it seems a bit of a coincidence. The timing and all."

"Well, at the time I didn't think so . . . but now, coupled with this report . . . are you saying? No . . . did someone intentionally alter my report?

"I know it sounds a little farfetched, but a lot of things have been strange ever since I started looking into this case."

"I really don't know how my report got changed, or who changed it" said Dr. Kirk. "Would your office have retained a copy of the original report?"

"Yes, of course. But it's been fifteen years. I'm not sure how long physical records are kept. I'd have to check the archives."

"Could you do that for me?"

"Sure."

"Another question. The file reflects that Megan was raped, yet there was no rape kit test results in the file either. Wouldn't there have been a DNA analysis?"

After a considerable pause, Dr. Kirk said, "There should have been. I recall one *was* done. But, if I remember right, there were issues with the DNA from the rape kit. I can't recall what they were. I definitely did put something about it in the report." She opened the report and looked it over. "But I don't see it here."

Sawyer's instincts kicked in and she realized she was on to something much bigger than she had originally thought. It didn't appear that mistakes were done, but rather, it was beginning to look intentional. She stood up and began pacing, then stopped, realizing what was going on.

"Your report was intentionally altered to make sure my brother *would be* wrongly convicted!" exclaimed Sawyer.

"This is sounding both crazy and plausible," said Dr. Kirk.

"You have to keep this quiet, Dr. Kirk. How soon can you check your archives?"

"I'll do it right away," said Dr. Kirk as she rose from her desk. "This might take some time, though. Please wait here," she said as she headed out the door.

Sawyer nodded, then reached for her purse and took out her phone. She tried Mason again. Voicemail. She then called Xander and relayed everything she had just learned, also voicing concern that Mason was missing. Xander told her he would head back to Rainbow River after he finished up in Court down in Saint Pete and completed his motion papers for her case. But it wouldn't be for a couple of days.

Twenty minutes later, Dr. Kirk returned. Her hands were empty, and the look on her face told Sawyer all she needed to know.

“I’m so sorry Sawyer. But there is no file in the archives. The clerk downstairs advised me that files are ordinarily held for twenty years. But, when I looked for where it should be, based on the year of closure, it was gone. I did note, however, that there were other files from the same year that were still on the shelves. I’m starting to believe your farfetched theory. Someone not only intentionally changed my report, but also removed the physical file. But, who would do this?”

“I can tell you right now, my suspicions revolve around former Sheriff Marshall.”

The doctor gave her a quizzical look as she walked around the desk, “Sheriff

Marshall? I don’t think he even had access to the file.”

“Well, I was told by some of the kids who were at the river that night, that it was his son Winston who gave out the OxyContin. So, my guess is that he covered up his son’s involvement, to protect him.”

A heavy silence followed. Then she breathed a dramatic sigh. “Jesus. I can’t believe my mother was nearly killed over a report.” She searched through her filing cabinet. “Back then we used an outside company to perform our DNA analyses. I will try to contract them and see if they have records of the testing from back then. I can use those records to recreate my report.”

Sawyer nodded, still sullen. “How soon can you do this?”

“I’m doing it right now,” said Dr. Kirk, as she picked up the phone.

“Thank you. Just be mindful about Marshall, I know he still has connections inside, so be careful, and please call me as soon as you get any information.” Her mind went back to Mason, “I need to take care of something else right now.” She stood, collected her file and turned to leave.

"Sawyer, you're not the only woman who's been taken advantage of here," she confessed softly. "I would never have trusted Sheriff Marshall, but I was young and didn't know this could happen."

"We were all very young back then," said Sawyer as she got up to leave.

Dr. Kirk dialed the number as Sawyer left the office.

34

 Sawyer returned to her car and called Mason once again. Voicemail. Dread turned to panic.

The only thing that made sense to her was that after receiving A.D.A. Nelson Vasquez's call he took it upon himself to confront Travis. She knew right then that she had to head up to the cabin and see, but she also knew that she couldn't do it alone. So, she called Vasquez.

"Nelson, it's Sawyer Greer. I think we have a problem. Mason has gone missing. Ever since you told him what you discovered about Travis Conrad, he's been off the grid. Something in the pit of my stomach tells me he went to the cabin to confront him."

"That does not sound good," he said. "But please don't think you can go there by yourself."

"I don't plan on it. I was just seeing if you secured a warrant yet?"

"No, I'm still looking for Conrad's college roommate."

"Can you do something for me?"

"I could question Conrad as a pretense, but it will take me three hours to get there."

"That would be great. In the meantime, I will see if the local sheriff can help us."

"Just promise me you won't go there alone."

"I promise, just hurry."

Sawyer called ahead to announce her arrival and quickly drove to the Sheriff's Office. She knew Sheriff Bursey from some of the cases she had worked on. And while she didn't know him well, she was confident that he was an honest man, unlike his predecessor, Sheriff Marshall.

Sheriff Bursey was anxious to speak with Sawyer and greeted her in the lobby. He led her back to his office. "How are you feeling?" he said with a compassionate tone evident in his voice. "That was some accident you had last week." He offered her a chair.

"It hurts a lot worse than it looks, but I've got more important things to discuss with you."

She proceeded to lay out in detail her meeting with Dr. Kirk and then quickly tied it all into Sandra Payne's murder, and then Mason's disappearance. Sheriff Bursey listened on intently, growing visibly angrier as Sawyer revealed all she had discovered.

"You're blowing me away with all this, Ms. Greer. I never would have suspected that Sheriff Marshall was capable of such corruption. You'll have to forgive me if I don't just accept what you're saying as gospel." The steel in his voice grew with every word.

"But you must agree there's substantial evidence. At least enough for you to look into this further."

He pointed at the file she held in her lap. "I'll need to get a copy of the toxicology report, and if Dr. Kirk is able to obtain the DNA and rape kit test results, I'll need to see those as well."

"Of course. But first we need to get up to Conrad's cabin right away" Sawyer pleaded.

At the risk of making her feel as if he didn't believe her, he said, "Before we race up there with no real evidence, why don't we try to track Mason's cell phone?"

Surprised, she said, "You have the ability to do that from here?"

Bursey smiled, "We've gone all high tech, Ms. Greer. All I need is his number and we can triangulate."

Sawyer provided Mason's number. Bursey got up and motioned Sawyer to follow him. She took up behind as he led her into a room with computers stationed in a row of cubicles. He handed the number to a staffer.

"Can you ping this number and get me a location?"

The staffer nodded, looked up at Sawyer and then turned to the computer and punched the keyboard with ferocity. The screen flashed and blinked through a series of commands until a grid map loaded. Minutes later, a red dot appeared on the map and Bursey leaned in to pinpoint the spot.

"Looks like a real remote area up about a half hour north of here. Not many homes there, just a few hunting cabins and a lot of woods and forest."

Sawyer practically jumped out of her shoes. "That's it! He's there. It's Travis's cabin. I was up there last week. We have to go! Right now! He could be in danger."

"Alright, calm yourself down. Let me round up a few deputies and we'll head up there. You can stay here."

"No way, Sheriff. I'm coming with you. I need to see Mason."

Bursey took her by the shoulders and stared into her eyes. Seeing the intensity, he nodded and said, "Fine, but if there's any trouble, you'll need to stay in the cruiser."

She bobbed her head and followed him as he went quickly into the pit and approached two deputies who were standing by a desk. It was the same two deputies who had handled Sawyer's car accident. Murphy and Delfino.

"Let's go boys, we're taking a ride up near Ocala National Forest. Hunting country. Missing person. You met him. The guy who called in Ms. Greer's car accident last week."

"Oh no, not these two. They arrested me for no good reason." She put up her hands and shook her head.

Delfino said, "No offense, ma'am. We were just doing our jobs."

Sheriff Bursey said, "It's fine, they're good men. Delfino's right, they had no choice. You had a firearm without a carry permit."

She grabbed Bursey's arm, "Can I talk to you in private, please?"

Bursey gestured to the men and walked off with Sawyer. "What's the problem?"

Sawyer whispered, "How can you be sure they aren't influenced by Marshall? They were very quick to arrest me."

Bursey laughed, "Trust me, I know these boys, been working with them for years now. They're solid. They weren't even around when Marshall was sheriff. No need to worry."

Sawyer clenched her teeth, "I hope you're right Sheriff."

"Okay boys, we'll take two cruisers, just follow us."

Murphy was dumbfounded. "She's coming?"

Bursey nodded, "That's right, Murph. Now let's get going."

"Copy that." He shook his head, turned, and followed behind.

35

Mason had been using his knife and digging notches into the walls of the pit. He wasn't making much headway, though. He had been able to get about five feet up, but with nothing to hold on to, he wasn't able to climb more than a few feet. Covered in dirt, he sat down to rest. He was weary, and with lack of food or water for almost two days, he didn't have the strength to continue. It was broad daylight, but he drifted off to sleep.

A half hour later the two vehicles pulled up to Travis Conrad's log cabin. It was situated at the end of a long dirt driveway and surrounded by deep woods that formed a semi-circular perimeter two hundred feet from the cabin and the barn that sat to the left of it. A small pond with clear water was located to the right, a hundred feet from the cabin. Leaves, hay and patches of St. Augustine grass littered the ground that surrounded the structures and ran up to the woods.

The three men exited their cruisers cautiously and sidled up to the cabin. Sawyer remained behind. Murphy went left around the cabin, Delfino went right, and Sheriff Bursey knocked on the door. They looked through the windows. It was empty. The three then headed to the barn and checked it out. Power and gardening tools were neatly stored on shelves and in racks along the walls. Bales of hay lay in one corner and an ATV was parked in another. No sign of Travis or Mason. They called out but received no response. Nothing seemed out of place.

Sawyer couldn't sit still and as the men exited the barn, she raced towards them. She was still fifty feet away when they reached the cabin. She held up her phone and shouted, "I'm calling Mason."

Sheriff Bursey was the first to hear it ring. He pointed towards the sound and found the phone hidden beneath some hay. He held it up.

Sawyer yelled, "That's his phone, he has to be here somewhere."

Murphy kicked at the front door, but it wouldn't budge. Both deputies began kicking at it and it finally broke open. They searched in vain while calling out for both men. The place was clean.

Murphy said, "No vehicles on the premises. It doesn't look good."

Sheriff Bursey took off his cowboy hat and rubbed his forehead. "Let's spread out boys. Check the woods and don't let him get the upper hand on us." He replaced his hat and pulled his pistol. The two men drew their guns as well.

Sawyer followed Bursey as they walked along the perimeter of the forest. The transition from open space to dense woods was quick.

In short order, Delfino called out, "Tire tracks over here." He went down on one knee to examine, as the group raced over. "These are pretty fresh, Boss."

Bursey holstered his weapon and bent down to look. He brushed his hand over the track marks. "Looks like the tires wiped away the dead leaves and branches. Can't be more than a few days old." He stood and pointed into the woods. "Looks like they headed that way." He indicated deep into the forest.

The tracks made a trail into the forest that was easy to follow.

Murphy was ahead of the group. He stopped to survey his surroundings then called out, "I got me some fresh broken branches. Looks like the tracks make a turn around these here trees."

Sheriff Bursey yelled ahead, "We're on your six. Just keep moving. We'll catch up." He looked back at Sawyer who was struggling. She was not accustomed to traversing deep into the woods and she was still suffering from the injuries she had sustained in the car accident. She was slowing the men down. She tripped and fell, letting out a painful shrill. Delfino ran back to help her, but she was clearly not in any condition to keep moving forward.

Delfino said, "I knew she shouldn't have come, Boss. She's holding us up."

The sheriff looked towards Murphy who was still following the tracks. He then turned back towards Sawyer and asked her, "You think you can keep up, Ms. Greer?"

Putting on a brave face, despite the pain, she said, "I'll be okay, Sheriff. Just keep moving. We'll see where these tracks lead." She forced herself forward.

Bursey grabbed her by the forearm and helped her a few feet further.

"I've got this, Sheriff. I'll be fine. You can let go."

"Okay, if you say so."

The three still lagged behind Murphy who was picking up speed.

He reached a large dead tree trunk and climbed over it. Up ahead, he saw a hole in the ground and approached it cautiously. Peering over it he could see a man sprawled out at the bottom. He called out "Mason Walcott, is that you down there?"

Mason came awake with a start. "Yes, I'm down here. Can you get me out of here?" Murphy shouted back to the group, "Found Mason! He's here!" Bursey started running, Delfino followed, and Sawyer trailed from behind.

Mason shouted, "You guys better watch out for Travis!"

"He set you in this hole?" asked Murphy.

"Travis was chasing me and shooting. I fell into this pit he made. Can you get me out of here?"

Bursey arrived and looked into the hole. "Jeez. Travis must have thought he could bag an elephant."

"Guys, I could use some water, some food."

Bursey said, "We're gonna need a rope." He turned to Delfino who had just arrived. "You've got to go back to the barn and get some rope. I saw some hanging on one of the racks in there."

"Ten-four." Delfino turned and took off running.

Sawyer made her way over and looked into the hole, "Oh my God, Mason, are you okay?"

"I knew you'd track me down," said Mason.

"You shouldn't have gone off alone, without telling me."

Mason chuckled, "Hindsight's twenty-twenty, and you were otherwise detained." He stood and began dusting off his clothes. "And I kinda wanted to impress you."

"Well, at least we found you and you're alright."

"If you didn't catch Travis, he's still out there. That creep left me here to die. And he admitted killing Sandra."

Sheriff Bursey said, "First we've got to get you out of there, son. Then you can give us the lowdown."

It took another half hour for Delfino to return with the rope and get Mason out of the hole. He then relayed his entire interaction with Travis to the shock and dismay of all, especially Sawyer. Hearing about her brother's homosexual encounter was difficult, and she knew she would have to deal with it.

By the time they had extricated Mason from the trap and returned to the cabin, Nelson Vasquez had arrived with his own backup, two police officers from Tallahassee. He introduced Officer Jake Brinson as the senior officer and Officer Trent Tucker as his partner.

Turning to Sheriff Bursey, Sawyer said, "As I explained to you on the way over here, Mr. Vasquez is an A.D.A. in Tallahassee. He has been looking into the cold case murder of Sandra Payne."

Mason addressed Vasquez, "Let me bring you up to speed, Travis Conrad admitted to me that he killed Sandra Payne. You should have enough evidence now to lock him up."

Bursey said, "Looks like we got a lot more'n probable cause." The men started laughing.

Mason said, "The last thing Travis said to me was he was going away for a few days and planned on returning once I was dead. Then he was going to bury me in the pit." He gazed from Bursey to Vasquez to the other officers.

Bursey said, "We got enough to check his cabin. Maybe we'll come across some cell phone bills, get his number and track him like a deer in the woods. We can also run a trace through DMV and see what he's driving."

Officer Brinson nodded, "I got a feeling we're gonna collar this creep real soon."

Mason said, "My SUV is parked in the woods, up the road a bit."

Bursey said, "Come with me to your vehicle. Then we can meet up at the station for a formal statement." Turning to Murphy and Delfino, he said, "Once you locate Travis Conrad, call it in. This guy's a real nasty S.O.B."

"Copy that," said Murphy.

They retrieved Mason's SUV. Sawyer said, "Are you sure you're okay, Mason. You've been through a lot."

"Yes, I'm fine. It's been a crazy few days, but I'm alive. And right now, that's all that matters." He turned and smiled at Sawyer. "Like I said before, I knew you'd come looking for me. I couldn't stop thinking about you." They hugged.

She leaned back, "When I couldn't find you, I panicked. I'm so glad you are alright, you really had me worried."

They got in the car. Sawyer took the wheel, and they began the journey back to Rainbow River. She patted his shoulder and accelerated onto the highway.

"Things just didn't go as planned. So, what's our next move?" asked Mason.

"Well, I met with the M.E. who did Megan's autopsy, and together we went over the report. It turns out that there are a few issues with it, so I'm going to find Chad's defense attorney."

"Do you know who he is?"

"Yes, a Public Defender named Raymond Youngblood."

"Should I come with you?"

"No. I don't want to spook him, so when I find him, I'm just going to play nice and see what I can learn. Besides, you need to make your statement, sign it, then get some rest. Take a day or two, and I'll get back with you once I've had a chance to speak with him."

36

Sawyer had no trouble tracking down Raymond Youngblood. He had been a fledgling attorney with the Public Defender's office at the time of Chad's arrest. And, because Chad's parents couldn't afford counsel, he was appointed to represent him.

Youngblood had given up the practice of law only a few years into his career. He had taken over his father's business running a car wash and detailing center called "Suds & Buff" in Tampa. He stepped into it when his father died, and he turned it into a successful and very lucrative establishment. He was never much good at being a lawyer, so this was a godsend for him. He was young, energetic, tall, and exotic looking, with a tight build and mixed features, chiseled by the gifted genetics of a white mother and black father.

He had originally chosen the law profession because he wanted to help the underprivileged, having grown up in an impoverished neighborhood. However, he never really took to it well, and was more than grateful to take over his father's business after his untimely death.

Sawyer introduced herself, and Youngblood brought her to his office. It was well-appointed with old car memorabilia, photos of great classics from the 1960's, an old Coca Cola soda machine, a jukebox, a refrigerator from a bygone era and various other antiques.

"Nice place you have here Mr. Youngblood," Sawyer said, trying to break the ice without hinting at where she was headed with her interview.

"Thanks. My dad was a real antiques buff. After he passed on, I continued the tradition. Whenever I can find something appropriate, I snap it up." He gazed around the room proudly, then turned back to Sawyer. "Please, sit down." He motioned to a bright yellow couch, that somehow fit the decor. "So, you told me on the phone that you wanted to speak about the case I handled for your brother back when I was with the P.D.'s office."

"Yes, and I'm hoping your memory will help me with what I'm trying to do."

"And what would that be?"

"Honestly, I am trying to have his conviction overturned, and I have come across quite a bit of evidence that has led me to believe he is innocent."

"Well, I do remember the case. It was one of my first losses. As an attorney yourself, I'm sure that resonates."

Sawyer gave him a nod, "I haven't had one yet, but I can sympathize."

He smiled, showing perfectly aligned, bright white teeth, "Consider yourself lucky. For me, losing that case, when I believed with every fiber of my being that Chad Greer was innocent . . . that just put me in a tailspin." He modestly ducked his head, "It was why I gave up practicing law.

After that, I felt I just wasn't good enough. I was too afraid to take on other cases. I couldn't bear to see someone else get convicted when I was certain they were innocent."

"I am sorry to hear that," said Sawyer.

"Then, my father died suddenly," said Youngblood, a tear coming to his eye. "He was the one who pushed me to stay in school, make something of myself. But, you know, it's funny, the things that death does to you. Makes you think, what am I doing all this for? This shop was everything my dad had worked for. So, I took over."

Sawyer thought about the right words to say, then said, "That must have been difficult."

"It was. But once I got over it, I fell in love with this place. Every day I work here I feel like I'm continuing my dad's legacy."

"Mr. Youngblood. I'm here to tell you that your instincts weren't wrong. The evidence I have uncovered leads me to believe that my brother, your former client, was innocent."

"Really?" said Youngblood.

"I hope you can help me to try and get my brother out of jail."

"Of course. If that's true, I'll do everything I can."

"Good. Now, one of my first questions . . . there were a number of kids that were part of the group that night who never made statements to the police. And information they had, never made it to the case file. One of the most curious was Winston Marshall, the Sheriff's son. I know he was there, because other witnesses I spoke to told me so. They also told me he handed out OxyContin pills to everyone. Yet none of that came up at trial."

Youngblood's eyes widened, "Really? OxyContin? That's news to me. That's the first time I'm hearing of this. Why didn't Chad tell me?"

"Apparently the kids all made a pact, because they didn't want to get in trouble with their parents. But more importantly, what about Winston Marshall? Didn't any of the kids tell you he was there that night?"

He nodded, "Yes, I was aware he was there that night, and I talked to him, but he didn't have anything much to say, other than that he saw Chad and Megan leave the bonfire and go off into the woods together. Like all the other kids, he told the same story. Except for one girl, Sandra. She did tell me that she saw Megan alone, crying. But then, while I was conducting my investigation, the DNA results came back pointing to your brother. Megan had his skin under her fingernails. And once that came out, the witness statements didn't much matter." He looked up at Sawyer.

"Okay, so tell me more about Sandra."

"Well, she would have made a good witness, but she committed suicide before trial. The judge wouldn't let me introduce anything she said. Rules of procedure. I'm sure you know."

"Yes, and that is a whole other story itself. You see, she did not commit suicide, she was murdered."

"Murdered?"

"I'll get back to that. But first, tell me this, I know that her boyfriend at the time, Mason Walcott, was there too, why didn't you have him testify?"

"Similar problem. He didn't actually see Megan talking with Sandra. He only saw a car drive off. He didn't see Chad get into the car, so his testimony would have been pure speculation, hence, inadmissible. Another thing that frustrated me about the practice of law, by the way."

"So, you didn't feel you should put him on the stand at trial, or any of the other kids either?"

"It made no sense. As I said, all of them told basically the same story. They saw Megan and Chad leave together. That, coupled with the DNA, really hurt. So, parading them out to confirm what we already knew, wouldn't have helped. In fact, it probably would have made matters worse."

"Why do you say that?"

"Think about it. It was bad enough that a few kids testified to seeing Chad and Megan leave together. A few more making identical statements would have just added insult to injury. And, what made things worse was when Chad was first interviewed by the Sheriff . . . before the body was found . . . he had scratch marks on his face."

"Yes, I later became aware of that."

"But did you know that when the sheriff asked him how he got the marks, Chad told him, and your mother was a witness, that he received the scratches during the basketball game that day. So, that lie, coupled with the clear DNA evidence, made the case almost unwinnable."

Sawyer interjected, "Which brings me to my next question. Did Chad ever explain about the scratches?"

"Yes, he did. Chad told me that he and Megan broke up that night, and when he tried to calm her down, she scratched him. But I couldn't take the risk of putting him on the stand to tell that story, because it would have made things worse. And, as you know, putting the defendant on the stand at his own trial is very risky to begin with. Then he would have had to try to explain why he lied to the sheriff about the scratch marks. It would have opened the door to almost anything."

"I see, so what about the test results from the rape kit?"

"What about them?"

"Well, I met with Dr. Kirk, the M.E. who did the autopsy. She told me that the DNA from the rape kit test was inconclusive."

"To my recollection, I didn't see *any* results from that testing. I just assumed it was all part of the DNA from the scratches, and so I didn't inquire any further."

Sawyer's expression changed from acknowledgment to surprise and then to anger.

"Honestly, that would've been one of the first things that I would have questioned, if I were defending the case."

"That's debatable. There were other circumstances. And, as I said, the DNA from the scratch marks were the biggest focus of the case on the prosecution's side. And we just couldn't refute it."

Sawyer thought for a bit. "I must say, your memory of the case is quite good. How is it that it is so fresh in your mind?"

"Well, when you asked to meet with me, I went back and looked over my case file."

Sawyer jumped out of her seat, "You mean you have your case file!"

"Yes, and it has haunted me for years, but I can't seem to let it go," he confessed. "I mean, look around you, many of the antiques you see here were my father's. He was a collector. I guess I became one, too. They remind me of him. And the case file, as painful as it is, reminds me of a time before all this." He spread his arms out as a gesture of the place his dad had built.

"That's remarkable." Sawyer exclaimed. "Would you let me go through it?"

"Most certainly, of course. If I can be of any help to you and to Chad, please be my guest." He pointed to a closet behind her. "I keep it in my safe in there. You can have it, and if it helps to get Chad out, that would be very cathartic for me as well."

37

Sawyer and Mason sat around her kitchen table where Youngblood's file was spread out.

"I'm glad you're feeling better and able to help me with this, Mason."

"Yes, and it feels good knowing we helped to solve Sandra's murder. I just hope they find Travis soon. The guy is a loose cannon and if he finds out I'm still alive, he'll go berserk."

"Well at least we can focus on Chad's case again. With what I've uncovered recently, it's clear he's innocent."

Mason hesitated, a forlorn look on his face, "Sawyer, there's something I need to tell you, and I didn't want to say it while we were still with Sheriff Bursey and his men."

She looked deeply into his eyes, "You're scaring me. What is it?"

"About Chad. Another thing that Travis said."

"What did he say? Tell me."

"Well, he suggested that Chad left his house that night and went back to the river and killed Megan."

"That's impossible. Chad told me he passed out in Travis's house and didn't wake up until morning."

"Yeah, and Travis told me the same thing. That he passed out and didn't wake up until morning, so he couldn't say for sure if Chad woke up at any point and went back to the river."

"Oh, come on, Travis was just trying to deceive you."

"No, I don't think so. I mean, the guy wanted me dead, and he admitted to killing Sandra, so why lie about that?"

"But he didn't say he knew for sure, just that he slept through the night, and didn't know any better, right?"

"Yes, true, but the two of them were very worried about their secret coming out, and Travis intimated that he was motivated to take care of Sandra because he thought Chad took care of Megan."

Sawyer was becoming angry. "I don't believe it, so let's just keep going for now, I want you to hear me out and look at the file yourself."

"Of course. And don't get me wrong, Sawyer, I'm still with you on this, completely. Just leave open the possibility that what you find out, may not be what you started looking for."

She held his gaze for a moment before reaching for a stack of folders that she pulled from the file. Thumbing through the tabs, she said, "I'll keep an open mind, but let me fill you in a bit on what he told me."

Mason nodded, "I'm all ears."

Sawyer told him of her entire conversation with Youngblood, then added, "So, I asked him about Winston Marshall, and why there was no witness statement from him, and why he didn't put him on the stand."

"And what did he say?"

"He gave me the same answer over and over about all the witnesses . . . that they had nothing to add and would only hurt the case, because they would all testify that they saw Chad and Megan leave together." She handed him Youngblood's summary. "Take a look, I'm going to pour us some wine."

He opened the folder and began to read.

Sawyer worked her way around the kitchen, pulled glasses from the cabinet, a corkscrew from the drawer, and a bottle of wine from the fridge.

Mason continued flipping pages, "I see what you mean here, he's basically conceding that all the kids said the same thing. But they all seem to have left at different times. Eric Vanguard was one of the last ones to leave and he ran into your dad in the parking lot. He was looking for Chad."

She stopped turning the corkscrew and looked up, "Yeah, I remember that. When Chad didn't come home, my mom practically had to beg him to go out to look for him."

"Speaking of that, you never really talked about your dad."

"Not much to say," she lamented, "He wasn't much of a father to either of us. He worked a lot, drank a lot, fought with Mom a lot."

"Sorry, I didn't mean to bring up bad memories."

"No, it's okay, I got over it. He took off when I was fifteen, and never even bothered to come back and visit. He left my mom to deal with all the bills and didn't really care at all that Chad was sitting in jail for something he didn't do."

"Sounds like a great guy," Mason said, sarcastically.

"Old news. Mom got over him quickly and found a new guy, who treated me and my mom very well. We lucked out. Unfortunately, he died while I was in law school."

"Well, join the club. My mom took off on us when I was seven and left my dad to take care of me. He did the best he could, but he had to work all the time, so I was on my own a lot. I practically had to raise myself. I even learned how to cook by the time I was ten years old."

"Too bad we don't get to choose our parents." Sawyer popped the cork and began to pour. "Anyway, keep reading, maybe you'll spot something I missed." She walked over and handed Mason a glass of wine.

He continued reading for a time, then stopped again. "So, explain to me why he wouldn't let Chad testify about how he got the scratches on his face."

"It's a tough call. You see, Chad had lied to the Sheriff at first, and told him he got the scratches during the game. So, if he took the stand, the prosecution would have said something like 'are you lying now or were you lying then?' Either way, he was lying at some point, which goes to his credibility. Plus, once he is put on the stand, they can ask him all kinds of questions, and most defense attorneys don't like to take that chance. You never know what could come up."

"I see, but if it were me, I'd have wanted to take the stand and tell my side, especially if I hadn't committed the crime."

"Look Mason, it's much easier to be a Monday morning quarterback. But I do get what you're saying." Sawyer took a sip of wine.

"Tough call, either way, I suppose. But tell me more about the autopsy?"

"Okay, so here's where it gets interesting," She put the glass down and her demeanor moved from acceptance to determination. "The report leaves out anything having to do with the OxyContin. We know that had to have been done by, or at the direction of Sheriff Marshall, to protect his son."

"Which means he was aware of the Oxy and his son must have been the one who supplied it."

"Exactly."

"So, do you think that means that Winston also killed Megan? And then Marshall blamed it on Chad to protect his son?"

"It's as good a theory as we've got. But also, they buried the rape kit test.

Apparently, it came up inconclusive."

"Meaning what?" asked Mason.

"I don't know for sure, but I think it means that the DNA didn't match the DNA under Megan's fingernails."

"Which would suggest that Chad was telling the truth."

"So, you're thinking that the rape kit test DNA might match Winston?"

"To me, he's the logical suspect. Otherwise, why would the sheriff cover it all up?"

"Makes sense. So, what now?"

"Right now, we have to wait. Dr. Kirk is reaching out to the DNA lab that performed the testing to get copies of the results, because the M.E. file doesn't have them."

"Okay, but then we have to find a way to get Winston's DNA to match it with."

Sawyer flashed a wide smile and raised her wine glass in toast. "One step at a time. But at least we're moving in the right direction."

38

Fifteen Years Earlier . . .

He came out of the woods and began walking along the shore at Rainbow River. The moon lit the night sky and when he reached the Big Rock, he saw Megan sprawled out on the rock outcropping. She was out cold and had no top on.

He climbed up and hovered over her. She lay still.

He whispered her name and waved his hand above her eyes. She didn't respond.

He knelt down and began massaging her breasts. That didn't awaken her either.

He reached down, unbuttoned her jeans and removed them, along with her panties. She was completely naked, and he became erect. Quickly, he undressed and lay down beside her. He began caressing her breasts again. Slowly, he moved his hand down between her legs and fondled her.

Megan's body responded. Slowly she came awake, though still very drunk and high on OxyContin.

She whispered, "Chad, you came back. I knew you would. I knew you would."

Ignoring her, he felt that she was ready and climbed on top, inserting himself roughly. The two began grinding, and within a minute, he exploded and rolled off.

Still in a fog, and not fully alert, she turned to look at him. Blinking her eyes, she tried to focus. Even with the moonlight, she still wasn't sure of what she was seeing. She stood up. He did as well. Still trying to focus, she squinted, and in an instant registered what had just happened. "Wait, you're not Chad, you're . . . you're . . . oh no! What did you do to me?"

He grabbed her by the shoulders. She began to struggle and shout.

She cried out, "Let me go, let me go!"

He released her and she fell backwards, stumbling and falling off the rock outcropping. As she fell backward, she smashed her head on the edge of the rock and tumbled into the river.

He stood at the edge of the rock looking down into the water as she began to float away.

In a panic, he gathered his clothes, dressed, and took off into the woods.

39

Sawyer let Mason continue to sleep and dream. It was already 10:00 a.m., but he needed his rest. She made a few calls and cooked breakfast. Mason awoke to the smell of a real morning meal.

He sat up on the couch, stretched his arms over his head and yawned. "Good morning," Sawyer said, flashing a wide smile.

Mason stood, "Smells good. Why didn't you wake me so I could help out?"

"You looked so comfy, I didn't have the heart to." She noticed again how good he looked in jeans and a plain white t-shirt that accented the contours of his build. Before he caught her looking, she turned away.

"I did need the extra sleep. Thanks."

"Go wash up, it'll be ready in a few."

Mason headed to the bathroom while Sawyer scrambled the eggs and prepared plates for each of them.

By the time he returned, the table was set and the food had been served. Mason sat down and shoveled a fork full of eggs into his mouth. Speaking while chewing, he said, "Yum, this is good. What'd you put in these?"

"It's my secret recipe, shredded Munster cheese and turkey mixed in with the eggs. It was my favorite, growing up."

"Well, now it's my favorite too," he said, with a wicked grin, "I could get used to this."

Sawyer thought to herself how nice it would be to have a man around the house, and Mason seemed to check all the boxes, but as soon as the thought crossed her mind, she shook it out of her head. For her, the timing wasn't right. She took a sip of orange juice.

"While you were sleeping, I called Xander and brought him up to date on everything. He was happy to hear you're alright. He was planning on driving up today, but since you've been found and I'm safe, he said he would just file his motion to dismiss electronically with the court, and the prosecution. He also emailed me a copy."

"So, how does it look?"

"I haven't had a chance to read it, but Xander says it's a slam dunk winner, and that I shouldn't have anything to worry about."

"What else did he say?" Mason was fishing for something. He was feeling a tad jealous, but he wasn't sure why. Xander was much older, and not even in the picture. But he still felt threatened after seeing how they interacted at the hospital.

Sawyer didn't notice the double meaning in Mason's question. "Well, he said that I should apply for a carry permit as soon as possible. The problem is, first I have to do the training and get my certificate, and then it's a ninety-day waiting period while they check me out."

"Yeah, for me it was easy. Since I'm a vet, all I had to do was show proof of status and honorable discharge, and while it took a few months, I got mine some time ago."

"Really, I didn't know you had one."

"Yup, I usually don't carry, but I probably should, with everything that's going on right now."

"Especially since they haven't caught Travis yet."

Nodding, he wiped his mouth with a napkin and tossed it on the table. "I'll tell you what, why don't we take a little break today.

I'll get my gun and we can go to the shooting range. I'll teach you a bit about shooting. While we're there, you can fill out the forms and see about lessons for the certification."

"I'd like that. Thank you." A warm sensation overcame her. She knew she was looking forward to spending some down time with Mason, but she refused to let him in on how she felt.

While at the shooting range, Mason showed her how to assemble and disassemble the pistol, how to load cartridges, and how to use a speed loader. Sawyer was only accustomed to a six shooter, where the bullets were loaded into a revolving cylinder, instead of in the stock with a magazine. He also showed her how to use the slide and how to check the chamber for a round.

She watched him intently as he went through the motions of teaching her. The more she followed his hands as they moved over the weapon, the more intense her excitement. She focused on his biceps, as they flexed when he held the gun, then pointed and fired at the target. It was a huge turn on for her.

Mason handed her the gun, then said, "Hold it out in front of you with both hands. Keep one hand on the stock, with your index finger at the trigger, but don't put your finger on the trigger, until you're ready to shoot." He stood behind her, reached around with both arms, and placed her hands in the proper positions. Then he put his hands over hers. His mouth was behind her ear. "Now look through the rear sight and line it up with the front sight and your target. Then squeeze the trigger. Just get ready for a recoil." He held her hands steady as she pulled the trigger.

The sound and recoil gave her a start. She laughed, and let Mason take the gun and place it on the counter. She turned around while Mason still had his arms around her. They looked into each other's eyes and Mason moved to kiss her. She didn't resist and responded passionately. Their tongues found each other and shared a moment. Then she gently pulled away.

"Not here Mason. Not now."

He smiled, "It's all good. I'm just happy you're finally letting yourself go."

Grinning, she stood up straight and said smoothly, "Don't think this means you're getting me into bed so quickly."

"Quickly? We've known each other for weeks already."

"Exactly," she jested. "I can't let you think I'm easy."

"By the time you think I'm ready to cop a feel," said Mason, "I'll have more wrinkles than a Chinese Shar Pei."

"And even then," Sawyer retorted with a chuckle.

40

Sawyer's phone rang. It was Dr. Kirk. "Is this good news or bad news, Doctor?"

"A little of both," she hesitated. "First, the bad. The DNA lab switched computer systems about ten years ago and they only have paper copy records dating back after that. Those are in storage, so they will have to try and dig them up. It will take time."

"Nothing is easy."

"I know, but on another front, I was able to track down Dr. Cavanaugh. He's retired, but he lives locally. He says he's willing to speak with us, but he would rather it be in-person."

"When's that?"

"We can go today, if you'd like."

"That would be fine, I'll come and pick you up at your office."

Cavanaugh's home, a brick, two story colonial set back on a nicely manicured property, was on the outskirts of town. They pulled into the driveway and made their way to the door.

A short, fragile man of about seventy-five answered. He was hunched over and feeble with a face of grey pallor, and dark circles under his eyes. He wore a nasal cannula and wheeled an oxygen tank behind him.

"Good afternoon, Liam," Doctor Kirk said, "It's been a while, but it's so nice to see you." She smiled sweetly at the old man.

He wheezed when he spoke, "Good to see you too, Heather." He looked over at Sawyer. "So, you're the one making the big fuss, I gather." He turned and shuffled back into his house. "Come in, and close the door behind you." He coughed and cleared his throat.

"How have you been, Liam?"

"Just take one look at me and you won't have to ask again," he wheezed and coughed. "You'd think I would've been smarter about smoking all my life, being a doctor and all."

"Bad habits are hard to break," said Heather. "How long have you had that tank?"

"Ahh," he waived his free hand, "Almost three years. I'm fed up with it already. I'm gonna die soon. Good riddance."

"Oh, don't say that."

"Why not? It's the truth. And frankly, I'm ready to go. Living like this is no picnic. My wife died last year, so now I'm all alone. Looking forward to the afterlife though, if they don't send me to hell for the shit I've done."

Heather looked at Sawyer, "Is this the beginnings of a confession?"

"Call it what you will, but after you phoned me, I did a little soul searching. I'd forgotten about the case until you brought it up. Then all these bad memories started filling up my brain, or at least what's left of my brain." He wheezed and coughed again.

Sawyer cut in, "So, Doctor, what can you tell us about my brother's case, and the toxicology report?"

Bile filled the back of his throat, "You cut right to the chase, don't you, Missy?" he grunted. "I like your spunk."

Sawyer smiled weakly, "I'm just anxious to find out the truth already. I've been digging around this case for quite some time and just hoping that someone will finally be honest with me about what happened."

"Of course, of course. Please come in and sit down, give an old man some time to suck in some air." He offered them the couch in his den.

"Thank you, Doctor."

He gritted his teeth, "And don't call me Doctor! I haven't been one in many years. Besides, I can barely take care of myself now." He sat down and knuckled his oxygen tank. "Need this fool thing, just to breathe."

Heather said, "I'm sorry you're suffering like this, Liam. Is there anything I can do for you?"

"Nah, I'm just a biding my time, nothing anyone can do. Sometimes I think I'll just turn off the tank and let happen what may."

Sawyer was unflappable, "So, sir; about my brother . . ."

"Yeah, yeah, I'll get into it in a second." He pointed towards the table beneath the window. "Over there. Saved it all these years. I don't know why, but you ladies can have it all."

Sawyer got up and moved over to it. Taking it in her hands, she sat back down and put it beside her. "Can you tell us what it says?"

He wheezed, "How's about you ask the questions, and I'll answer as best I can."

Sawyer looked at Dr. Kirk for direction. Heather nodded, "Sawyer is the lawyer, so I'll—"

"Really?" said Liam, "Sawyer, the lawyer?" He chuckled then started coughing until he put his breathing mask on. Then, removing it again, he said, "I'm sorry. Go on."

"Yes, so, Doctor Kirk and I went through the file I have from the D.A.'s Office, and she pointed out to me places where the report was altered. It seems that information was cut out of the report. Information that would have helped my brother."

Cavanaugh nodded. "Go on."

"Well, there was no mention of OxyContin found in Megan Miller's body, yet she had taken a number of pills. At least that's what my other witnesses have told me. Also, and more importantly, the DNA results from the rape kit test are not referenced or mentioned and are nowhere to be found."

He swallowed hard, "Yeah, yeah, that's about right. And you can thank good ole' Sheriff Marshall for that. I'm sure you figured that much out." Sawyer and Dr. Kirk nodded. "You see, he, and that piece of garbage, Cole Hanratty, the 'Rat' aptly named for sure, were looking for an easy win in court. They didn't want any interference. They told me that they had the suspect." He coughed and wheezed again. "And I saw the DNA from the fingernail scrapings, which pointed to your brother. So, when the DNA from the rape kit came back and it was inconclusive, they asked me to bury it." He pulled on his nasal cannula. "Damn thing don't give me enough air." He tapped the tank valve and drew a deep breath. "So, the argument was that somehow the fact that because the body floated in the water for some time it corrupted the sample, and rather than give the defense anything to hang their hat on, they made me deep six it."

Sawyer rose from the couch and stood over Cavanaugh, "And you just let them?"

"The fact was though, that I also believed your brother committed the murder, because of the scrapings, so I didn't feel too bad about it back then."

"But that's what trials are for. You can't just do something like that and ignore evidence."

"It's a bit more complicated than that. You see, back in the day, before this case, I was pulled over for drinking and driving. I would have lost my job and my respect in the community. So, Sheriff Marshall did me a favor, made it all go away." Another cough and wheeze. "No one ever knew about it. I thought the guy was doing me a solid because he was a stand up kinda guy. Boy did I get that wrong. He hung that over my head for years."

Sawyer pointed angrily, "So, does your file have the actual report, or the edited version?"

"Nah, I held onto the proper one. Figured I might need it someday. You never know with assholes like the Rat and Sheriff Marshall. I needed something to hang over their heads, too."

"And the rape kit DNA test is in there?"

"Yep. Along with another sample."

Dr. Kirk cut in, "Wait a minute, Liam. I was the one who was supposed to testify, and I knew there was a rape kit DNA test. And while I didn't know exactly what the problem was at the time, I still would have testified that it was inconclusive."

"Frankly, Dr. Kirk, I don't know why you didn't testify."

"How did they know you would have to substitute for me?"

"That, I don't know. But those two assured me that I would be the one testifying."

Kirk looked at Sawyer, then back at Cavanaugh, "Liam. Do you remember why I couldn't testify?"

"Of course. You had to take a plane to New York. Your mother was in an accident."

Sawyer cut in, "We think that Sheriff Marshall was somehow behind that accident."

Liam sat back. This had never occurred to him. "I don't know how they could've done it. They were in Florida the whole time."

"We understand, Liam," said Dr. Kirk. "It was a bit of a stretch for me to believe it, too."

"No, no," Liam said, waving his hands. He was deep in thought. "I don't know how I know it. Maybe it's just a feeling, but somehow I know your mother's accident was no accident. I have a strong feeling they were behind it."

"Would you be willing to testify to all this?" asked Sawyer. "Except for the car accident. I don't think we can get them on that based on a feeling."

"And face those two no good pieces of shit?" He coughed uncontrollably, then caught his breath. "Absolutely!"

41

A.D.A. Nelson Vasquez finally received the warrant on Travis Conrad based on his findings and Mason Walcott's statement. It was almost dark out when he checked in with his two deputies, Brinson and Tucker.

Brinson answered his cell, "Vasquez here, I just wanted to let you know that we have the warrant on Conrad, I'll text it to you." He punched in a few commands and the warrant was on its way. "So, can you bring me up to date?"

"We're still working with Delfino and Murphy. They headed back to Rainbow River yesterday. They've going to triangulate Conrad's cell phone. Though, he probably turned it turned off." He looked out the window of Conrad's log cabin as he sipped his coffee.

"Well, what's next?"

"We've got our cruiser hidden behind the barn. We'll grab him when he returns."

Tucker was watching the news, sitting comfortably on the sofa. He turned to look at Brinson. "Did you hear something?" he asked, as he turned off the flat screen.

Brinson nodded, "I've gotta go. There's something outside the cabin." He hung up the phone and turned out the light.

Both men went into combat mode. Brinson gestured to the back door and Tucker took off. He pulled his service revolver and exited into the growing darkness.

Brinson remained behind. He took out his pistol and slunk low by the fireplace.

Travis had driven past where Mason's SUV should have been. It was no longer there. Concerned, he pulled into the woods, grabbed his rifle from the trunk, and hiked his way towards the cabin. From the edge of the woods, he could see a light on inside his cabin.

As he made his way closer, he saw the TV playing through the window. He bent down low and quickly got closer. He was able to make it around back, and when the door opened and Tucker came out, he took his rifle by the barrel and swung the butt of his rifle at Tucker's head. He connected hard, and Tucker went down. He crushed Tucker's skull with a few quick jabs.

Brinson heard a 'thwak' and crawled away from the fireplace towards the sound. Sensing movement inside, Travis pulled back and pressed himself up against the wall of the cabin.

Brinson didn't want to call out, in case Travis was out there, but he also didn't want to leave Tucker to fend for himself.

He thought for a second and decided his best option would be to crawl towards the front door and exit that way.

In seconds he was outside. He circled around to the side of the cabin where the pond lay. It was almost completely dark by then, and the moon wasn't able to shine through the clouds. Because of this, Brinson couldn't see too well. He kept his back pressed up against the cabin and moved slowly along the wall.

Travis heard the front door open and took off for the barn. Silently, he made his way inside. He cursed himself, thinking he should have killed Mason when he had the chance. But he wasn't going to be taken alive. If they wanted him, they were going to have to come after him, and kill him. He wouldn't go down without a fight. His mind raced as he looked around trying to figure out his next move. He had the ATV, so he could try to make a fast getaway to his pickup. But he didn't know how many other cops were out there, or where they were positioned. It would be foolish to go crashing out of the barn riding the ATV, but it would be even worse to just wait for them to barricade him.

His heart pounded against his chest. He took a steadying breath.

His mind raced as he considered his options. He started formulating a plan.

He would sneak out the secret escape hatch in the rear, and head into the forest. He knew the woods very well, and he knew he could make his way around and get back to his truck without being caught. He didn't think they would be able to track him in the darkness.

Brinson made it to the back of the cabin and saw Tucker laid out on the ground. He scanned the area all around as he slid over to him. Not seeing anyone, he bent over the body. Tucker's skull was crushed. Blood covered his face.

"What the fuck? Holy fucking shit! Damn!" exclaimed Brinson.

He checked for a pulse . . . No. Tucker was dead.

Panicked, Brinson called Deputy Murphy and asked for backup.

They were almost a half hour away, but would get there as quickly as they could.

Travis moved the hay bales, found the secret hatch, and exited the barn. He found the cruiser hidden there, took out his knife and slashed all four tires. Then he entered the woods and began to make his way back towards his pickup. It was completely dark, but he knew where he was, and how to get where he needed to go. He moved slowly and cautiously so as not to alert whoever it was that may have been in his cabin.

Murphy and Delfino were on their way within minutes and flew down the highway at over one hundred miles per hour. At that rate, if they didn't crash, they'd make it in twenty minutes.

Delfino called Sheriff Bursey on a private line.

"Sheriff. It's all fucked up. He beat Tucker to death with a blunt-edged object, probably the butt-end of his rifle. That's what it sounds like. Brinson's freaking out. I'm with Murph and we're headed back up to Conrad's cabin."

"Are you fuck'n tell'n me Conrad beat Tucker to death?!" he shouted. "How the fuck?"

"Boss, Brinson is in deep, deep shit. He's all by himself."

"Fuck! Okay, get up there and if you see that fucker, nail him with every clip on your belt and don't say nothing to nobody. Bust your bodycams if ya hafta . . . I wanna watch an M.E. count the bullets in Conrad's body."

"Copy that."

Brinson heard movement in the woods but was unable to see anything. He stayed low and purposefully covered the distance towards the sound.

Slowly, the moon began to shine, as the clouds passing overhead gave way.

Brinson saw only a shadow moving deeper into the woods but going in the direction of the main road. He figured that Conrad had probably parked his truck away from the cabin and was headed for it now. He turned and ran to the barn to retrieve his cruiser, but when he got there, he found the tires slashed. Muttering a series of expletives, he turned back and, with gun drawn, set off down the driveway, figuring the direct route would get him to the main road faster.

When he reached the end of the driveway the clouds returned, and it began to rain.

Brinson took the main road and set off in the direction of the highway, figuring that had to be where Conrad had come from, and where he would have parked his vehicle.

Travis propelled himself through the woods picking up speed, thankful for the rain and its masking effects on the sounds he made moving forward. It still wasn't easy, and as the rain intensified, his clothes went from damp to saturated in minutes.

Murphy exited the highway and turned onto the main road that led to the cabin. The rain came down in earnest now, and with little visibility on a road that seemed to have been cut right through the forest, he had to slow down to a safer speed. The wipers flapped back and forth on the highest setting, but still couldn't clear the torrent from the windshield fast enough. He put on the flashing lights for more illumination.

Travis reached his pickup just as he saw flashing lights coming towards him. He didn't want to open the door and have the interior light go on, so he waited beside the truck. Then he heard footsteps coming down the road from the other direction.

He was caught in the middle and decided it was time to do a John Wayne. He came up to the road, pointed his rifle in the direction of the cruiser, and fired. The round went through the windshield between both men, narrowly missing them.

Murphy slammed on the brakes and skidded onto the shoulder.

Brinson heard the blast and saw Conrad standing by the side of the road.

"Drop the fucking rifle, Conrad!"

He fired a shot at Travis Conrad.

Conrad spun around and pulled the trigger.

Brinson dove to the ground and fired multiple shots in Conrad's direction.

Murphy and Delfino exited the cruiser, pulled their guns and kept firing as though they had a thousand rounds. They crouch-ran along the treeline.

Conrad saw an opening and jumped into his pickup truck. He started it, jammed it in gear and floored it. The wheels spun out, the vehicle lurched forward, and hit the pavement still spinning. Now, coming directly at Murphy and Delfino, Conrad pointed his rifle through the open driver side window, and fired at the cops.

Murphy and Delfino kept shooting at Travis' truck until a round hit Conrad, he lost control, the truck went sideways, rolling and flipping over and over before coming to rest on its side.

42

Former Sheriff Chuck Marshall and retired D.A. Cole Hanratty paid a visit to Dr. Liam Cavanaugh. He wasn't expecting company, but when he looked at his cell phone that was paired with his Ring doorbell video camera, he knew precisely who they were and why they were there. Before he answered the door, he snapped a picture through his phone, turned on his cell phone recorder, and hid it beneath the pillow on his sofa.

He shuffled to the door toting his oxygen tank. He let the men in and ushered them to his den.

Wheezing, he sat on the sofa and said, "Please, sit down and tell me, to what do I owe this intrusion, gentlemen?"

"Don't play dumb with us, Cavanaugh," Marshall said firmly, as he stood over the old man. "I'm sorry, but I don't understand." Cavanaugh squinted and shook his head.

"Look, we know who came to see you the other day. We just want to know what you said?"

"Who's them?" asked Cavanaugh, convincingly.

Hanratty interjected, "C'mon Liam, what have you done?"

He coughed, "I've done nothing. What have you done?"

"The women, what did you say to them?" asked Hanratty.

"I must be missing something. Who are we talking about?"

"Hey old man, unless you want me to hurt you real bad," Marshall said as he reached over and grabbed Cavanaugh's brittle hand, "I suggest you stop fucking around." He squeezed just hard enough to hurt, but not too hard where he might break something.

Cavanaugh yelled out in pain, "Stop that!"

"Then talk."

"Okay, okay, easy now." He drew a deep breath and hacked up phlegm. "Yes, my protégé, Dr. Heather Kirk, and her friend, Sawyer Greer, were here. So what?"

"So, they just paid you a casual visit," said Marshall, "Is that what you expect us to believe?" Marshall reached out and pulled Cavanaugh's nasal cannula from his nose. "Talk, old man, or die from lack of air."

Cavanaugh reached out to Marshall and tried to grab the cannula. He started wheezing and opened his mouth to draw in air.

Marshall reinserted it. "Now talk!"

He continued drawing deep breaths and wheezed when he spoke. "They know everything."

Figured it out all by themselves, I didn't have to tell them anything."

Hanratty chimed in, "What's everything?"

"The report, they know it was altered. And they know you buried the rape kit test results."

"Did you confirm that?"

"I didn't have to."

"Then why would they have bothered to come to see you?" asked Marshall.

"To see if I would testify."

"Really, so now you're going to put yourself on the line," said Hanratty. "Because you are just as guilty."

"Look at me!" he wheezed, "I'll be dead before they put me in jail. But you two, well, that's a different story. You boys have a few good years left in you. So, you'll enjoy them behind bars."

"Not if I can help it," said Marshall. He reached out and pulled the cannula out again.

"Turns out you won't be testifying after all," said Hanratty, chuckling.

Cavanaugh tried to stand up and take the cannula from Marshall. Marshall pushed him back down onto the sofa. "We're gonna watch you take your last breath."

Cavanaugh began to struggle. He opened his mouth and tried drawing in air, but the phlegm in his throat prevented him from getting enough oxygen.

They watched as he wheezed and gagged, suffering for the last ten minutes of his life.

When they were sure he was dead, Marshall wiped the cannula clean and took Cavanaugh's fingers and clasped them around the tubing so that his were the only prints that would show up if anyone checked.

43

Mason showed up at Sawyer's apartment holding his hands behind his back. When she answered the door, a mischievous smile spread across his face.

"What's with that silly grin?"

He brought his hands around. "These are for you." He gave her two wrapped boxes, one much heavier than the other.

She smiled, "Really, now what did you do here?"

"Aren't you going to invite me in?"

She stepped aside, "I'm sorry, please come in."

Sawyer carried the boxes and placed them on the kitchen counter. She looked at them and then back at Mason.

"Go ahead, open them." He gestured towards the packages. "Open the heavier one first."

She removed the wrapping and opened the box. Inside was a carrying case. She opened it. "A gun?" her eyes widened. "You bought me another gun?"

"I thought you might need some protection at home. You won't be able to carry it with you, but at least you'll have it here, just in case."

Sawyer didn't know whether to laugh, cry, thank him, or throw him out, so she just stared at the pistol. She stammered, "I, I, I don't know what to say? I was sort of expecting candy." She laughed uncomfortably.

"It's alright, I simply wanted you to feel a little safer at home, especially if I'm not here."

"I get it, and thank you for your . . . a . . . thoughtfulness?"

Mason chuckled. "Ok, now open the other one."

"I'm a little afraid to. I mean, how do you outdo a gift like that?"

"Just open it. It'll make more sense when you do."

She reached for the box, ripped off the wrapping paper and saw that there were two smaller boxes. One was a handheld taser, the other a pocket size pepper spray canister. She turned to look at Mason. "So, what are you now, an arms dealer?"

He laughed again, "I'm worried about you with everything that's going on, and I thought you should have some protection. You know, something that you can carry with you, until you get your carry permit for the pistol."

She burst out laughing. "That's the most thoughtful set of gifts I can ever remember receiving," she said, the sarcasm evident in her voice.

Returning the sarcasm, he said, "That makes me feel . . . uh, appreciated?"

"No really, I understand where you're coming from. Don't get me wrong, the thought behind all this makes a lot of sense."

"And you'll promise to carry the taser and the pepper spray whenever you leave the house?"

"Yes, I promise."

"Good, so fill me in. What are we doing today?"

"Well, as I said on the phone, Dr. Kirk and I are going to meet with Sheriff Bursey and my boss, D.A. Crenshaw." Sawyer pointed to the stack of papers on the table. "I've got everything from all the files sorted out and I'm ready to present them with my case to obtain arrest warrants for Marshall and Hanratty."

"That's a big step."

"It is, and I want you there for moral support."

Sawyer and Mason were the first to arrive at the D.A.'s office. Dr. Kirk arrived along with Sheriff Bursey a few minutes later, and all were brought into the conference room.

Crenshaw stood at the head of the long mahogany table and addressed the group, "I've already been briefed by Ms. Greer over the phone. But I haven't seen any of the evidence. I'm going to let her present her case." He moved aside, "Ms. Greer, the floor is yours."

Carrying her file, Sawyer stood. She walked over to Crenshaw and took his place.

"As you all know, I have been looking into my brother Chad Greer's conviction for the murder of Megan Miller fifteen years ago." She took a nervous breath. "Throughout the process, I have been met with resistance. And perhaps resistance is an inadequate adjective. In fact, my life has been threatened and my home invaded. I have been arrested and I have been accused of acting in a conflict of interest with my position as a Marion County A.D.A." She looked at Crenshaw.

"Get to the point, Counselor," said Crenshaw.

"I am getting there, have some patience."

Sheriff Bursey said, "Let Ms. Greer talk."

"Thank you. So, my investigation led me to a number of witnesses. From the kids who were at the river the night of the murder, to the Medical Examiners who conducted the autopsy and testified at trial, to the Public Defender who represented Chad at trial. I have also collected files from the P.D., the D.A., and most recently, from Dr. Liam Cavanaugh, who was the head of the M.E.'s office at the time." She looked at Mason for support, and he nodded his head. "What I have found is that the autopsy file was altered, critical information deleted, and the rape kit test results removed and never introduced at trial. This can be corroborated by Dr. Kirk and Dr. Cavanaugh. In fact, Dr. Kirk and I interviewed Dr. Cavanaugh the other day, and he admitted to us that Sheriff Marshall and D.A. Hanratty conspired and colluded with him to tamper with the evidence and suborn perjury. They actually forced Dr. Cavanaugh to lie at the trial." She held up a folder from her file. "Contained in here is Dr. Cavanaugh's original file with the actual and correct autopsy and toxicology report as well as the autopsy and toxicology report that Sheriff Marshall and D.A. Hanratty used to obtain the conviction at trial. That file failed to include the fact that Megan Miller had ingested a toxic quantity of OxyContin. In fact, it made no mention of OxyContin in her system at all. And I have discovered that Sheriff Marshall's son distributed the OxyContin to all of the kids that night. It is my belief that Sheriff Marshall's son, Winston Marshall, was the one who murdered Megan Miller, and that Sheriff Marshall covered it up."

"That's a very bold accusation," said Sheriff Bursey. "And I'm curious about the rape kit test.

What happened with that?"

"I will leave that to Dr. Kirk to explain."

Dr. Kirk added, "I conducted the autopsy and reviewed the DNA report from the lab. My recollection was that it came back inconclusive."

"Meaning?" asked Bursey.

"Meaning that the sample used could have been corrupted because the body had been floating in the water."

"So, how do you propose to link this to Winston Marshall?" asked Crenshaw.

Sawyer responded, "Dr. Cavanaugh's file has another sample which can be tested for a DNA match."

"Well, I suggest you get that done before making any accusations against anyone."

Dr. Kirk said, "We are working on that. I have already submitted the sample to the DNA lab for testing. We should have results soon."

"Very well," said Bursey, "Please continue, Ms. Greer."

"Yes, so, as I was saying, Dr. Cavanaugh admitted to us that, at trial, he used the altered reports, under duress, at the direction of Sheriff Marshall and with the assistance of D.A. Hanratty."

Sheriff Bursey cut in, "Excuse me, Ms. Greer, but has Dr. Cavanaugh agreed to testify to this? Because he's a co-conspirator and will be subject to arrest and prosecution."

"Yes, he has agreed to testify," said Sawyer.

"Good, I will need to meet with him in person to confirm his side of the story. And if it coincides with your account, I will ask D.A. Crenshaw to seek warrants from the court for all three men. In the meantime, I will need to examine your file," said Sheriff Bursey.

"I will need to review the file as well," said Crenshaw.

Dr. Kirk stood up. "Sheriff, I was there. I heard what Dr. Cavanaugh said, as well."

"I'm not disputing what he said, I just need to hear it for myself, so that I can do my job properly."

"Well, how soon can you go see him?" asked Sawyer. "We need to arrest these men as soon as possible. I don't feel safe. And frankly, I'm concerned for my life."

Mason said, "Sheriff, not to change the subject but, do you have a status on Travis Conrad's condition? I understand he is still in critical condition in the hospital."

"He's still in a coma and under twenty-four-hour surveillance. One of my men is stationed outside his room, and he is handcuffed to the bed. He poses no risk to anyone at this time." He turned to Sawyer, "And to answer your question, as soon as we wrap up this meeting, I'll head over to speak with Cavanaugh, and take his statement."

Sawyer asked, “May I go with you Sheriff?”

“If you insist.”

Mason was still on edge. “One more thing Sheriff, whatever became of the girl who died in the cell while Sawyer was incarcerated?”

Bursey said, “After further investigation, we learned she was a habitual drug user. Friends of hers confirmed it wasn’t the first time she overdosed on drugs. So, it was ruled an accidental death.”

44

Sheriff Bursey and Sawyer arrived at Dr. Cavanaugh's home and rang the doorbell. There was no answer. Bursey knocked loud and hard. Still no response.

Sawyer said, "That's strange, his car is in the driveway. He must be home. I'll try his phone." She punched in his number. It started to ring.

"Wait, I hear something," Bursey said. "It's his phone, I hear it ringing inside."

Bursey tried the door. It was unlocked.

They went inside and followed the sound of the ringing phone. It led them to the den where they found Cavanaugh sprawled out on the couch, his cannula hanging from his neck.

Sheriff Bursey checked for a pulse. There was none. "I'm afraid he's dead."

Sawyer lifted the pillow beside Cavanaugh and found the ringing phone.

"Oh no, this is awful. We were just here the other day," she breathed a heavy sigh. "I know he wasn't well. He was having trouble breathing, so it makes no sense that he would just take his breathing tube out of his nose?"

Bursey said, "Maybe he had a heart attack," he said, shaking his head sadly. "I need to get the M.E. here." He called Dr. Kirk and then he called for an ambulance.

Sawyer looked around the room. "I don't like this, Sheriff. Something is wrong with this picture."

"Please Ms. Greer, don't start with your conspiracy theories again. Look what happened in your prison cell. As bad as it was, it turned out there was no plot to poison you."

"Well, what about my car? That was no accident. Someone sabotaged my brakes."

"That still remains to be seen."

"Come on, Sheriff. Can't you see what's been happening ever since I started investigating my brother's case?"

Checking the flow valve on the tank he said, "Oxygen is still flowing. This looks to me like an old man who was clearly very ill, and who just died of natural causes."

She looked forlornly at Cavanaugh's body and adjusted his head to a more comfortable position. "Yeah, and right after he agreed to testify against Marshall and Hanratty."

"It's a stretch. How would they even know about that?"

"How did they know about any of what I was doing?" she said brusquely. "I am sure they have their ways. Maybe an informant? Maybe they have been following me? Who knows? I just think this is too coincidental." She looked at the phone she was holding and placed it on the coffee table.

"Well, let's just wait for the M.E. to evaluate and make her report."

"Fine, but in the meantime, isn't there something you can do?"

"I'm afraid not, Ms. Greer. We don't have enough evidence. You're an attorney, you know that whatever Cavanaugh told you is hearsay, and inadmissible in court. We needed to hear it directly from Cavanaugh. And even more to the point, your testimony would be suspect to begin with. After all, you're Chad's sister."

"Yes, I know," she pleaded. "But we also have Dr. Kirk's testimony. She heard it as well."

"Still hearsay. But we will look into the evidence you brought us and discuss it with D.A. Crenshaw to see what can be done."

Looking around the room, she said, "With all due respect, Sheriff, and I'm not trying to tell you your job, but, shouldn't we treat this place as a crime scene?"

"Look, Ms. Greer, this truly appears to me to be an unfortunate and sad end to the doctor's life. He was old, sick, and infirm. I mean, the man had to wheel around an oxygen tank."

Grudgingly, she said, "I know, it does seem that way, but with everything else that has been going on, don't you think a little caution is needed here?"

Placing his hands on his hips and scanning the room, Bursey nodded and said, "Alright, Ms. Greer, it goes against my better judgment, but I'll get a crime scene team in here." He pulled out his phone and made the call.

Dr. Kirk completed her autopsy the following day and was ready to issue her report to Sheriff Bursey. He arrived at her lab anxious to hear what she had to say.

As they stood over the body she said matter-of-factly, "Dr. Cavanaugh was a very sick man. He had lung cancer, a very weak heart, and numerous other ailments I don't need to detail here. But it is clear that the level of oxygen in his blood was so low that it killed him. Basically, he died from a lack of oxygen, which precipitated the heart attack."

"So, was there any evidence of foul play?"

"Sheriff, I can't really make that determination. How the nasal prongs came out of his nose is pure speculation. Could they have fallen out while he dozed on the couch? Sure. Could he have taken them out in an attempt to commit suicide? It's possible. Could someone have physically removed them? Well, that's also a possibility. But I can't tell from my examination. The only thing that is a little curious is he has a bruise on his left hand. I don't recall seeing that when I met with him the other day."

"And so, what would you make of that?"

"Also, difficult to say. You see, as people age, they bruise more easily. He could have simply banged his hand on something, or perhaps someone could have shaken hands with him and squeezed a bit too hard."

"I see, but nothing that you would consider suspicious?"

"No, but the timing of his death gives me pause. But that's not a medical conclusion."

"Well then, I guess all I can do is wait for the crime scene boys to give me their report."

"It would seem so. I'm sorry I can't give you clearer answers Sheriff, but if there is anything else I can do, please let me know."

"Will do, thank you."

Sheriff Bursey met with his crime scene chief in the conference room at the Sheriff's Department. Sergeant Tyler Dean was the senior officer and lead investigator. An assertive man of many talents, his appearance belied his capabilities. Mid-forties, short and thin with a crew cut, deep set brown eyes, and a thin mustache, he looked better suited for a desk job. Still, he knew well how to de-construct a crime scene.

Dean began, "Sheriff, we went over Cavanaugh's home thoroughly. The place is clean. Nothing was out of place, no signs of a struggle, no fingerprints, other than those of Cavanaugh himself. We checked the tank and nose prongs for prints. They were clean, other than prints from Cavanaugh, that is."

"So, that's it. Death by natural causes?" asked Bursey.

"Unless the autopsy uncovered something else, my findings are pretty clear. Just one thing that remains to be done before you relinquish the body to next of kin."

"What would that be?"

"We charged up his cell phone and I would just like to open it up and see the most recent activity. I don't expect much, but it's part of our routine. So, we just need to get his fingerprint on the phone to access it."

"Makes sense. Since the autopsy is done, why don't you head over there now and wrap it up."

"Copy that."

Dr. Kirk led Sergeant Dean into the autopsy lab. He gently took Cavanaugh's left thumb and pressed it on the phone. That didn't work. He walked around to the other side of the table and tried the right thumb. The phone came to life and he inspected it, first checking to see the most recent calls. The one from Sawyer was the latest call, and that was made at the time of discovery of the body. The second call was from Dr. Kirk apparently to set up the meeting with herself and Sawyer. The call prior to that one was two days earlier and the caller ID read 'Hannah Cell.' Dean had previously learned that Hannah was his only daughter. He then checked the photos, gasped, and nearly dropped the phone when he saw the latest photo.

"Is everything alright Sergeant?"

"Check this out. It's a photo from his iRing app. Do you recognize these guys?"

Dr. Kirk looked at the photo. "Oh my God, that's former Sheriff Marshall and former D.A. Hanratty. So, they did show up at the doctor's home."

"Yeah, and there's a new sound recording." He pushed play and heard the entire conversation with Marshall, Cavanaugh and Hanratty. The evidence was clear and damning.

"Holy shit! I've got to call Sheriff Bursey."

Within a half hour, Bursey and Dean were at Crenshaw's office playing the phone recording. That, in conjunction with the photo, were all Crenshaw needed to go to court and seek arrest warrants for both men.

Meanwhile, Bursey called Murphy and Delfino. He advised them to locate Hanratty and bring him in for questioning. He intended to track down Marshall and do the same.

45

Sheriff Bursey arrived at Marshall's residence without any backup.

Marshall was a large and imposing figure. Adorned in his beige cowboy hat and chewing a wad of tobacco, he answered the door. "Bursey, what brings you here?"

Bursey was not intimidated. "Don't look so surprised. You know why I'm here."

"Haven't a clue." He spat a wad of juice into the flower bed beside the front door.

"Calm, cool, and collected. Your trademark, of course. I'm here to bring you in for questioning."

"Questioning? About what?" He stepped outside, closing the door behind him.

"Do you want to do this here? Or perhaps it would be better if you came down to the station and we talked like men?"

"We can talk like men from right here, Bursey." He rocked on his heels impatiently.

"Well, either way, you're coming with me. But let me read you your rights before we begin."

"My rights!" he shouted angrily. "What is this?"

Bursey read him his rights. "Now, are you ready to talk?"

"I must be missin' something here. What are we talkin' about?"

Bursey pulled his shoulders back and pushed out his chest. "Okay, for starters, when was the last time you saw Dr. Liam Cavanaugh?"

"Cavanaugh? I ain't seen him in years. Why you askin'?"

"We found him dead at his home yesterday."

"And so how does that involve me?"

"I'll ask you once more, will you come with me peacefully," he pulled his pistol, "Or do I have to pull rank and cuff you?"

"Are you accusin' me of something, Boy?"

"Hands where I can see them," Bursey ordered, as he reached for his handcuffs.

"You sure you wanna be doin' this, Sheriff?"

"I'm glad you remember I'm the sheriff here, not you. That was a job you gave up some time ago and have apparently dishonored as well." He raised his pistol. "Hands where I can see them."

Marshall raised his palms up in mock surrender, "Easy now, Sheriff. Don't be pointin' no gun at me."

"Turn around."

"Okay, Sheriff. I'll come peacefully. You don't need no handcuffs. But from the way you're talkin' to me. I'm not sayin' another word. Let me just go inside and call my lawyer."

"Not a chance, Marshall. Come with me now, and you can call your lawyer from the station." He motioned for him to turn around. "And I will have to handcuff you. You know the drill."

Marshall chewed hard on his tobacco and spat again, then he turned in apparent acquiescence to Sheriff Bursey.

Bursey holstered his weapon, and as he reached out to cuff Marshall, Marshall spun around and threw his fist directly at Bursey's nose.

Bursey was prepared, released his grip on the cuffs and dropped down below the punch. Marshall's punch whizzed over Bursey's head. Bursey planted himself and threw a right cross that landed firmly on Marshall's jaw. Marshall stumbled backwards. Bursey followed with a left-right combination that sent Marshall to the ground.

Then, Bursey pulled his pistol and aimed it at him. "Big mistake, Marshall," he chuckled, "I guess you forgot I was base boxing champ in the Service. You're too old and slow for the likes of me." Bursey rolled Marshall onto his stomach. "I'm taking you in," he said as he put his knee on Marshall's back while pointing the pistol at his head.

46

Murphy and Delfino confronted Cole Hanratty at his home. When he heard the doorbell, he looked out the front window and saw the two deputies. A knot formed in the pit of his stomach as he thought about his options. He could head around back and grab his car from the garage and just run. But where would he go?

He was too old to run, but too young to spend the rest of his life in jail. He thought for a moment. He didn't actually kill Cavanaugh, Marshall did that. Maybe he could make a deal? He used to be very good at negotiating when he was in the Prosecutor's office. Perhaps those skills could come in handy now. First, he needed to know what they knew. He wouldn't be so foolish as to offer anything until he knew what he was up against.

He moved to the door and opened it. Smiling through yellowed and crooked teeth, he said, "Good afternoon gentlemen. What can I do for you?"

Murphy spoke first. "Sheriff Bursey has asked us to bring you down to the station. Please come with us."

"Can you tell me what this is about?" Sweat glistened, accentuating his pock-marked face. "We don't have that information. The Sheriff just asked us to bring you in."

"Am I under arrest for something?"

"Did you do anything to warrant your arrest?" asked Delfino.

"Warrant is an interesting word young fellow. Do you happen to have a warrant?"

"We do not," Murphy said. "But we will have one shortly. So, if you don't wish to accompany us peacefully, we will wait here with you until the warrant is issued, then we will cuff you and take you in. The choice is yours. Either way, you're coming with us."

"Quite alright, Officers. I'll come with you now. Just let me get my phone."

Delfino said, "Okay, we'll come inside with you, just make it fast."

The three went inside. Hanratty got his phone, and they escorted him to the station.

Upon arrival, the Sheriff put Marshall in a cell, and Hanratty was placed in an interrogation room. Neither knew the other was there. He let both of them stew while waiting for the arrest warrants.

Carrying a folder, Sheriff Bursey went inside to question Hanratty first.

Standing over the table he said, "Mr. Hanratty, this is to advise you that I have in my possession a warrant for your arrest. But before I begin, I want you to know that we are being recorded." He took a breath. "And now I would like to read you your rights."

"Record all you want, Sheriff. I know my rights."

"Be that as it may, the law requires me to read them to you." He proceeded to read him his rights. "Now that the formalities have been taken care of, do you wish to have an attorney present during this questioning?"

Hanratty snarled, "I am a lawyer. And there isn't a better one in this town, so I'll be representing myself."

"Are you sure you want to do that?"

"Yes. Now get on with it. What am I being charged with?"

Sheriff Bursey sat down, put on his glasses, and opened the folder. Scanning the page he said, "Let's see here. The first count is murder. You are charged with the murder of Dr. Liam Cavanaugh." He looked up waiting for a comment.

Hanratty didn't flinch.

"Count two, you are being charged with tampering with evidence in the capital murder case of Chadwick Greer."

Again, no response from Hanratty.

"Count three, you are being charged with suborning perjury during the trial in the capital murder case of Chadwick Greer."

Hanratty remained stoic.

Bursey removed his glasses and said, "Do you have anything to say for yourself?"

Hanratty took a deep breath, crossed one leg over the other, placed his palms on the table and asked, "Are we finished here?"

"So, does that mean you have no response. Not even an 'I didn't do it?'"

"Look Sheriff, when you started this interview, the first thing you said was, and I quote,—'You have the right to remain silent'—end quote. I took that literally."

"Fair enough. You'll be placed in a holding cell until arraignment." He gathered his folder and stood. "Just one more thing before I leave you. I want to remind you that Florida has the death penalty, and we will be speaking with former sheriff Chuck Marshall, whom we already have in custody. Since you are both charged as co-conspirators on all counts, if the D.A. chooses to make a deal with either of you, the first one to talk will be offered life without parole. The death penalty will be taken off the table."

As Sheriff Bursey walked towards the door, Hanratty mulled over what he had said. "Just a minute, Sheriff. I am entitled to know what sort of evidence you have against me on these charges."

Bursey turned and gave Hanratty a half grin, "You are, but if you aren't willing to talk, it can wait until arraignment. Meanwhile, my next stop is to talk with Marshall."

"Well, if you are willing to provide me with a little information, perhaps I could be convinced to cooperate."

Bursey sat back down and ruminated before he spoke. "Okay Mr. Hanratty, let's start with this." He opened the folder and pulled out a date and time stamped snapshot of Marshall and Hanratty at Dr. Cavanaugh's front door. He slid it over to him.

Hanratty looked it over and slid it back to Bursey. "And this tells you what?" he asked, arrogantly.

"That you were at the scene of the crime."

"Well, it doesn't prove anything."

Bursey smiled and took out a copy of the recording. "Would you like to listen to this?"

"What is that?"

"Just a recording of the entire murder of Dr. Cavanaugh. Apparently, you weren't aware that he had his cell phone recorder on from the moment you walked through his door."

Hanratty's boldness was short-lived. He wiped the beads of sweat that had formed on his forehead, swallowed hard and said, "I don't believe it."

Bursey turned it on and let it play, watching as Hanratty's expression went from defiant, to shocked, to hopeless.

After the tape concluded, Bursey waited a long minute while he let Hanratty absorb what he had just heard. Finally, he spoke. "So, why did you do it?"

"I didn't do it, and that tape doesn't prove I did it either. So, before I agree to tell you anything, I want D.A. Crenshaw here with a written agreement setting forth the following: First, death penalty is off the table. Second, if I testify to anything having to do with the Greer conviction, I'm offered an overall plea deal on all charges of five to ten years. Possible parole after five years, that is. I'm getting old, and I can't spend the rest of my life in jail."

Sheriff Bursey got up and said, "I can't promise you anything, but I'll get back to you."

47

"Did you hear the news?" Sawyer could hardly contain her excitement.

"What are you talking about?" asked Mason.

"Come inside, quick." She grabbed his elbow, pulled him through the door and led him to the den, speaking rapidly as she walked. "Marshall and Hanratty were arrested! Crenshaw secured the warrants and Sheriff Bursey has them both. Believe it or not, I was right. They killed Liam Cavanaugh."

"What? Really?"

"Yes, it's all on tape. Cavanaugh had his phone recorder on the whole time they were there."

"That's unbelievable."

"I know. I'm still in shock myself."

"Wow," his broad smile was followed by a firm embrace. "You did it!" He picked her up and spun around. Letting her go, he looked deeply into her eyes, took her face in his palms, and kissed her on the lips.

She absorbed the kiss then pulled away softly. A wave of sadness played across her face. "It's still nothing to celebrate. I mean a man was killed because of all this."

"True, yes, I am sorry, I didn't mean to . . ."

"It's okay, I'm excited too, and torn between emotions. I still don't know whether to jump for joy or bawl. I feel terrible that my visit to see him ultimately caused his death. But, at the same time, he was a part of the conspiracy that put Chad in jail."

"So, he got what he deserved."

"Don't say that. I mean, sure he should have been punished for what he did, but from his point of view it wasn't ill-intended. He honestly believed Chad was guilty."

"Don't go making excuses for him just because you're feeling a little guilty," Mason insisted. "The man still broke the law."

"I know, but still."

"Hey, I get it, too. But now you can secure Chad's release. Right?"

She sighed, "It's not that easy. We still have to establish that they not only withheld evidence, but that the evidence would have changed the conclusion of the jury. To do that, we still need the DNA, and if the DNA does not match Chad's, then we have enough to demand a Hearing and secure his release."

"So, how much longer before the lab gets you the results?"

"Soon, I hope."

48

Hanratty looked drained and defeated as he paced back and forth in front of the mirror. The pores on his face were even more pronounced and the hair on his head more slicked and greasy than just a few short hours ago. He really was starting to look like a man-sized rat. Sheriff Bursey and D.A. Crenshaw continued to watch him through the one-way mirror.

Bursey said, "Is it worthwhile to give him what he wants to get him to talk? I mean, we already have enough evidence to convict him and Marshall. And frankly, I'd like to see the two of them rot in prison for the rest of their lives, even if you can't get the death penalty to stick."

"It's a tough call, and while from the tape it sounds as if Marshall was the one who removed the nasal clip, Hanratty can still say that he had no idea that Marshall intended to kill Cavanaugh."

"But he's an accessory nonetheless, right?"

"Yes, but I'm thinking about the Greer case, too," said Crenshaw. "If we can get him to go into detail about that, it will certainly help with reinvestigating whether that was a wrongful conviction, and I could use more on that front."

"So, we have to negotiate with this fuck trumpet?"

"It would make things easier."

"Well, it's your call. How do you want to proceed?"

"The agreement I drafted gives him seven and a half to fifteen years. He's sixty-seven now, so best case scenario: he's out at age seventy-five. But making the deal also depends on what he can tell us about the other case."

"Alright. Let's get in there."

As the door opened, Hanratty spun on his heels. "It's about time. I've grown tired of waiting."

Forcibly restraining himself, Sheriff Bursey said, "Really, Hanratty, you're in no position to complain or make any demands. So, sit down and shut up. I've had just about enough of you."

"Whatever," mumbled Hanratty. He eyed Crenshaw. "Are we in agreement on the terms?"

Crenshaw tossed the agreement on the table. "It's all there, not exactly what you wanted, but we can offer seven and a half to fifteen years."

"Not acceptable. I told the Sheriff, five to ten."

"Look, Hanratty, it's going to be difficult enough selling the judge on this, so be happy and take what you can get. But it's all going to hinge on what you can tell us about the Greer case."

Hanratty sat down and scanned the papers, not fully reading them, but flipping the pages to the operative clauses. He knew where to look. He'd been on the other side of the table many times before. "It says here that my pension is forfeited. That's not going to work."

"You can't expect the government to fund your pension while you sit in jail."

"Sure I can. I've earned it. I put in my time. That's my money."

"That's debatable," said Crenshaw.

"You work with me on the pension issue, and I'll consider the extra time. But I'd like a first parole hearing after five years."

"Seven and a half and we cut your pension in half. But you need to give us all the details on Greer."

"Seven and a half and give me three quarters pension, I'll spill everything on the Greer case, and as a teaser, I'll tell you right now that this was all Marshall's idea. From day one."

Crenshaw looked at Bursey. "Let's talk outside."

The two men left.

Once outside the room, Crenshaw said, "I think we can work with that. Do you have any other feelings on it?"

"I don't know. I really hate giving in to this piece of shit. Just looking at him makes my skin crawl. But if he can give us Marshall and help with the Greer matter, I suppose it's worth it."

"Okay, I'll make the changes and be back in a few minutes."

Crenshaw returned with the revised agreement and Hanratty reviewed it more thoroughly. Satisfied, he signed, and pushed it over to Crenshaw for his signature. Crenshaw signed and then turned on the recorder.

"First, tell me what went down at Dr. Cavanaugh's house. Then I want to hear all about what happened with the evidence on Greer."

Hanratty massaged his chin with his thumb and index finger.

Looking up at the ceiling he said, "Marshall called me and said that he found out that Sawyer Greer and Dr. Kirk had paid Cavanaugh a visit. He was very concerned about what Cavanaugh might have said, so he asked me to accompany him to talk to the doctor."

"Did he say how he knew this?"

"He did not, and I didn't ask. He picked me up and we drove to Cavanaugh's home. He never indicated to me that he intended to kill him. Otherwise, I would have never agreed to go with him."

"Why were you so concerned about what the doctor could have said?" asked Crenshaw. "Well, that goes back a ways." He stretched his legs under the table and clasped his hands behind his head. "After

Marshall began investigating the Greer case, he became convinced that Chad Greer was the culprit. He based it on the fingernail DNA and the scratches on the kid's face."

"Tell us something we don't know."

"Well, the toxicology report came back with a finding that the decedent, Megan Miller, had a toxic amount of OxyContin in her system. And he knew his son was the one who supplied the drugs. He confided in me that he found a vial of the pills in his son's truck, and that he didn't want that to interfere with the trial. He firmly believed that Greer was guilty, and so did I, so rather than muddy the waters and add a twist to the evidence, I let him bury it. He got Cavanaugh to alter the report and then it was given to me for my case. I never saw the original report."

"Why would you compromise your office that way? You're supposed to uphold the law, not circumvent it."

"Look, the kid was guilty, and it made my job that much easier. No harm, no foul."

"And how can you be so sure he was guilty?"

"Come on, the kid had scratches on his face. The DNA matched. He lied to the Sheriff about how he got the scratches . . ."

"Okay, so then how did you know that Cavanaugh would be the one to testify to the report? It was Dr. Kirk who conducted the autopsy and wrote the report, so it would have been her job to testify at trial."

"That you would have to ask Marshall. He just assured me that Cavanaugh would be the one to take the stand."

"Alright, then what about the rape kit?"

"Ahh, the rape kit." He sat upright and rubbed the back of his neck. "I asked Marshall about that, and he told me that the DNA from the test was corrupted from the seawater, so we would just have to rely on the fingernail scrapings."

"And you didn't feel the need to investigate that any further?"

"No, not at all. Marshall was leading the investigation, he's the one that provided me with the evidence I needed to take the case to trial, and if he said the evidence was corrupted, I believed him."

"Yes, but that information should have been provided to defense counsel. Under the law, they were entitled to all evidence, good or bad, and that alone could have raised some doubt with the jurors."

"Exactly why Marshall didn't want that to get out. And frankly, the P.D. on the case . . . what was his name, Young . . . something or other . . . Youngblood, that's it. He was green, didn't have much experience, so it was easy to convince him that all we had was the DNA from the fingernail scrapings. He was nervous enough about the whole case, so it was easy to slip that by him. And that made things much easier."

"So, you took advantage of inadequate counsel as well?"

"I was just doing my job. I can't be held accountable if the other side is incompetent."

Sheriff Bursey cut in, "You're a real piece of shit Hanratty."

"As I've said repeatedly, as far as I'm concerned, and I'll believe this to my dying day, the kid was guilty. He got what he deserved."

Crenshaw said, "Okay, so what happened at Cavanaugh's home?"

"Well, Marshall took the lead there. You've got the tape. I had no idea he was going to pull that thing out of Cavanaugh's nose and let him die. I didn't want any part of it, but there was no way I could stop him."

Sheriff Bursey said, "There was nothing on that tape that sounded like you trying to stop Marshall."

"Look, you know Marshall as well as I do. You worked with him for a few years before he retired. When he sets his mind to something no one can stop him. And I didn't need that kind of grief. The man's an animal."

Crenshaw looked at Bursey and said, "I need some time to review all this, and I still want to talk to Marshall, so keep him in a holding cell, separate from Marshall, and don't let on to Marshall that we have Hanratty here."

Bursey nodded, "Will do."

49

Sawyer received a call from Dr. Kirk asking to meet at her office. The lab technician wanted to bring the DNA results personally and explain what he found. She and Mason couldn't get there fast enough. Upon arrival they were brought to Kirk's lab where the DNA tech had already spread out some paperwork and charts on the table.

Dr. Kirk greeted them and introduced Ryan Decker, the lab technician.

"Ryan, since this is your area, can you explain to Ms. Greer what you have found?"

Ryan nodded and said, "Just to bring you up to date, there are two main types of DNA sequencing. The older, classical chain termination method is called the Sanger method. That is what was originally used back fifteen years ago when the DNA in this case was analyzed. Since that time, newer methods have been developed that can process a large number of DNA molecules more quickly. They are collectively called 'High-Throughput Sequencing,' or HTS techniques, or 'Next-Generation Sequencing,' or NGS methods." He looked around the room. "Are you following me?"

Sawyer and Mason nodded their heads, though they had no clue what he was talking about.

"Good. So, we are able to use low concentrations of DNA to obtain reliable sequencing reads. Due to recent advances, we are now much better equipped to sequence every DNA within a sample.

Mason interrupted, "Excuse me, but could you explain what sequencing means?"

"DNA sequencing is the process of determining the sequence of nucleotides within a DNA molecule. Every organism's DNA consists of a unique sequence of nucleotides. Determining the sequence helps us compare DNA between organisms. This can help show how the organisms are related."

Mason shook his head, "This sounds like rocket science to me."

Sawyer dug her elbow into his side and whispered, "Let the man finish."

"Yes, so we were able to get a clear picture of the DNA sequence from the rape kit, despite the fact it has been sitting around for quite some time. And we were able to compare it to the results from the original skin under the fingernails of the victim, and the results are very strange. You see, there are a large number of long stretches of DNA and segments that match the two samples. However, they aren't the same person. My conclusion is that the DNA sample from the rape kit is a male and a close relative of the sample from the skin under the fingernails."

"What!" Sawyer nearly jumped out of her shoes. "What are you saying?"

"That whoever it was, the two are genetically related. Either a brother or a father."

"That can't be. Are you trying to tell me that my father is the one who raped and killed Megan Miller? Oh my God!" Sawyer began pacing the room frantically.

"Are you sure?" asked Mason. "Is this really accurate, could there be a mistake or something?"

"No mistake, sir. The DNA doesn't lie."

50

After she located where her father lived, Sawyer wanted to go in alone. The trailer park situated at the edge of Ocala National Forest was a grungy place. The mobile homes there were tattered and run down. Chadwick Greer's was no exception. If anything, it stood out.

Sawyer stared blankly at her father's trailer. Momentarily paralyzed, she was unable to raise her fist to knock on the door. She hadn't seen him in at least thirteen years, and the dread she felt just thinking about what she would say to him made her blood run cold.

She spun her head around looking for support and assurance before banging her palm loudly on the door.

A thick, gravelly, smoker's voice came from within, "Go away. I ain't takin' no visitors today."

Sawyer knocked louder.

"If ya don't git, I'm gunna have ta come out there and kick the shit outta ya." Sawyer kicked at the door.

It swung open and a man with long, grey hair and a heavy, grey beard stood at the entrance. Looking down at Sawyer, he said, "Who the fuck are you?"

Defiantly, she said, "What's the matter, don't you recognize your own daughter?"

Greer squinted as he scanned her from head to toe. "Izzat you Tom Sawyer?" A hint of a smile exposed blackened front teeth.

"The name is Sawyer; no 'Tom' before it. And you know I always hated when you called me that."

"You wuz a Tomboy, so the name fit. Still does, seein' as how yer dressed."

Ignoring the comment she said, "Aren't you going to invite me in?"

"I ain't seen ya in a long time, and I don't got no money, so what's yer business here?"

"I'm not looking for money, I just wanted to talk," she said sweetly.

"Well, it ain't too clean in here, but suit yerself."

Holding the door open, he stepped aside. The inside was just as run down as the outside suggested it would be. The stench of cigarettes and warm beer was offensive. Empty beer bottles spilled over the top of the garbage pail, a half empty bottle of Vodka stood on the counter, and dusty curtains hung open to a dirt covered window.

Greer removed old newspapers that lay on a green recliner, he brushed the seat cover, then patted it. "Y'all can sit here." He pulled a wooden chair from beneath a small table and sat across from her. "So, what ya wanna talk about?"

She wanted to make him feel at ease, but just the sight of him made her sick to her stomach. In spite of herself, she smiled, "How have you been?"

He bellowed a laugh, "Look around ya. If that don't say how I've been, then I dunno what else would." He scratched his armpit, then wiped his hand on his grease-covered jeans.

She eyed him up and down, noted his bare feet and the once white Wife Beater undershirt. "Well then, have you given any thought to how Chad and I have been doing all these years?"

"Haven't thought much about y'all. Why?"

"I don't know, I guess I just figured that you'd think about us once in a while."

"Okay then, how are y'all doin' and how's yer mom?"

Avoiding eye contact, she said, "Jeez, you didn't even know she died."

"Well, that's too bad, I guess. Good riddance is all I gotta say about that bitch."

"How can you say that? You were the one that ran out on us."

"Not so, she ran me out. There's a lot you don't know, Tom Sawyer."

"Stop calling me that!"

"Whatever. So then how are y'all doin'?"

"Not that you care, apparently, but I'm doing fine. I became a lawyer."

"Well good fer y'all. At least someone in the family made something of themself."

"Aren't you going to ask about Chad?"

"What's to ask? Besides, ain't he in jail?"

"Yes, he is, and, honestly, that is the main reason why I came here today."

"Really? What's that all about?"

"I was wondering if you ever felt guilty about what happened to him?"

"Why should I feel guilty?"

"You tell me. Isn't there something you'd like to say after all these years?"

"Not sure what yer gettin' at here."

"I think you do."

"Sorry, but I don't."

"Okay, let me make myself a little clearer. You see, I've been investigating Chad's case because he is innocent, and I'm trying to get his conviction overturned."

"Yeah, so? How does that involve me?"

"Like I said, I think you know how."

"Yer twistin' me up girl."

"Let's try it this way. Do you remember going out to look for Chad that night?"

"Yeah, but I never found him."

"Where did you go to look?"

"I went around to a bunch a places I thought he might be."

"Did you go to Rainbow River?"

"I believe I did. So, what of it?"

"Well, did you happen to run into anyone there?"

"I don't remember."

"How about Megan, did you find her?"

He shuffled uncomfortably in his chair. "What is this? Where y'all going with this?"

"Just answer my question."

"Course I didn't run into her."

"Are you sure, because I've uncovered evidence that you did."

"How so? What kinda evidence?"

"I'll get to that. But with what I've found, it's clear to me that you know exactly what I'm talking about."

He pointed at her, "You better mind yerself girl, cause I'm not likin' what you're a sayin.'"

"You know, it looks to me like you've been punishing yourself for years because of what you've done. I mean, look at yourself, look around you. Don't you think it's time to come clean?"

He jumped up sending the chair backwards into the refrigerator. "Are you accusin' me a somethin'?!" he shouted.

"Dad, please, the time has come for the truth."

"You want some truth Tom Sawyer, well, I'll give you some truth." He kicked the chair away from the refrigerator, opened it and took out a beer. Twisting it open he said, "I ain't yer dad. Never was. Surprised yer mom didn't tell ya after she threw me out." He took a long swig.

"What are you talking about?"

"You ain't my kid. Yer mom was a whore. She went out on me and got herself knocked up by some cowboy." He slammed the beer bottle on the counter. Foam rose up and poured over the top.

"Are you serious?"

"Damn straight I am."

"So, that's why you were always so cold to me."

"Bullshit, I did my best. I put in sixty-hour weeks to put food on that table."

"Well, your best was pretty sad. Besides, half the money you made went to the bar."

Chadwick slammed his hand on the table, startling Sawyer. "Listen here, Tom Sawyer. I know you'll never understand what it means to be a father. Even though I wasn't your father, I was still yer father. Ya hear? I still stuck in there with yer whore mother as long as I could, try to raise you two best I knew how, 'til I couldn't no more. Still, at some point you got to take responsibility for yerself. That's what my Daddy always told me."

"So, what was your excuse about Chad. Why'd you treat him so bad?"

He waved his hand at the air, "Ahh, he probably wasn't my kid either. Damn fool playin' pecker games with other little boys. He couldn't have my blood runnin' through him after seein' that kinda shit."

She looked at him, speechless and horrified. "You're an awful human being, I can't believe there was a time where I actually cared about you."

"Screw you, and him, and your mother, too!"

"So, then, admit it, admit that you raped and killed Megan Miller."

"Y'all better watch yer mouth if ya know what's good fer ya."

"Go ahead, set yourself free, tell me what happened that night."

Shouting, he said, "Ya know what, I'm gonna tell ya, then I'm gonna kill ya!"

"Just admit it already!"

"Fine, yeah. Yeah, it's true. I did it with Megan Miller. But I didn't kill her. Who'd want to kill a piece o' ass like that? No . . . No . . . it was an accident. I found her layin' nekkid on the rocks, and she starts callin' my name. Next thing ya know we're doin' it, and she's into it, callin' my name again and again: 'Chad! Chad!' Then afterwards she gets up and starts hollerin,' saying I wasn't who she thought. Then she steps back and falls, hittin' her head on the rock, and into the river she goes. She was dead by the time she hit the water."

Chadwick sat down and started to cry, the guilt of the crime overwhelming him.

"And you just let her die like that? You cruel bastard!"

"Sawyer, ya gotta believe me. I thought she was dead. Maybe she wasn't. Maybe I could've saved her. Maybe it wasn't consensual . . ." The tone of his voice changed as he got up from sitting.

"But, you know what, Tom Sawyer," he said in a menacing manner, his voice turning from remorseful to angry, as he approached her slowly. "Neither you or your pecker lovin' brother knows what it's like to be a real man. But I'll show you. I'll show you what a real man is!"

Chadwick Greer lunged at Sawyer. Sawyer was ready. She pulled out her pepper spray and sprayed him right in the eyes. He stumbled backwards, banging his head into the refrigerator, and dropping to the ground.

At that moment, the door burst open wide. Sheriff Bursey rushed inside, followed by Deputy Murphy. Delfino stayed outside with his gun drawn while Mason remained in the car.

They pinned Chadwick Greer to the ground and handcuffed him. Looking back at Sawyer, Sheriff Bursey said, "We got it all. Good job."

As they were taking him out, Sawyer said, "By the way, Dad, Chad is your son, and unfortunately for him, he has your blood running through him. That's how we caught you. We matched his DNA to yours."

51

Sawyer waited outside the Marion Correctional Institution for Chad. Finally finished being processed, he walked out of the gate and ran up to Sawyer.

"You did it, Sis! You got me out. You're amazing. I don't know how to thank you. I can't believe I'm actually free. I love you so much, I think I'm gonna cry." He hugged her tight as tears formed in his eyes.

"Oh Chad, I'm so happy for you. I can't imagine the hell you've been through all these years, knowing you were innocent and no one believing you."

"You believed in me, and that's all that matters."

"So much has happened since I last saw you. I'll have to bring you up to date."

"No rush, I heard about Dad. I still can't believe it. What a piece of shit he turned out to be."

"That's for sure, but he'll pay for what he's done."

"I hope so."

"Okay, so what's the first thing you want to do?"

"I want a hamburger, fries and a coke from the Rainbow River Café, assuming it's still around."

"It is, and I want you to meet Mason Walcott, he's in the car waiting. He was of great help to me in getting you out."

"Then I owe him a debt of gratitude," he said, grinning ear to ear. "I'd like to thank him personally."

"You'll get your chance in a minute. I just wanted to see you alone first."

"You're the best Sis. Let's get outta here now. I don't ever want to see this place again."

52

"Face it, Sawyer. Ever since we met, we've been dancing around taking things to the next level," Mason reached out and took her hips in his hands and pulled her towards him, "Don't you think it's time?"

Sawyer looked away then turned and smiled. Looking deep into his eyes she said, "I know, I've been fighting it, too. But the timing just wasn't right."

"Until now. Just think about everything you've accomplished." He reached up, brushed the hair from her eyes and kissed her tenderly.

She embraced him and let her stoic exterior liquify in his arms. They opened their mouths and shared a soft exchange of tongues. He gripped her tighter and she responded, her hands squeezing the taught muscles of his back.

"I've been dreaming about this for far too long, Sawyer."

She put two fingers over his lips, backed up, took his hand and led him into the bedroom. She motioned towards the bed. "Sit."

He sat down. She positioned herself in front of him and slowly began unbuttoning her blouse. His eyes became glued on her hands as she went from one button to the next, finally opening her shirt and exposing her breasts. He reached up and cupped them as the ache in his groin intensified.

His fingers brushed softly over her nipples.

He pressed his head up against her belly and kissed it.

She pushed his shoulders back and made him lie on the bed while she removed her top. He pulled his shirt off and she climbed on top of him. They kissed passionately again, stopping only to unzip each other's jeans.

Once naked, she straddled him and as he inserted himself, she groaned. They began moving together holding each other tightly. The kisses became more urgent as the sensations between their legs grew unbearable. The release was as intense as they both knew it would be.

Afterwards, they lay facing each other. Mason touched Sawyer's face and said, "That was wonderful, the perfect ending to a crazy day. I'm so proud of you and all you've been able to do."

"I couldn't have done it without you. Thank you for everything."

"We make a good team." He kissed her gently on the lips.

53

Three Days Later . . .

Travis Conrad lay in a hospital bed, his left arm cuffed to the rail. Still in a coma and heavily bandaged across the chest, his stillness made him look like a body at a wake. He was on life support and his chances of survival were quite slim.

In the hospital hallway a little aways from Travis' hospital room, Sawyer, Mason, and Chad came to a stop.

"Are you sure you want to do this, Chad?" asked Sawyer, concerned for her brother's emotional well-being.

"I'm not sure," said Chad, tilting his head down a bit.

"If you need us," said Mason, "we'll be right outside the door."

There was an officer stationed at the door. Chad approached him. "Chad Greer."

The officer nodded to Chad. "Yeah, I know. Take your time." He opened the door and let Chad enter.

When Chad first saw Travis in the hospital bed, he almost didn't recognize him. Gone was the young teammate he knew from the basketball team. Here, before him, was a totally different person, one who obviously had lost his way.

Chad approached the chair in the corner, but decided it was best not to sit. What he wanted to say wouldn't take long and if he sat he might need help getting up.

"It's not easy for me to come here and speak to you, Travis. I know you probably can't hear me, but it's been a long time. A real long time. In my fifteen years in prison, I had a lot of time to think. It's strange. You think you're sick, you're a deviant, sicker than my old man. And everybody makes snide remarks about . . . you know. I had a lot of alone time, with my thoughts as my only company. Some convicts made friends in the can. But I didn't. I couldn't. My time was for me, waiting every day for those bars to open and for me to be set free from a crime I didn't do; I could never do. But, I can't be free unless I confessed to the worst crime you could do to a friend. I'm sorry what it did to me. And what it did to you. I'm sorry I wasn't strong enough to . . . to accept what I am . . . what I meant to you . . . what you meant to me. I know why you killed Sandra. It wasn't because you hated her. It wasn't even because she could expose us to everybody. If I wasn't in jail for what my old man did—that crazy drunk shit-for-brains—you would never have . . . ended Sandra's life. I hope you know, they're never gonna forgive you for what you did to Sandra. But it wasn't Sandra you were choking. It was rejection . . . all of the rejection . . . you felt. And I only added to it. I'm the real criminal, the real killer. Yeah, I know, Travis, they'll never ever understand what happened. Only that my dad killed Megan and you murdered Sandra in cold blood. Like the Replacements used to sing, 'The ones who love us best are the ones we'll lay to rest.' I hope and pray you don't die. But maybe it's better that way. Too many people hate your guts. You know I could never hate you. But I'm through lying to you, or Megan, or my sister, or my mother who died while I was in prison. And whether you wake up from all of this insanity and serve your sentence in this world or serve your sentence in the next, both of us are convicted killers. I killed the best part of you and you took it out on Sandra. That's my crime, too. So, I finally confessed to the crime I *actually* committed. We both killed Sandra. I hope she forgives us in the heavens above."

As Chad left the room, Travis remained unresponsive. One would think that he hadn't heard anything that Chad had said. But, if one looked very closely, from his right closed eye, a tear formed as Chad closed the door to the hospital room. A single lonely tear streamed slowly down the side of Travis' cheek.

Epilogue

Rainbow River Gazette
by Mason Walcott

Fifteen years ago, an innocent young boy named Chad Greer was convicted of murdering his girlfriend, Megan Miller; A murder he didn't commit. He spent all those years in jail because of the corruption and incompetence of the Sheriff's Department, the D.A.'s office, the P.D.'s office and the M.E.'s office. Corruption at the highest levels of local government has finally been uncovered, and a decade's old case has been put to rest.

Former Sheriff Chuck Marshall has been indicted on a number of charges including murder, falsifying records, hindering prosecution, assaulting a police officer, and tampering with evidence material to a criminal investigation. Former D.A. Cole Hanratty has entered into a plea agreement with the D.A. where he will serve seven and a half to fifteen years for his role as a co-conspirator with former Sheriff Marshall. The details of his agreement have been kept confidential as part of the plea arrangement. However, he will be required to testify against Sheriff Marshall at trial. It has come to light that the disgraced sheriff, colluding with the disgraced D.A., and now deceased M.E. Dr. Liam Cavanaugh . . . who was apparently murdered by Marshall . . . buried evidence that would have altered the outcome of the case and vindicated the accused Chad Greer.

Tremendous credit must be given to A.D.A. Sawyer Greer for digging deep and putting in the time and effort to uncover the truth and set her brother free. And as part of her investigation, she was also responsible for bringing two other murderers to justice. First, Ms. Greer helped to solve a cold case involving local girl, Sandra Payne, who was thought to have committed suicide while attending school at Florida State University. Through Ms. Greer's efforts, she zeroed in on another local resident, one Travis Conrad, who committed the crime. He is presently in a coma in a local facility, and on life support.

In addition, in a bizarre twist of fate, Ms. Greer also brought Megan Miller's real killer to justice. She discovered that it was actually Chad Greer's father, Chadwick Greer, Sr., who was the culprit. Greer, Sr. is currently incarcerated pending trial on the charges, but we are advised by a source, who prefers to remain anonymous, that not only is there DNA evidence confirming his guilt, but there is also a voice recorded admission which further inculpates the accused.

Finally, Chad Greer, Jr. has been freed from jail and is contemplating a suit for damages against the County, the Sheriff's Department, the D.A.'s office and the Medical Examiner's office. We will continue reporting this story as it unfolds.

Author Bio

Howard K. Pollack was born and raised on Long Island. A Brooklyn Law School graduate, he has had a distinguished career as an attorney for over 35 years. While he enjoys practicing law, his first love has always been writing. Beginning simply as a hobby in high school, writing has grown into a passion that has become a dominant force in his life.

His titles include the thrillers EVERYWHERE THAT TOMMY GOES (2014) and UNMASKED (2022), THE FEARLESS FOURSOME (2023), a coming of age story for young teens, and SO YOU WANT TO BE AN AUTHOR?, a writer's guide to becoming an author. WHERE THE RIVER RUNS RED is his third contemporary thriller.

A message from Howard: "I hope you enjoyed my book, and if you did, please put a review out on Amazon." You can get in touch at HowardKPollackAuthor@gmail.com

www.ingramcontent.com/pod-product-compliance
Lightning Source LLC
LaVergne TN
LVHW100522110826
845146LV00002B/739

9798990009639